Acclaim for *The Lewellyns From Vincennes*

"Doctor Reece has done it again. His fourth novel is a page-turner in a midwestern three-generation family memoir. This story has all the triumphs, foibles, joys, sorrows, and redemption one could hope for. The narrative brilliantly reflects the wider world by showing how wars and external events profoundly affect individuals and whole generations on a personal day-to-day level. It is hard to put down such writing when one intimately feels tears of sadness and of joy, as well as emotions of jealousy, hopelessness and relief that comes from overcoming impossible odds. This is a winner!"

– James Lijlestrand, MD

———

"A wonderful story of the lives of a family in the 1900's punctuated by whirling events of world history. The characters come alive through Reece's narrative and dialogue, so that you feel both sadness and happiness for the main characters. Everyone will love Sarah, cheer for Martha, and waver through a myriad of feelings towards Jack. It's an interesting and enjoyable book."

– Judy Singer

———

Praise for Robert Reece's *Strong Medicine*

"During a long and productive medical and academic career, Dr. Reece never lost his capacity for outrage at injustice and corruption. In *Strong Medicine,* he summons Dr. Tom Barrett and other people we learned to care about in his last novel, *Double Blind Double Cross,* to embody and express his outrage at the wrongdoing of so much of Big Pharma, to prove the enormity of the consequences of the wrongdoing, and to design a roadmap for correction. Dr. Reece tells an absorbing story, and, after reading it, it is impossible not to share his outrage."

– Judge Richard Cohen

———

"Patients in the U.S. often face insurmountable expenses when paying for prescription drugs, with huge profits accumulating for drug companies and their executives. In his third novel, Dr. Robert Reece explores this critical issue while creating interesting characters and developing personal interactions among them."

– Robert Block, MD, past president
The American Academy of Pediatrics

———

Praise for *Double Blind Double Cross*

"In *Double Blind Double Cross*, Dr. Robert Reece wields a talented pen. His memorable characters jump off the pages, keeping the reader up late into the night. I highly recommend it!"

– Steven Manchester, #1 bestselling author
The Rockin' Chair and *Twelve Months*

———

"In *Double Blind Double Cross*, Robert Reece deftly weaves the devastation of war, the quest for medical discovery and the big business of drugs into an engrossing, unpredictable and ultimately satisfying adventure story."

– David Kerns, author
Fortnight on Maxwell Street, Standard of Care

———

About *To Tell The Truth*

"Dr. Robert Reece's moving novel is fiction based upon non-fiction. We judges grapple daily with the dilemma he depicts, as do jurors. Reece's book, besides entertaining and enlightening, is a tool for all Americans. It helps all know that the world of science has finally established not only that the world is round but also that abusive head trauma in infants and children is a scientific reality-without plausible denial! Thousands of physicians agree. Perhaps a dozen criminal defense medical witnesses would disagree. The latter testify, earning $12,000 a day in court, that infant head trauma has other causes... And presumably also that the world is flat. Reece's book supports the reality of abusive head trauma. Let there finally be justice for all, including children!

– Judge Charles D. Gill
Connecticut Superior Court

—

"I just finished Dr. Reece's novel this morning. I already have a long list of people to whom I plan to personally recommend it – including judges. There's great potential for this book to help inform the public at large."

– Melissa L. Currie, MD, FAAP

"This book is an excellent story and a commentary on those who would subvert our justice system. As a *Law and Order* fan, this book is in that vein. It opens with a tragedy and walks the reader through the issues culminating in a criminal trial. This is a solid character and issue study with a grounding in real life drama and science. I own all of Dr. Reece's books. His other books are outstanding textbooks of child maltreatment science. However, like *Law and Order*, it is this book that engages your emotions to teach life concepts.

– Mary Case, MD

———

"Bob Reece has written a compelling story, addressing an issue familiar to physicians who care for children, but important to all of us. A baby dies, and the question of a sad, natural death weighed against a homicide becomes a quagmire of truth and lies inherent in the justice system assigned to determine guilt or innocence as the baby's case winds its way through an all-too-real courtroom drama. The narrative of witnesses in the courtroom and tactics of attorneys brings the reader face-to-face with a startling reality: sometimes criminal cases are influenced by more than "the truth, the whole truth, and nothing but the truth."

– Robert W. Block, MD, FAAP, professor emeritus, pediatrics
The University of Oklahoma School of Community Medicine
Child Abuse Pediatrician and past president (2011-2012),
The American Academy of Pediatrics

THE LEWELLYNS FROM VINCENNES

ROBERT M. REECE

To My Family

Also by Robert M. Reece

To Tell The Truth
Strong Medicine
Double Blind Double Cross
About Ben

CONTENTS

Chapter One

Dear Doctor

1897

THEY CALLED ME CYRUS. I was born headfirst. My twin brother Jack slid out several minutes later, not headfirst but one foot at a time, followed by the rest of him. Jack and I greeted the world at home during an oppressive humid summer day in western Indiana. Before the turn of the century children were most often born at home. Papa was there, but he told me years later he didn't do anything but watch, restraining himself -- hard for him -- as Edith, the midwife, did her job well getting us twins into the world. Papa had taught her how to help mothers have their babies and she'd eased many mothers through this rude process. Was she nervous, delivering her mentor's twin boys?

Mother (we were never allowed to call her Esther) knew Edith and trusted her to get the job done. Papa said Mother was her usual stoic self as she bore down when told to. Edith told us when we were older that each one of us came out easy, screamed right away, and were put to Mother's breasts as soon as the cords were cut and clamped.

Mother had another boy about a year later, named him Andrew. From the start he was a strange little being, cried a lot, and took up much of Mother's attention, right after he was born and forever, it seemed to Jack and me. She spent most of her time looking after him. He never seemed right to us. But he didn't bother us either, seemingly preoccupied and uninterested in everyone except Mother.

Dr. Jeremiah Lewellyn was well-known in the community of Vincennes, Indiana and beyond. He was Dr. Lew and our Papa. He always seemed a giant to us boys, but he was only of average height. His thick hair was like those ebony keys on the piano he loved to stroke. His bushy eyebrows over wide-set eyes and a narrow nose kept rhythm with his lips, rising and falling, as he spoke with staccato cadence in his deep baritone. And when he sang, well, those eyebrows were out of control.

In his white stiff- front shirts, celluloid cuffs, snap on bow ties, and polished high black boots, he was the archetype country doctor. Tightly disciplined in all things, his only breach in rigid self-control was a voracious devotion to sweets. This resulted in a constant war between himself and his office scale where he weighed himself every day after breakfast.

He was always in a hurry. He drove his horse hard to get to house calls in corn country around Vincennes.

A practicing family doctor for a decade, he was a familiar and beloved figure bouncing along in his horse-drawn buggy, visiting patients at rambling farmhouses scattered among the corn stalks farmers grew all over Knox County. He made rare diagnostic mistakes, causing him to have periods of dark self-recrimination, but everyone knew he did his best, that was what counted. When Papa himself got sick, everyone was upset. But I'm getting ahead of my story.

We enjoyed living in a spacious red brick Tudor-style house on Elm Street in Vincennes, this midwestern town with sprawling lawns and backyard barns for horses and buggies. It was one of the nicer homes in a neighborhood populated with merchants who had prospered because of an accident of nature. Our river, the Wabash, was a haven for fresh-water mussels. Someone realized that the shells of these mollusks could be harvested and put to good commercial use. Special tools were used to punch out circular discs to fashion "mother of pearl" buttons for shirts, blouses, jackets, and dresses. For many decades, manufacturing these buttons was the major business enterprise of Vincennes.

When we were about five, Jack eagerly joined Papa as he went on house calls. I was a little squeamish – well, truth be told, very squeamish -- about sickness and injury. I didn't like seeing distressed people, or smelling the attendant odors of illness, and death was only a vague idea in my young mind. But Jack immersed himself in Papa's medical books and equipment when the office was empty. His immaculate office matched Papa's temperament, so Jack always returned everything he touched to its exact original position. Jack sniffed jars of alcohol, cough syrup, throat swabbing solution, Merthiolate, and various salves and ointments. He cautiously turned instruments over in his hands, feeling the cold steel and smooth texture of forceps, hemostats, and probes. When Jack got older, Papa taught him how to sharpen hypodermic needles on a whetstone and boil syringes in a stainless-steel sterilizer. Jack spent many blissful hours there.

I wasn't interested in any of it. While Jack puttered in Papa's office, I learned to read. Jeanette, the clerk at our library, spotted me, this little boy, wandering around in the stacks one day, while Mother searched for a book. She pointed me towards books used by schools to teach kids how to read. I was in love with the printed word, stories, and characters. This enchantment grew as I got older and led to my lifetime of writing.

Jack knew how I felt about sick people, but he still couldn't resist regaling me about his experiences with Papa, who told him all about his patients, how they lived, their families and illnesses. He stressed how important it was to know about the daily life of patients to understand how they'd respond to his advice. Papa taught Jack how he went about making his diagnoses. But with all this, he was always sensitive to Jack's feelings and fears. I overheard him saying, "Now Jack, I don't want you to be scared by what you see, but you'll learn a lot. I hope you'll get interested in medicine. If you become a doctor, you could take over my practice when I get old and gray."

But Jack, despite the warnings, sometimes got scared by what he saw. I was sure glad I wasn't there with them.

"This kid," Jack told me in intimate tones one night as we went to sleep, "maybe ten, lives on a farm out near the river. One of his chores was to muck out the stables. Awful job, but he did it 'cause he had to.

"One day he got sick, and his pa didn't know what he had, so he called Dr. Lew. When Papa went into the house, he told me to stay in the buggy since he didn't know what the boy had. I waited and waited a long time.

"After a while, he came to the door and waved me to come in. I went into this dark room that smelled like dead rats. Over in the corner this boy laid on a straw mattress, his back all arched up. Until my eyes got used to the dark, I thought the kid was smiling. But he wasn't smiling at all. His jaw was tight, with his lips pulled back away from his teeth, spit comin' outta his mouth, and moaning in pain.

"I looked away and Papa took me back out to the buggy, then he went back in. I saw him talking to the boy's Pa. It took a long time. When he came back to the buggy Papa was frowning."

Jack whispered to me, "I remember he said to me, 'Maybe I shouldn't have shown you that boy, but you need to know about this one disease because it's so common out here in the country. He has what we call tetanus, or lockjaw. You saw his mouth, right? Looks like the person is smiling, but it's far from that. It's called risus sardonicus, and it's the hallmark of lockjaw. He must've stepped on something sharp in the stable that punctured his skin and it got infected with a germ that causes a kind of paralysis. There's an anti-toxin serum to counteract it, and I gave him some, but it's probably too late now. Poor boy. And his poor father. I don't know this family. I'm not even sure there's a mother with them. They're dirt poor and barely making ends meet.'"

"I asked Papa if the boy was gonna die."

"Papa said, as he looked up—and away from me, 'I'm afraid he is.' He brushed a tear away."

Another time, Jack said they'd seen this woman complaining of awful belly pain. A man she lived with sent for Papa because she thought she might have a bad appendix, something one of her friends died of last year. On their way to see her, Papa told Jack intestinal flu was going around. He suspected she might have it, accounting for her belly pain.

When they got to the house, Jack said the man was in the front yard waving to Papa to hurry. "He dashed into the house, with me trailing behind."

I was getting a little queasy, but Jack kept talking.

"Papa asked the woman where it hurt as we watched her writhing in pain. She was shaking her head from side to side, talking nonsense. We both could see she was pale as a ghost. He quickly looked her over, saw purple rope-like veins in both legs. He turned and asked the man about them."

I didn't want to hear anymore. But Jack continued to tell me his story anyway. "The man told Papa that she always got them when she was with child.

"Papa, all of a sudden looking very nervous, asked if she was pregnant and the man told him that the midwife told them she was a couple of months along."

"Papa's face fell, his brow wrinkled up. He pressed her distended belly low down. She again screeched in pain.

"Then Papa quickly decided to get her to the hospital. He asked the man if he had a wagon to carry her to the hospital. The man said he only had a horse and buggy. Papa hurried to help him get his woman into the buggy. He told the man to follow him to the Vincennes Hospital as fast as he could go because the woman was in big trouble.

"They tore into Vincennes Hospital, took her directly to the operating room." Jack sat up and stared at me. "You know, Papa's not a surgeon, and I was scared, but he explained later he had no choice but to scrub her belly quickly, have the nurse drip ether into a gauze mask and operate.

"Papa told me afterwards that blood had boiled up out of the hole he'd cut in her belly, and after he groped around inside her, he found the problem: a baby was growing in the tube – he called it the fallopian, or something like that, and the tube had broken and was bleeding like crazy."

Jack stopped talking for a spell, and despite my practically turning green, he went on to tell me that instead of the baby growing in the womb where it should've been, it was growing in the tube leading from the ovaries –that's where the eggs are made-- to the womb. In other worlds, the fertilized egg got stuck in the tubes, never made it to the womb where it's 'sposed to get planted and grow.

"By then, most all of the blood in her body had gathered in her belly."

I pulled a pillow over my head, but Jack continued, not noticing that I was trying not to listen. "Papa said that as the woman died, he was so frustrated that he threw his mask and scalpel to the floor in that operating room, startling the nurse. She picked them off the floor, cleaned up the room and arranged for someone to take the woman downstairs to the refrigerator."

"Then Papa gathered himself and went out to give the bad news to her man who, Papa said, just stared at the floor, didn't cry, 'as is common with men 'round here', Papa said, and 'he showed no emotion.'"

"Papa said the man told him she was the second woman with child he'd lost, that she was a good woman and didn't deserve this and that he'd pray for her."

I was close to running out of the room, but Jack kept on talking.

"Another time, Papa said we were going on what he called 'a mission of mercy.' We drove to what he called the County Poor Farm where he took care of ill and weakened folks, mostly feeble-minded and really poor. We saw this pitiful man who snarled viciously when I looked at him, fighting the ropes holding him in a chair. Papa told me that the lesson here was how I should appreciate that some people are more fortunate than others."

Papa explained everything to Jack. Maybe that's why Jack wanted to be just like him. He'd go to medical school and carry on his life of caring for the sick. But that was never to be.

Chapter Two

In My Merry Oldsmobile

1905

"HORSELESS CARRIAGES are catching on," Papa announced at dinner. "You know, about five years ago a fellow named Olds started making them. People tell me, because I'm a doctor and need to get places fast, that I should have one. I don't know what they cost. I'm going to look into this."

Jack and I darted glances at each other and smiled. Both of us thought we knew all about automobiles. We were in second grade and boys talked a lot about horseless carriages. Young people are always ahead of their parents about such things. We hoped Papa would get one, and we'd get to show it off to our friends. We were pretty sure he would because he'd been talking about horseless carriages for some time.

A few weeks later, without telling any of us, Papa rolled into our driveway with a brand-new black Oldsmobile. It was a sight to behold. We all piled into it for a ride. Mother didn't come. She claimed she had to take care of Andrew, our little brother who was now going on four years. We thought the real reason was that she didn't approve that Papa would spend good money on this new-fangled contraption.

The one thing Papa didn't like about the car was the starting crank. He'd set the magneto, run to the front of the car, engage the crank, and turn it as hard as he could. Usually nothing happened. He'd do it over and over until the blasted thing started, then he'd scurry back to adjust the controls so he wouldn't have to do it again.

He loved to take us out in his new toy. People called them machines rather than automobiles, horseless carriages, or cars. That's what they really were – machines. Some said they should be outlawed because they scared the bejeepers out of horses. Papa took care of several people who got injured when their horses got spooked, making their carriages run off the road, landing their occupants in a ditch. There were complaints about their loud noise, and how exhaust fumes stunk to high heaven. These same people never complained about horse manure aroma hanging in the air all over the streets. Maybe they were used to that odor, since manure was spread on their fields as fertilizer.

The reason Papa got the machine, he explained, was to get to patients faster. Although he had a home office, most patients lived out in the country on farms and only had a horse and buggy or wagon to carry their sick family member to his office. Papa had a telephone earlier than most people in Vincennes, but with a few exceptions, his patients didn't. They would send someone to tell him he was needed. Some of his in-town office patients would complain that he'd drop everything, leave them sitting in a dressing gown on the exam table, if one of his farm patients sent a runner to fetch him.

His doctor bag was enormous, containing duplicates of many office instruments. These had been sterilized in boiling water and carefully wrapped in sterile towels and packed tightly in his bag. He also had pills and capsules to dispense for different ailments. These were kept in small compartments on the inside of the folding top of his valise.

One of the stories he told, maybe made up, was about when he was the new doctor in town. He arrived at a farmhouse on a house call, stumbling as he got out of his carriage. He dropped his bag, and it sprang open, scattering pills of all sorts on the ground. Roaming chickens in the yard eagerly gobbled them up.

The next day, the farmer let him know that several of his chickens were found dead in the hen house the next morning. He feared the worst: his practice would never get past this horrible beginning. But just the opposite happened.

Word got around that the dead chickens proved that Dr. Lewellyn had powerful medicines. His practice thrived after that. At least this was the story he told, prompting many laughs. Looking back, I suspect this was part of a country doctor's mythology.

In 1908, Papa bought another car, this time a Model T Ford, a machine made by factories owned and operated by Henry Ford. It was much cheaper than his Oldsmobile, only $850. It wasn't as grand, but much more serviceable. Papa also liked Henry Ford's philosophy of making cars "for the people" and paying his workers a fair wage.

Jack and I were now in fifth grade. We were curious students and did well in our studies. Jack was better at math and science, but I was way ahead of him in reading and history. Even so, Jack was very smart and knew a lot of things outside of math and science. He was interested in politics and United States history. He could name all the presidents and even our Indiana senators and local congressman.

As for me, when not playing games with neighborhood boys, I was at the library, devouring all manner of books. Mother thought I wasted my time doing this and I should be learning how to "do things you can make a living at" instead of being a bookworm. She took the fun out of everything.

About Mother. She was a gaunt and humorless woman, pretty much interested in herself, Andrew and the house. She never paid much attention to Jack and me. We went about our lives without interference or even attention from her. We wondered why Papa had married her in the first place. She seemed so flat, so disinterested in everything, especially us. We never saw any exchange of affection between Papa and Mother. The good thing was we had Papa, who played with us, read to us, showed us how to do things and took us places.

Often, in the evenings, he played our beautiful grand piano. He told us he'd learned how to play in college, often had a fine time with friends, playing and singing popular songs of the day.

We joyously joined in his habit of singing. We sang sometimes in unison but, as we learned more, in harmony. Barbershop quartets were the rage, and we started using those standard close harmonies. Even when we were in the car, we'd all tune up, lean our heads back and give out with "Lida-Rose," "Harvest Moon," "Dear Old Girl," "Comin' Round the Mountain," "Alexander's Ragtime Band," and other simple tunes. Singing in the car became a family tradition, one we all looked forward to.

Papa did have some idiosyncrasies. His habits were fixed. He always dressed the same, even when we went fishing or on camping trips: black three-piece suit, white shirt, bow tie and highly polished, dark boots. These outings only took place when he was able to get another doctor to look after his practice. His patients always came first.

In summer that year, we regularly rode our bicycles to the Wabash River and frolicked in the water, cooling off from sticky summer heat. Our river marked the boundary between southwest Indiana and Illinois. It was a fast-moving river as it ran by Vincennes. The riverbanks were yellowish-brown clay and in summer had a moldy smell that clung to your skin long after swimming. The water was usually cloudy, and loose twigs and small branches floated on its foamy surface. Tiny leaves from the locust trees fluttered down onto the river surface like snowflakes.

Frequent boats of all sizes could be seen since the Wabash poured into the Ohio River and the confluent streams ended up in the Mississippi River. The Wabash was a water highway for moving all manner of goods. It was also an easy place to dump waste from farms and emerging industries along its path. Swimming there was fraught with annoyances- oil slicks, loose boxes, debris.

We rigged up a rope from one of the overarching shoreline trees. We ran, hanging onto it until we swung out over the deep water, letting go at precisely the right time. We taught ourselves how to swim -- well, we had help from older kids who also swam there.

No girls ever swam there, so often we'd go skinny-dipping. As adolescence approached, we'd compare our privates and check on the growth of our pubic hair, a ritual of adolescent boys. Once, one of the older guys brought some cigars and we all took turns drawing cigar smoke into our mouths until coughing fits stopped most of us from continuing. The older boys convulsed with laughter watching us as hacking turned our faces red.

During one lazy summer afternoon, an unfamiliar boy came to where we swam. He was about our age, lanky, blond, and very white. No one knew him. He was shy, didn't talk to anyone. We had no idea where he lived or where he went to school.

We soon lost interest in him, but when he undressed to go swimming, Jack said he'd noticed darkened areas on his skin, some making curved lines, maybe bruises, on his back and a few flat ones on his face. He slipped into the water quietly. We exchanged glances, but no one said anything, and soon our focus was on playing marbles on the soft clay of the riverbank.

Everyone was absorbed in our game, but someone realized that he hadn't come back out of the water for a long time. At first, we just looked at the spot where he'd gone in, then became alarmed that he was nowhere in sight. We rose as one, our hearts racing, and rushed into the water to find him.

In a few seconds, two of the older boys found him floating face down in one of the eddying pools near the shore and quickly dragged him ashore. He was pale and lifeless. Jack rushed to him and began artificial respiration that Papa had taught him.

After a few chest compressions, the boy sputtered, coughed, and threw up a lot of water and weeds, along with the sour smell of stomach juice. Then he began breathing and crying. Our small crowd stood silently, trying to take it in, to understand what had just happened. When he recovered enough to stand up, we asked his name.

"I'm Eugene Wainwright," he stammered, looking sheepish.

"Where do you live?" Jack asked him.

"That way," pointing to the road.

"Should we get in touch with someone to let them know you had a close call?" Jack said.

"Nope, I'm fine," he said as he snatched up his clothes and hurried for the road.

We watched him leave and wondered about what we had just witnessed. Was it an accident? Or what?

"What were those marks on his back?" one of the boys asked Jack, knowing he knew a lot about medical things.

"Don't know for sure, but to my mind they looked like bruises from whip marks. The things on his face looked like he'd been whacked."

When we talked about this in ensuing weeks, we thought maybe he was trying to drown himself. We'd never know for sure, but we soon found out more about Eugene Wainwright.

A couple of months later, Papa was called to the hospital to see a kid who'd run from his home and came there because he was hurt and didn't know where else to go. He told Papa he'd been beaten by his father. He had several broken ribs and a swollen face with both eyes shut. His name was Eugene Wainwright.

Papa bound up his chest with tape, cleaned the wounds on his face and called the police. Papa told us later that Eugene had been removed from his father's care and sent to a new home. We never saw him again.

Chapter Three

Libera Me

1910

PAPA HAD ALWAYS been a good driver, whether in a buggy or his Model-T. He took pride in his careful steering and deliberate speed, and avoidance of other vehicles, livestock, or rabbits. He joked about how the rabbits would sit and stare as he drove toward them, then, at the last minute, they would jump away. Possums, squirrels, and raccoons, he always said, were the dumbest of all the small wild animals, because once they started across the road, they were determined to get to the other side, ignoring wheels bearing down on them. He studiously avoided hitting skunks. He'd done that once and it took weeks to clean the stink off his car.

But recently he showed signs of carelessness. His car bumped into the barn door one evening as he was coming home from a house call. We wondered if he'd been drinking. But we knew he wasn't a drinking man. The other thing was that lately he seemed to lose his balance getting up from the dining room table or his favorite easy chair. He wobbled and swayed as he climbed stairs, tightly gripping the banister. We heard him knocking into the walls heading for the bathroom during the night. When Mother asked him about why he had to pee so much during the night, he said impatiently that he was getting older, that's what old men did in the night.

Despite eating large quantities of food at mealtime and snacking in between, he'd steadily lost weight. He gulped down large quantities of water, coffee, and tea. We worried about him, but when anyone said anything about his health, he exploded in irritability. Typical of doctors, I found out later. Nothing can happen to them. They think they're immune from diseases that only afflict patients.

One day he and I were going downtown to pick up Papa's trousers at the tailor shop. They were being taken in at the waist because he'd lost so much weight. He was a fastidious man, and the thought of someone seeing him in baggy, ill-fitting clothes, rankled him.

I walked with him from the house to his car, but he suddenly turned off the path and made a beeline toward a tree. He opened his trousers and relieved himself on the ground. I was surprised and embarrassed, because he'd always been modest about such things.

"I'm sorry, but I had to go real bad," he said. He proceeded to his car, told me to get on in and we went to the tailor shop. He tried on the altered trousers which now fit perfectly. I had to admit he looked better in his taken-in pants. When we got home, we walked past the place he'd peed on the ground and there was a swarm of ants over the area. He stared at this for a few moments. You could tell this was a "Eureka moment." He slapped his forehead, turned to me and said,

"See that, Cyrus? Those ants are feasting on the sugar in my urine. That explains what's been going on with me for weeks-- my weight loss, my hunger, my thirst -- everything. I should have recognized the symptoms of diabetes. I'm a good doctor for others, but not for myself. As an old saying goes, doctors who diagnose and treat themselves have an ass for a doctor and a fool for a patient. I guess I simply didn't want to admit that anything was wrong with me."

I didn't know how to respond to this. In retrospect I'm glad I was ignorant about how serious diabetes was back then, before the discovery of insulin.

Over the next several months Papa continued to practice but he was always exhausted. He went to Dr. Holt, a specialist in Indianapolis. Papa said he tested his urine using a new chemical called Benedict's solution. He said that when Doctor Holt added Benedict's solution to the test tube containing his urine, the mixture turned brick red. Dr. Holt told Papa that was a sure sign he was losing lots of sugar in his urine. Papa told me it was then he knew for sure that he had diabetes. He'd read everything he could get his hands on about it.

Dr. Holt advised a special diet, which Papa followed carefully, but it made little difference. All sorts of things were going wrong. He had more and more trouble reading and as his vision began to fail, he could no longer drive. Now all his patients had to come to the office. Everyone knew that Dr. Lew was sick and dying. Many tears were shed as patients settled their bills at the end of their visits.

In January of 1910, Papa was turning from a patient he'd just examined when he fell against his desk. Mother and I rushed into the room to help him up and I watched, shocked, as she tried to move him onto a chair. Desperate for help, she telephoned Lucille, a neighbor, to come. When she arrived, Papa was unconscious on the floor and the two of them were unable to rouse him. They called Dr. Holmes, one of Papa's closest associates, who took one look and quickly told Mother he needed to go immediately to the hospital in Indianapolis.

There were few ambulances in those days. A hearse was the nearest approximation, so Mr. Reynolds, the local undertaker, was called to take him to Indianapolis, about 100 miles away. We wondered why Mother didn't go with him, but Jack said it was because she wouldn't leave Andrew with anyone else. I couldn't stand still at the door watching our dear Papa being taken away to an uncertain future in the big city hospital. Mother and Jack were pacing around, Andrew was playing on the floor, unaware of how sick Papa was.

Mother rose to the occasion and gathered us in the living room. She was a devout presbyterian, and she had us all bow our heads as she said a prayer. I can't remember what she said in that prayer, but Andrew, Jack and I all cried as she spoke. After the prayer, she told us God would guide us and we should all get to bed, say our own prayers, and be ready for tomorrow. She tucked us all in that night-- the first and only time I can remember being tucked in by her. There we were, thirteen years old, being tucked in by a mother who had paid us little attention until now. I suppose I should have felt thankful, but I didn't. All I could think of was Papa. I was so scared.

Morning came after an uneasy night for both of us. Jack was up first, dressed and in the kitchen. When Andrew and I went down to breakfast, Jack and Mother were talking quietly. As we sat around the table, Mother asked us to put our hands on the table and join them together in a circle. She prayed again and then said,

"During the night, around 2 o'clock, I got a telephone call that Papa died at the hospital. He is with God and Jesus now." She gulped and then closed her eyes for a moment. But then she went on, to tell us the doctors did the best they could. "But diabetes is incurable. Doctor Holt told me he didn't suffer, so that's some comfort. He would want us to carry on with our daily tasks. I will do what I can to make your lives easy, but we'll all miss Papa, each of us in our own way."

I asked Jack what he and Mother were talking about when we came down.

"She said I'd have to get some kind of job to help with expenses," Jack said.

"What about me?" I asked.

"You'll continue in school. I won't."

"Why is that?"

"I don't know why," Jack said, and walked toward the door. "That's just the way it's gonna be. Mother has spoken."

"That's not fair!" I shouted. "If you're gonna go to work, so am I."

"No, you're not. That's that, so there should be no further discussion. And don't ask Mother why. She's upset enough by this."

I was determined, however, to talk with Mother. It wasn't fair to make Jack quit school to work and for me to continue on, as though that was the natural order of things. I waited and picked my time to talk to Mother. It would have to be after the funeral and things had settled down.

Usually, funerals were a few days after a death back then, but Papa's was delayed since his body had to be brought back from Indianapolis and then prepared for burial. We were in deep winter now and that meant that the burial would be delayed even longer until the grave could be dug in frozen ground. Jack and I went back to school while we waited. For Jack it was a doubly sad time. He didn't tell his classmates he wouldn't be coming back to school, and I certainly didn't want to be the messenger of that ugly news.

On the day of the funeral, we dressed in our Sunday School clothes and went to church for services. The minister spoke about the terrible loss of our beloved Dr. Lew being taken from us. He extolled his virtues to a weeping congregation. For us it only made our sadness worse, hearing how much would be missing from our lives.

When the service ended, we got into the undertaker's car with Mother. It was behind the hearse and led a procession of cars and buggies going to the cemetery. There we had to endure more eulogies and watch our precious Papa being lowered into his grave. Each of us was instructed to scatter a handful of icy soil onto his coffin when it settled into place.

Jack was stoic. I was not. I sobbed noisily and Jack gave me an annoyed look. After the funeral, we went home where friends and neighbors brought an abundance of casseroles, cakes, and breads. Some of the friends and neighbors were tearfully hugging my mother, while others were laughing, recounting some of the good times they had with Papa. To me that seemed disrespectful. I would learn as I got older that this behavior was common at funerals. It wasn't dishonoring the deceased, but a complex emotional response to loss, a release of feelings. I guess it was an attempt to accentuate the good times that Dr. Lew had brought into their lives, and maybe that dispelled their own fear of dying.

When they all had gone home, I planned my conversation with Mother.

Chapter Four

What Dreams May Come

1910

SNOW LENT QUIET to the town during night-time. I floated in and out of wakefulness, wandering, lost in a grove of trees with twisted branches and furrowed trunks, waking with a snort, heart pounding against my chest, ringing in my ears. I sat up in bed and looked for Jack. He was not in his bed. Panicked, I jumped up in the dark and bumped into him, staring out the window. He kept me from falling and said,

"Whoa, there brother. Hard to sleep, isn't it? You okay?"

"Bad dreams. What woke you up?"

"Same. Just can't believe this." Jack took a deep breath. "I dreamt Papa walked through our front door, just like he always did, pulled down his pipe from the mantle, stuffed his favorite tobacco into it, lit it with a kitchen match, filled the room with that familiar smell."

"I don't know what we'll do without him," I said, choking on the words.

"Me, neither. It's so hard. Maybe we ought to talk to Reverend Bill. Mother can't help. She has her own sadness to deal with."

"What's Reverend Bill gonna say to make it better? Can't bring him back from the dead, can he?"

"No, course not. But I bet he knows other kids who've lost their pa. Maybe he can tell us how to think about it, so it doesn't hurt so much."

He turned to me.

"You want to sleep with me? Maybe it'll help us both get back to sleep."

"Okay. Good idea."

We got into his bed, pulled covers over us, and the warmth of our two bodies together allowed us to slip back into sleep.

Mother was up early. We smelled bacon cooking and went downstairs to the kitchen in our pajamas. Mother looked at us, saying nothing, motioning us to sit down and eat. After we finished eating fried eggs, bacon, and toast, I lingered while Jack went back upstairs to dress.

"I wanted to talk to you about Jack quitting school to work," I said.

"Well, you may as well know what the real world is all about," she said curtly. "Your father wasn't good about money. Lots of his patients didn't have money, so he gave them free care," she threw her hands in the air, exasperated. "We've always had to live hand-to-mouth. He never put anything aside, didn't carry any life insurance. All we have now is this house, some furniture, his office equipment, and that damned car. So, we have to sell the house, move to something smaller, Jack has to get some kind of job to earn money so we can eat. That's just how it is."

"Well, why only Jack and not me too?"

"Jack knows how to do a lot of things that can make some money. He was learning about your father's profession. Maybe he can get a job with one of the other doctors in town as an apprentice."

"Well, I want to help too. I could get a job too."

"You don't know how to do anything, now do you?" she said with a wry smile. "All you do is read books, dream about faraway places, and play games with your friends." She spoke this all, not directly to me, but into the kitchen air.

It was so hard to hear what she was saying to me. I knew she wasn't interested in Jack or me, but I hadn't thought she really disliked us. I sat there, stupefied, unable to form any words to argue with her. I jumped up from the table, charged out of the room and ran upstairs. Jack was coming down and saw how angry I was.

"Wow, what's goin' on?" he said.

"I can't talk right now," I snapped, but immediately realized this wasn't Jack's fault. I told him what Mother had said to me and yelled out, "I hate her!"

Jack was startled at my outburst, tried to calm me down. "She's upset about Papa. Give her some time and she'll be better."

"That's not it, Jack! She said Papa wasn't good about money and we had to sell this house. I knew she never loved him, and I know she doesn't love us. The only ones she cares about are herself and that damned Andy." I stormed into the bedroom.

Jack followed me. "Look, Cyrus, we're all sad and worried about what comes next. Don't blame Andy for getting her attention. He's kinda different, you know, and maybe he needs her attention more than we do.

"I'm really okay with quitting school, getting a job. I can study at night, keep up with learning, especially if you'll tell me what you're doing in school. And remember, we'll take care of each other."

I looked at Jack and knew what he said about taking care of each other was true. We'd always been close. Now was the time to make sure we stuck together. But I knew what he said about being okay with quitting school and getting a job, was pure balderdash, trying to make me feel less guilty.

As days turned into weeks after Papa died, Jack and I found ways to raise each other up. We went to Reverend Bill because we didn't know what else to do.

"Although death takes away a loved one, it doesn't take away the relationship we had with them," he said. I remembered that.

Jack talked to some doctors in town who knew Papa to see if they would take him on as an apprentice, but they had to take on Papa's patients, leaving no time to oversee and train him. One of them suggested he ask Stanley Baum, our local druggist, if he could give him some work.

Papa had been friends with Mr. Baum. He and the town's doctors played poker together twice a month, and Baum filled prescriptions from all the doctors, despite their illegible handwriting. So, Jack walked into Baum's Apothecary to ask him about working there. Jack told me about how nice Mr. Baum had been to him. He recounted exactly how the conversation had gone.

"I introduced myself and asked him if I could talk to him. I'm sure he wondered what I wanted to say to him, but instead of asking me out there in the store, he showed me into his little office and said he'd be glad to talk to me. He reminded me of the good times he'd played poker with Papa and his friends at our house. He put his arm around me and asked me how our family was doing. I told him we were making it. I was nervous, but after a little while, I told him I'd get straight to the point. I asked him about a job at the drugstore."

Jack told me Mr. Baum didn't answer right away. You could tell he was trying to figure out what I could do.

"He said I was a little young, but he didn't say 'no' right away. He said he'd think about it, to come back tomorrow. I thanked him and as I left, I gave out a big sigh of relief. I was really nervous."

Jack looked at me and said, "I felt better than I have since Papa died, just getting a chance to talk to a nice adult. Can't wait 'til tomorrow to see if he'll take me on."

"Did Mr. Baum talk about how much he might pay you?"

"Well, no, it never got to that."

"Can I go with you tomorrow? I'd like to see the drugstore and meet your possible new boss."

Jack pulled on his ear, considering this. "I don't know, Cyrus. Don't want anything to mess this up. I'll tell you what happens." It was no, without it being said. But anyhow, if he got hired, I could see the drugstore later.

Jack and I heard some commotion in the front yard. When we looked out there was a man pounding a sign into the frozen ground in the middle of our front yard. We ran downstairs to look.

For Sale by Owner the sign read. *Come Get a Tour.* Well, that was sure quick. Things must be worse than she told me, I thought. We went back inside to find Mother.

"A *For Sale* sign is going up in our front yard. You know that?" I asked.

"Of course, I know it," she said in her usual impatient and irritable way. "I told the bank fellow to put it up. We need to plan ahead."

"But if someone wants to buy it, where we gonna live?" Jack asked, and for the first time there was rising anxiety in his voice.

"Cross that bridge when we come to it. It'll take some time to sell this place." Mother turned to go back to the kitchen. "I've got to make dinner now. Come down in a half hour." That was the end of that conversation. We didn't speak of it during a silent dinner.

The next day, Jack got up early, got a bath, put on his best shirt and trousers, and headed to Baum's Drugstore. For his interview, he said. I would've loved to be a fly on the wall for that, but I knew I'd have to wait until Jack got home to find out how it went. When he finally did get home, he was smiling. He grabbed my hand pulling me upstairs to our bedroom.

"I got the job!" he laughed. "Start next Monday! I can't wait. You should see this place. There's a long soda fountain along one wall with round leather-covered stools in front of the counter. There are racks of bottled cures for everything. Carter's Little Liver Pills, Lydia Pinkham's Vegetable Compound, stuff to make hair grow on old men's bald heads, all kinds of things. Mr. Baum works behind a wall making pills, ointments, and elixirs. His wife is cashier and bookkeeper, but I'll be the only other employee. That's what they called me, an employee. I'll be that guy behind the soda fountain with a high white hat and apron when I'm not busy with stocking shelves and arranging a special table he calls his sales platform. That's where he puts different things that appeal to women, you know, like creams to make them look younger, and hair stuff, lipstick, and rouge."

"Wow!' was all I could say. So, he was going to be a working man while I continued school. What was I gonna tell the kids at school?

Mother's prediction that it would take time to sell the house was wrong. She had an offer in a week, from one of the doctors Papa knew. He'd been at our house for dinner and poker games, so he already knew and liked the house. I guess he also figured patients in Papa's practice would keep coming there, so the practice would come with the house.

Jack and I were sad thinking about leaving our house, the only home we'd ever known. We had so many memories and leaving this place was still another loss. Mother, on the other hand, seemed buoyed by the quick sale. Where we would go next was still up in the air. She scoured the newspaper for rentals. Thinking about living in some cramped apartment was a gloomy thought, to say the least. We were used to a big yard, a barn and lots of room inside our house.

Jack fretted about what Mother had in mind about Papa's car. He finally got up enough courage to ask,

"What are you gonna do with the car?" dreading the expected response.

"Sell it. I can't drive so it's no use to me. Besides, we need the money."

"But I could drive it," Jack blurted out. "I'll need some way to get to Baum's for work. Please don't sell it."

"You're too young to drive it."

"There's no law against a thirteen-year-old driving a car! We drive tractors and buggies. Why not a car?" Jack said, feeling more desperate by the minute.

"Because I've decided to sell it, that's why. That's the end of it."

And it was. She told Jack to move the car out to the curb, then she put a *For Sale* sign on it too. He considered refusing to move it, but decided against it. There was no bargaining with Mother. She was in charge of our lives. Everything.

That night Jack and I were in bed with the lights out. I heard Jack sighing over and over.

"What's on your mind?" I asked.

"A lot. I have to quit school, so I'll never be a doctor. And Mother doesn't even say she's sorry for selling the house, the car, our furniture, even the piano, which I was teaching myself to play. And that minister didn't help at all. Where is this so-called God? If there were a God, all this would've never happened. When I saw those patients with Papa, sick and dying people with horrible diseases, it was then I realized there couldn't be a God."

"I'm really sorry," was all I could think of saying. "I miss Papa too, you know, but it wasn't fair you had to quit school and go to work."

"But that's how it is," Jack said. "Now I have to work as a flunky in a drugstore in this backwater town, don't get to learn things I need to know to be like Papa. I'm really angry, sick, and tired of always getting the short end of the stick."

I'd never heard Jack talk this way. He'd always been a rock, accepting whatever came his way. But I realized tonight just how down he was. And I didn't know how to make it better for either of us.

Jack started at Baum's after the weekend. He left early, before I went to school. I still didn't know what I was gonna tell the other kids. When I got to school some boys came and told me they were sorry about my father's passing. I didn't cry once and was proud of that. But when I got home, the first thing I did was go to my room and cry, for a long time. I closed my door, put a sign on it *Keep Out!* because I didn't want Mother to talk to me. I was still really mad at her.

About a week later Mother told us that she'd found a place for us to live. It was across town, in a rundown area, a real change, since we'd lived all our lives in the best part of town. When Jack saw it, he proclaimed, "What a dump!" and flung his cap onto the ground. Mother gave him a sharp look but said nothing. At some level, she must have realized she shouldn't alienate him since he was now "the man of the house" bringing home a paycheck. She didn't care one whit what I thought. Andrew just watched and went on playing with his trucks.

We moved at the end of the month after selling the house, most of our furniture, and the car. We kept our beds, the kitchen table and chairs, but that's about it. We knew this was an awful comedown in our lives, on the heels of losing Papa. Jack and I went back to our minister, who tried again to help us get through this. Jack mostly ignored what he said.

Little Andrew didn't seem to understand anything of this. He seemed to be in a world of his own. Jack and I left him alone. Maybe this was not good for him, but we had no extra energy for our strange little brother. Besides, he had Mother nearly all to himself during this time. We never could figure out why she favored him over us.

One night after we moved, Jack was muttering to himself as he was trying to sleep.

"I can't hear you. What?" I said.

"I can't sleep, thinking about how different life is now that Papa is gone. I hate it here. Walking to the drugstore takes almost an hour. If she hadn't sold the car, I could be driving it there. I miss school and all my friends. And Mother is getting more far away every day. What's wrong with her?"

"I don't know. I've noticed it too. She must be worried and lonely. Andrew's been acting up too. I don't think he understood what death was, and now he's confused about everything -- no Papa, new place to live, Mother a mess. He's with her all the time, too. That's gotta be hard. Maybe we ought to try to play with him more and get him interested in something."

I raised up on my elbow to look at Jack. "So, how's the drugstore job?"

"Oh, the work is okay. I'm learning a lot about stock and selling stuff. Mr. Baum is really nice. I like him a lot. But it's not like school. I miss my old buddies. I miss seeing you, too. Could you come down to the store sometime? I'd like to show you what I'm doing."

"I miss you too. I'd love to come to the store someday after school. What's a good time?"

"Anytime is okay. I'll introduce you to Mr. Baum."

"Thanks Cyrus. Now maybe we can sleep."

Chapter Five

Let Me Call You Sweetheart

1911

TIME SEEMS TO HAVE a way of getting away from you. It was quite a while before I went to Baum's to see what Jack did there. But when I finally went, there was Jack, busy arranging bottles on a shelf. He stopped what he was doing, smiled, and came over, grabbed my arm.

"I wanna introduce you to Mr. Baum." He tapped on the Dutch door that led to a room where Mr. Baum compounded the pills and elixirs. Soon it opened and this friendly guy stepped out. He was not much taller than I, had a little paunch, wore his spectacles down at the end of his nose and had a gold tooth that gleamed when he spoke.

"So, you're Jack's brother, eh? I saw you at your house during poker parties. I sure miss those." His wife, who was working in a room behind the pharmacy, saw me, smiled, and came over to greet me.

"I'm Mrs. Baum, glad to know you, Cyrus. We sure like having Jack here. I understand you're twins, but you don't look a bit alike. Both handsome, of course," she said with a blush, "but different. Is Jack going to show you around?"

"Yes, I've been hearing so much about this place I wanted to see it for myself."

After this introduction Jack led me around the store. As he showed me the soda fountain, a couple of girls came in.

"Hi Reba, Maybelle," Jack said. "You want your usual chocolate milkshakes?"

"That chocolate milkshake is just what I'd like," said Reba, smiling and winking at Jack. Both girls were sparkling with life, and clearly becoming young women.

"Hi there, you work here too?" Maybelle said to me.

"No, just visiting my brother," hoping my blush was not obvious.

"This is my brother, Cyrus," Jack said, trying to shield me from further embarrassment. "These two young ladies are Reba and Maybelle." I smiled and nodded to them, trying not to appear interested in them. Then, Jack stepped behind the counter and made a big show of putting on his apron and hat before he began scooping ice cream into a metal container, tossing in rich cream and other "secret ingredients," as he put it. Then he pushed the cannisters under the mixer. Moments later, with a flourish, he presented the milkshakes to the girls.

"Thank you, Jackie," Maybelle cooed as Reba looked away.

I was astounded. Jack hadn't told me anything about his secret social life. These girls were in different classes in our school, so this was the first time I'd seen them. Then Jack excused himself to continue showing me around.

"You didn't tell me about your girlfriends," I whispered.

"They're NOT my girlfriends, just friends," he snapped. "So just watch it." I couldn't help but laugh at my brother's embarrassment.

"Okay, so Maybelle and I are interested in each other. But we haven't done anything," he whispered, then he burst out laughing. "I don't tell you everything that happens in my life."

"Well, here I am, feeling sorry for you since you can't go to school and you have this hidden life, wild women chasing you, and all I have is books and classes. Some deal!"

"Just don't tell Mother!"

Several days later Jack asked me if I would like to go with him, Maybelle, and Reba, to the "Red Mill." The local nickelodeon was called that because it was built as a replica of a Dutch windmill, painted red. For five cents you could watch a "flicker," since hand-cranked projectors made the pictures jitter on the screen. People flocked to watch these silent movies, usually watching Max Sennett films, like Keystone

Kops, and other slapstick comedies. Other movies were accompanied by a piano player sitting in an otherwise deserted orchestra pit, grinding out music, if you could call it that, supposedly to mesh with vaudevillian silliness or melodrama on the screen.

"Sure, I'd love to come. Does Reba know I'm gonna be her 'date?' I'd hate to spring that on an unsuspecting girl."

"Yeah, it's all arranged. We knew you'd want to come. And Reba thinks you're cute!"

We had an awkward time at the Red Mill. I did hold hands with Reba during the "flicker," but Jack was doing more than that with Maybelle. So, I concluded Maybelle could be considered his girlfriend. Turned out, their romance was short-lived, but at least Jack had some experience for when he went to Washington, D.C. More about that later.

Chapter Six

When My Ship Comes Sailing Home

1914-1915

I GOT A JOB delivering newspapers shortly after Jack started at Baum's. I delivered papers in early morning, and still got to school on time. When summer came, I cut lawns, getting 50 cents for front lawns and 25 cents for back lawns. Not much, but I felt better contributing at least something to the family treasury.

Mother did thank me, being a little more relaxed now that time had gone by since Papa died.

I felt really grown-up, reading newspapers before I tossed them onto porches. Each morning I'd scan headlines, and if they grabbed me, I'd read the whole column. It was 1914 and war in Europe was always frontpage fare. Even though battles were happening far away, I tried to keep up and understand the progression of events "over there."

Newspapers described the threat posed to four archaic ruling dynasties in Europe by commoners. The paper said these rulers were so self-absorbed they lost track of their countrymen, paying no attention to people who worked the fields and did everyday jobs to make their countries tick. But now these ordinary people were stirring to life, agitating all over the continent. Abe Lincoln once said, "God must love the common man because He made so many of them."

As months passed into years, I followed these events with great interest. Jack, however, was always dismissive of the news and refused to talk about it. "It's a problem we can't do anything about. Europeans have been fighting amongst themselves forever." At school, though, things were different. Students had spirited arguments, some advocating for going into the war, others strongly arguing we should stay out. I was a star in these discussions because I'd read the news each day before any of the others knew what was going on. My position was always to avoid getting into war.

One morning in 1914, as I was packing my canvas newspaper bag, a frontpage headline immediately caught my eye:

*Assassin's Bullets Kill Archduke Ferdinand
and Wife in Sarajevo*

At the library I found out that Archduke Ferdinand was heir to the throne in Austria. The newspaper article explained that by this act the assassin and his political clique sent Austria a blunt message: stop annexing Southern Slav provinces. They insisted these provinces should be part of Yugoslavia. As it turned out, this assassination would begin a chain of events that evolved into the World War.

Talking with Jack about impending war usually was one-sided. His attitude was representative of prevailing public opinion: getting into foreign entanglements was not part of the American dream. Wars like this were one of the things our ancestors had come to this country to avoid, he said, long-standing blood feuds that led to war and killed thousands of innocent people.

President Wilson said repeatedly that he'd keep the United States out of this "foreign war," gaining approval of most Americans who were averse to involvement in a fight in which they had no apparent stake. But after he was re-elected in 1916, he changed his tune. By the end of 1917 the US entered the war. On December 4, 1917 the first 5,000 troops left aboard the George Washington troop ship for Europe. But I'm getting ahead of myself again.

~~~

In summer of 1915, Jack saw an ad from Goodyear Tire and Rubber Company recruiting young men to be trained in the art of salesmanship. He applied for this, not expecting anything to come of it. A week later, an official-looking letter bearing the return address of Goodyear Tire and Rubber Company, Akron, Ohio, dropped through our mail-slot.
~~~

We've reviewed your application and are pleased to offer you a position for training in our sales department. Please respond no later than ten days from receipt of this letter.

"Cyrus, can you believe it? Here I am, an eighteen-year-old high school dropout, being offered a job with Goodyear, this huge important company. I'm gonna reply right away, not let this chance pass me by."

He sat down that night and wrote his acceptance letter. He was blinded by exhilaration and didn't know what this might mean in his life.

"How can I tell the Baums? I'm not even sure when the training begins. I'll wait a while before I talk to them. They've been so good to me. I feel guilty even thinking about leaving them."

When he got word that the training would begin the first week of the following month, he was stunned and thrilled at the same time. He dreaded speaking with the Baums, but he needn't have been. Jack said Mr. Baum was delighted that he got hired by Goodyear. He told Jack how much he and his wife had enjoyed having him at the store, that he had too much going for him to be only a soda jerk and stock-boy.

"Mrs. Baum had tears in her eyes when she said it was great news and she couldn't be happier for me. She also told me how much they'd miss me, that I was like the son they never had. That almost made me cry, too.

"She threw her arms around me and hugged me. I was touched, surprised and relieved," Jack said.

Before Jack left for his job-training, I graduated high school and got a job with the newspaper, not as a delivery boy, but working in the "big room" with reporters, writers, and editors. The room really pitched and rolled with all the phone calls, people running around yelling at each other and incessant clatter of typewriters. This is the life I dreamed about since I started delivering papers. I was now sure I wanted to be a journalist.

~~~

As Jack prepared to leave for Goodyear, my emotions were in a tangle. I felt selfish being sorry to see him go, happy for his opportunity, and scared, all at the same time. I knew life would be different for both of us. He and I had become inseparable after Papa's death.

Just before he climbed into the Greyhound bus with *WASHINGTON, D.C.* emblazoned above the windshield, we embraced and wept quietly. I have to admit I was a little jealous, but mostly I was glad he was getting this chance.

"I don't know how we can have singing at home without your baritone anchoring us," I said as he
~~~

shoved his bag onto the top step of the bus. I looked at him anew now that he was going away.

A handsome fellow, I thought. Standing almost six feet tall, a slender but strong frame, dark brown hair combed straight back from his forehead, blazing blue eyes that held on to yours as he regarded you. Those eyes were wide-spaced over his straight narrow nose, with bow-lips below. His chin had a single dimple in its middle. His clean-shaven face suggested a serious demeanor.

"I'll miss that too, but we'll find time later to sing together. You'll see. We'll sing "Sweet Adeline" better than ever!" With that hopeful declaration, Jack scurried into the bus before tears came again, for both of us.

About a week after he left, I got his first letter.

September 14, 1915

Dear Cyrus,

The lead teacher in this boot camp for us future aggressive hawkers was an over-enthusiastic former drill sergeant named Chester Cummings. Two hundred fifty pounds, at least, football player at 'Bama,' his feverish delivery was so offensive that I wondered what I'd gotten myself into.

I considered quitting, but what else was I going to do? So, I'm sticking it out.

How're you doing? Ever see Maybelle or Reba? Say hello if you do. I ought to write to Maybelle. Tell

Mother I'm doing well and will send some money as
soon as I get paid.
Love,
    Jack

As someone whose first love is language, I was impressed with his vocabulary. He'd always absorbed information rapidly. What he missed by not going to high school he made up for at night at home alone. He spent hours reading Shakespeare and poetry by English and Irish writers, things those of us getting a "proper education" at school had not even begun to study.

I wondered if there were some way for him to get a high school diploma so he wouldn't be discriminated against. He was smarter and more well-educated than anyone in my class.

His letters came less frequently as he finished his training. His first assignment to develop a territory in Bloomington, Indiana, started in a few weeks. I realized one of the reasons he'd been hired, despite his age and lack of formal education: he was a home-grown Hoosier, would fit in and understand the locals. He was also a guy who could talk a dog off a meat truck, a natural born salesman. He made friends easily, had a great sense of humor, and a laugh that shook his whole body.

December 15, 1915

Dear Cyrus,

I love Bloomington. I'm staying in a room and board place downtown. It's cheap and the food passable. It beats having to cook, buy groceries, and this way I don't have to buy pots, pans, silverware, and plates.

The best news is the company is giving me a car to use! A model T just like the one Papa used to have. It's not new, but it's in pretty good shape. Now all I have to do is whip up business for tires in this area, find a store for rent and set up a dealership. No problem, eh? It's sure better than being in training. But I'll say this for Cummings and the training: I'm prepared to do this job and I'm going to do my best.

I've already made some friends here at the boarding house, a couple of guys from Evansville, working in town. We've already been out to some local bars. Don't tell Mother, but I've started to smoke, too. Camels. Took me a while to get used to it, but now I really enjoy smoking. Calms me down and gives me something to do with my hands when I'm in a conversation.

My address is 2011 Linden Street, Bloomington, Indiana. Drop me a line when you can. Say hello to Mother and Andrew for me. Also, Maybelle and Reba.
Love,
Jack

Chapter Seven

Since We've Met

1916

February 10, 1916

Dear Cyrus,

I've opened the first tire store here and so far, there's been little interest from people in town. That will change soon, I'm sure.

The big news is that I met a young lady. Her name is Sarah Griffiths. She's a voice student at Indiana University.

I can't think of words to describe Sarah, but I'll try. She has thick brunette hair, worn down to her shoulders, wavy and shiny. Her eyes match her hair color, dark brown, and they light up her face, always smiling. She's about five and half feet tall, slender, shapely (you know what I mean!) and has a low and mellow speaking voice. Which is funny, since her singing voice is soprano with a high range. I'm going to her recital next weekend and will tell you how it goes.

She'd fit right into our family singing sessions. I hope I won't embarrass her with my amateur piano playing, but I hope she and I can sing some old favorites together. When you visit me, I'll introduce her. I know you'll love her almost as much as I do. And brother--no cutting in on this gal!
Love,
Jack

~~~

March 15, 1916

Dear Jack,

Got your letter. So glad you've met Sarah. She sounds great. I promise I'll not try to woo her! Of course, if she just naturally falls in love with me at first sight, there's nothing I can do about it!

I have some time off next month. Would a visit then be possible?
Love,
Cyrus

~~~

March 25, 1916

Dear Cyrus,

Next month is perfect. I've moved into my own apartment so you can stay here. I'll pick you up at the bus station. My new address is 6018 Elder Street. I have a telephone! Number is AV 7110
Love,
Jack

~~~

"Welcome to Bloomington!" Jack boomed when I stepped off the bus. "Sarah's in the car and dying to meet you. We're going to our favorite restaurant. How're you feeling?"

"Fantastic. So good to see you," I said as we hugged. "I'm hungry as a horse, so I'm glad we're gonna eat soon."

We walked to the car and there was Sarah, looking just as Jack had described her, but better. Her smile looked as if she would break into song any moment. Her slender body slid out of the car gracefully, and I was soon enfolded in her arms, to my surprise and pleasure.

"I've heard so much about you, Cyrus, I feel like I know you already. Jack's so excited to have you here." She paused, drawing back to examine me. "It's true, you two don't look like twins, even brothers, but both of you are so good-looking!" Sarah said, laughing.

I could see why Jack was so in love with this stunning creature. She was guileless, so open, and warm. Her brown eyes sparkled as we sipped wine and gobbled up spaghetti and meatballs. After dinner we went to Jack's apartment. He offered cigarettes and we both declined, Sarah citing her singing voice as the reason, and I just said I wasn't a smoker.

"Tell me about yourself," I stammered to Sarah, unused to small talk with attractive young women.
~~~

"Well, not much to tell. I was born in Oakland City, Indiana, grew up with my younger sister Minnie, went to Miss Doherty's Girls High School. There I sang in the choir and was lucky to have lessons from the head of music. She recommended me for IU School of Music and here I am, majoring in voice. With a scholarship!"

"What kind of singing?"

"Basic voice training first, then we can specialize in opera or concert or pop. I'm singing all of them now, trying to figure out what's best for my voice and style."

"So, are you gonna be an opera diva?" I asked.

"Probably not. Opera consumes a person. I'd have to learn different languages.

"Besides, I'd like to have a family someday. I like to do so many other things besides singing. Outdoors things, gardening, and I love to work with fabric, needles, and thread."

"You should see how well she sews," Jack chimed in. "She made the curtains you see here, and that couch--see that slipcover--she made that. Fits like it was tailored for that sofa. Well, come to think of it, it was. She did it with her Singer sewing machine. Pardon the pun!"

Sarah seemed like everybody's girl next door. With a lot of talent, apparently, if the head of music advocated for her and she got a scholarship. But it was clear she wanted a full life, boding well for her relationship with Jack. I hope he doesn't blow it.

Typical brother's reaction, knowing your brother's faults.

We spent the rest of the weekend getting acquainted and then I heard her sing. Boy, was she ever good! Her high notes were clear, not vibrato, her breathing and phrasing impeccable. I couldn't see her singing popular tunes, or opera, but could imagine her as soloist for oratorios, choral groups, and church choirs. She'd be in high demand, not only for her superb voice, but her demeanor and beauty.

Chapter Eight

Over There, Over There

1916-1918

AFTER WRITING A thank-you note to Jack and Sarah, the first of many I'd send to them, I felt duty-bound to bring my brother up to date on current affairs since he kept blinders firmly tied on when regarding the world beyond the shores of America.

June 18, 1916

Dear Jack and Sarah,

Thanks for the lovely visit to your home. It was wonderful meeting you, Sarah, hearing you sing, and getting to know you. I hope this is the first of many such visits.

Jack, I suspect you haven't heard about our border war with Mexico since you don't read newspapers. This guy Pancho Villa is raising a ruckus at the American-Mexico border. All the girls are in love with him, he's so dashing and romantic. It's said that Villa's doing this to tease Wilson into a war. My guess is that Wilson, like any politician, will send troops down there to put a stop to this nonsense. Pancho has already gotten into New Mexico, and we can't have that. I think this will be a short little border war and we'll win it.

The other topic everyone in the newsroom is talking about is the Battle of Verdun in France. It's been going on for a few weeks now with no signs of abating. Trench warfare must be horrible. There are reports of rats scurrying around in trenches, gut and respiratory infections, and malnutrition in addition to the usual casualties of battle. Burial of the dead is delayed, and the stench of rotting bodies has to be overwhelming. I hope this ends soon.

Sorry to dwell on the ugliness of war, but that's what I'm reading and writing about each day in the newsroom.

Hope to hear from you soon.

Love,

Cyrus

~~~

Only a few short notes came from Jack over the next six months, and I assumed the reasons mainly were his love affair with Sarah, and his work which was going full speed ahead.

News of the war preyed heavily on my mind. The Battle of Verdun turned into a cataclysm, dragging on for almost a full year, with French and German
~~~

casualties each reaching nearly 400,000, ending with the failure of the German offensive. The very definition of a stalemate and a short-lived Pyrrhic victory for France.

Jack was prophetic about war in Europe. Both sides were losing large numbers of men in the flower of youth, and many civilians were caught up in these battles. Wilson, running for re-election, has been saying he's against entering the war, but some accuse him of politically motivated hesitation. He's reflecting popular opinion since most news accounts indicate little stomach for war.

In March 1917, Wilson took the oath for his second term. A month before, the Germans resumed their U-boat attacks in the North Atlantic, and we severed diplomatic relations with Germany. In April, Wilson, now secure in his re-election and out of patience with recent German behavior, declared war on Germany, sharply reversing his previous position of neutrality. By May, Congress passed the Selective Service Act, which authorized conscription of young men into the armed services.

Jack and I were sitting ducks for conscription. Jack went into the Marine Corps, sent first to Quantico Virginia for basic training. Then he was sent to Paris Island (Jack called it "Devil's Island") near Beaufort, South Carolina, for "advanced training," a euphemism for instruction in more effective ways of killing people. This was in late 1918, towards what turned out to be the end of the war. But our service was extended well into 1919.

I got pulled into the Army. After basic training, they discovered my writing skills and assigned me to a desk job in Washington. That suited me just fine. I had no desire to be cannon fodder. My only regret about being sent to Washington was that I missed out on living with Jack when he was working here for Goodyear.

His overseas duty was distinctly more unpleasant than mine. I sure didn't envy him and worried the whole time he was in Europe. Even though the politicians declared a cease-fire shortly after he got to France, his service went on and on. First, he landed in the western part of Brittany in a town called Brest, where many of the American troops disembarked. His journal entries about his time in the Marines were often laced with quotations from his inveterate reading. He kept these notes in a scrap book that got increasingly battered while in Europe.

Chapter Nine

Jack's War Journal

October 19, 1918

Sailed for France on the Pocahontas from Hoboken. The Pocahontas was a captured German vessel, so we changed her name to sound more American.

Before going aboard, we were well fed with sandwiches, cakes and coffee given out by the Red Cross. This was the climax of ten weeks strenuous training on Paris Island, the place God forgot.

From Oct. 19 to Nov. 3, 1918, we zigzagged our way across the Atlantic, keeping a keen outlook for submarines and other enemy craft. Each day became more monotonous and brought with it an undue load of unpleasant experiences. We lived more like animals than humans.

On Sunday morning November 3d, we sighted land and things began to take on a new light. In a few hours we would set foot on the soil of La Belle France and when we landed about noon, we were in Brest.

We were immediately taken to a Rest Camp about four kilometers outside of the city limits.

As my anxiety rose, I thought of a quotation from Shakespeare's **King Henry V:**

"O God of battles, steel my soldiers' hearts.

Possess them not with fear; take from them now the sense of reckoning, if the opposed numbers pluck their hearts from them."

Nov 4, 1918

With heavy rain, wet blankets, and the ground to sleep on, our outlook was dark. But we soon adjusted to these changes, except those who took sick. Regular military routine was followed, with plenty of police work to keep us busy. Nothing to eat but gruel.

November 11, at the 11th hour:

Magic news came that the armistice had been signed. What would that mean for me? Not much.

Nov. 17th,1918

Passed through Verdun today. Terrible results of shell fire. Miles of trenches, dugouts, and camouflaged roads.

I thought of more Shakespeare, King Henry IV:

"What is honour? A word... Who hath it?

He that died on Wednesday? Doth he feel it?

No. Therefore I'll have none of it.

Honour is a mere scutcheon."

Nov. 19, 1918

We marched all day. I somehow got separated from my company, but I found and rejoined them about 3 hours later. I was lucky to draw a hayloft to sleep in.

Nov. 20, 1918

Crossed line into Belgium. Arrived in Arlon about 8 PM. Billeted in Monastery.

Nov. 22, 1918

Marched all day and entered Luxembourg in the evening. I was now permanently attached to the 74th Infantry Company of the 6th Regiment Marines.

Nov. 28, 1918

Thanksgiving. Ate a Thanksgiving meal of corned beef and coffee at 3 o'clock.

Dec 8, 1918

Marched 42 kilometers and Landed in Ahrweiler, a pretty town, many restaurants, about 6 o'clock. A billet over wine distillery. Had beaucoup wine.

Dec 13, 1918

Reveille at 2 AM. We crossed the Rhine River at Linz and were billeted in Höningen for two days.

Jan 1, 1919

Slept the old year out. No sunshine. Everybody anxious to get home.

Jan. 2, 1919

Same damn thing as yesterday- rain and slop. Meals rotten as ever.

Jan. 5, 1919

Sabbath day in Hunland. It seems more like judgment day in a penitentiary. The Marine Corps is a good place for mules and other beasts of burden. If one has the tactics of a pickpocket or the talent of a magician, he might get a meal. If a plate of their gruel doesn't turn your stomach, it might make a good starter for that long-lost thing called a meal. The Marine Corps is a wonderful organization, according to their publicity agents.

Jan. 7, 1919

A full stomach would do lots toward making a man feel optimistic. Only the officers are allowed the privilege of feeling that way. According to newspapers, we're having a picnic in Germany. One hell of a picnic.

Jan. 10, 1919

Marched 14 K. to the machine gun emplacements. We stood by with frozen toes and empty bellies till his Majesty, the Major, inspected. After an insufficient meal, I went on guard.

Jan 11, 1919

I stood guard 1–5 AM but there was no relief in evening, so I stood more guard.

The Corps loosened up and actually sold 1 piece of Lind chocolate to each man who was first on the scene. The rest were out of luck.

I wish we could send sealed letters home. Newspaper men, who know as much about our condition as a hog knows about autocracy, show our plight to the people through rose-colored glasses. My sins have been many, but none so great as to deserve the punishment of time in the Marine Corps. Even criminals are allowed luxuries in a penitentiary.

Jan. 12, 1919

Another Sabbath. It seems that the gods frown on this country once a week on Sunday, for good reason. Some of these simple square heads still believe "Deutschland is Uber Alles!"

Nations are just like people--one is jealous of the other. Even after Germany is whipped, I suppose the Allies will fight it out among themselves in order to see who deserves most credit in the great struggle.

England is already jealous of the fact that America expects to have a navy as large as theirs.

Jan. 14, 1919

We missed drills today, much to my surprise and pleasure. For breakfast today we had three 1-inch cubes of beef for breakfast and 1 two-inch cube beef, spoonful of spuds for dinner. Gruel for dinner. The entire amount would not be equal to a square meal.

Jan 21, 1919

Still look forward to going home. Homesickness falls far short in describing our desire to get back. If Germany were the only country on earth, I would end my ancestral chain in the morning.

If outpost were our only duties, this life would be partly bearable. At last, my stomach was filled. Filled twice since Sunday.

Jan 22, 1919

Stood guard 11–1 AM. Had chocolate and lemon drops last night!!! Breakfast disappointing–the pancake batter refused to take shape of pancakes.

Home is the only subject attracting immediate attention. It's a darn good subject but just discussing doesn't bring it any nearer. The "Atlantic Cross" is the only decoration much coveted at present.

Never again will I refuse to eat "the rest of my pie" because the crust is tough. Anyway, we owe thanks to "spuds" and boiled meat.

Jan 24, 1919

Stood guard again. This is getting damned tiresome. Reminds me once more of Willie:

'Tomorrow and tomorrow and tomorrow,
Creeps in this petty pace from day to day,
To the last syllable of recorded time,
And all our yesterdays have lighted fools the way to dusty death.'

-William Shakespeare, Macbeth

Feb. 2-9, 1919

The stove was removed from the Brig on Feb 8. Another example of awkward attempts at military discipline. Quite consistent with democratic ideals!

While an investigation of the war department is taking place, a closer investigation of these little things could become a subject for discussion among the voters of America. A fair number of voters are here, and I think a lively discussion is taking place. There will be no blind casting of votes when they return. A society for the suppression of everything military would be endorsed by large numbers.

The war was won by fighters, not soldiers. If everybody had gone over the top in step and parade ground formation, the burial detail would still be busy. Instead, they went over to the cadence of machine guns.

Feb 10, 1919

Getting an average of four hours sleep nightly. The temperature is Zero and no fire except between the hours of 10–11 and 5–7. It' hardly soothing to frozen feet to be told 'This life will make either a man or a bum of you.'

What is the measure of a man? It must be his ability to withstand physical hardships.

Feb. 11, 1919

Passed another miserable night-watch. Breakfast this day was greasy gravy, a piece of bacon and a slice of bread. If we were training for a purpose, it would be interesting. But the war is over, why not go home?

Feb. 16

Haven't heard from home yet.

Feb. 18

Byer got sick. Fainted away in door of Sick Bay.

Feb. 28

Bath day. Heard from home, from Reba and Maybelle. Homesick as hell.

Mar 3

Wrote home to Brownie and Maybelle. When are we going home? The last letter I had from home was October 8th, 1918.

Mar 20

Company excused from drill on account of sore arms. Who will help us understand that our wonderful government fosters such an organization as the Marine Corps?

Mar 25

Started on leave with six others from the company. Went to Battalion Headquarters and heard a few hundred lectures on venereal diseases and prophylactics. After the inevitable wait in line for three or four hours we were loaded in trucks and went to Coblenz. There we had another lecture on venereal diseases and marched halfway across Germany to 2d Division barracks.

That night we spent two or three hours in line but were finally assigned to a third-class compartment on a German train. We slept in 'blanket hammocks, hat racks, seats and on the deck. After two days we arrived in Aix-les-Bains and were given a couple of dozen more lectures on venereal diseases and prophylactics.

Finally, we were given rooms at the Folliet. We celebrated the first night with Benedictine cognac.

Sleep, eats, and sight-seeing consumed the remainder of the time until we started back to Germany.

Apr. 12

The subject of going home is becoming more serious each week. Like dogs, we are denied information which would lead us to believe our return will come to pass within the next five years. To make a world safe for democracy requires more work than simply the overthrow of autocracy.

Just a word about the principles of an officer who will force a man to wash a ration wagon with a toothbrush. Another word about that same officer who will deprive a man of his liberties and privilege of shows because he refused to belong to a Fraternal Divisional Organization.

It was plainly stated that membership was not compulsory and because this officer was deprived a 100% membership sheet, he used the overbearing authority given him by the government to avenge himself. Surely there is justice somewhere for such cases as this. But where?

The question is, how did such derelicts, bums, and illiterates as these ever gain admission to ranks of commissioned officers? Why are they trusted with the liberties, privileges, and rights of the enlisted man? Why are they allowed to say to the enlisted men, "You have absolutely nothing to say, I can charge you with anything that I choose, and you have no protection whatever. My word goes."

Where does the old theory that 'all men are born free and equal' carry any weight? I cannot connect my early teachings of democratic ideals with militarism. Who is to blame? Not the government, surely. The men elected to run the affairs of the government are to fault. It must be them.

Apr. 22

Got a whole night's sleep. Hurrah! Aside from waking up five or six times because of cramps due to lack of springs and mattress it was a great night. There is one advantage of being on guard. You are awakened for a watch before the bunk has a chance to get hard.

Ran the 880-yard dash this morning. Of course, in hobnails there were quite a few who broke world's record. These athletics remind me of playing billiards on a cushionless table.

I took my third degree in extra police duty this morning. Our commanding officer is becoming more considerate. He called only one man a son of a bitch this morning. Secretary Daniels came thru our section last Sunday.

In one of the Infantry companies, a platoon of men was detailed to sit and read, write, and smoke. The object was, of course, to convey to the Secretary an impression that the boys are living on the velvet, enjoying life, and hoping that the Army of Occupation will be a permanent thing. Just remove the censorship or interview any of the boys personally and facts will be uncovered. Impressions are mighty fine for a little while, but facts are the only things which can't be removed.

~~~

When I finished reading his journal I was overwhelmed by Jack's complaining. After all, he was never in combat, not in real danger. But then I realized that he had witnessed firsthand the ghastly carnage of this war.

He took grim and horrifying pictures of dead bodies at Verdun, Somme, and other battlefields. His was a realistic assessment of egregious behaviors of some military officers. He experienced profound loneliness and bullying by officers leaving him embittered. He admitted he had it much better than many who lost their lives or had been seriously wounded. He survived without injury or disease. But he returned to the states a different person. Once home, Jack never talked about his time in the service. But his journal spoke volumes.
~~~

Chapter Ten

Here Comes the Bride

1919

JACK AND I MUSTERED out of military life in the summer of 1919. We got together in Bloomington to plot our next moves. Neither of us had a job and we were getting desperate. Mustering-out pay was meager, soon to run out for both of us. Jack wrote to Goodyear trying to get his old job back, but he hadn't heard back. I was looking for something with a newspaper and contemplated going to IU journalism school.

"I'm staying in Bloomington as long as I can," Jack told me. "Sarah's here, finishing her studies. I don't know what's up with Goodyear. They praised the hell out of me when I worked for them before. After serving in the Marines, you'd think there'd be a break for veterans." He sighed, looked down into his coffee cup. We'd met at a local greasy spoon for breakfast. My eyes stung from dense cigarette smoke as we sipped our too-hot watery coffee.

"Guess lots of guys back from the war are looking for work, so I know I'm not alone, but I'm getting pissed off," he said. "I'll never be able to marry Sarah if this doesn't change. The other thing is, it's really hard to find a decent drink with this damned prohibition crap."

"As Mr. Micawber said, something will turn up," I said. Jack scoffed and I realized how down he was. He lit another cigarette, rose from the table and headed for the door. "Let's find a place to live and go from there," I called to his departing back. "I applied for a job as a stringer at the Bloomington Herald. Hope that comes through."

"Sarah may be able to help us find a cheap rental," Jack said, turning around to face me, recovering a little from his gloom. "She's been here since before the war, knows her way around. She's staying in a rental room near the U with a nice family."

"Speaking of Sarah," Jack said, "I met her folks. Her dad's okay. Her mother seems not to like me very much. Guess she thinks I'm not good enough for Sarah. Maybe I'm not. Sarah's gonna graduate from IU and I'm a high school dropout with no future, no money, no prospects." He lit another cigarette. "But I'm crazy about her, want to marry her. Haven't asked her yet, but I think she knows I will. I feel like she loves me, but you never know. Since you don't have a girlfriend, you probably don't understand this."

What I did understand was how unhappy he was. I wished I had someone to love as much as he loved Sarah. But right now, it didn't seem to be in the cards.

Goodyear continued to be unresponsive, so Jack took a job in a drugstore. Back to that. He was sore about losing out at Goodyear, but at least he got paid something. I got a low-paying job with the *Herald*, so by pooling our two puny incomes we could afford a boarding house. We got bikes to get around.

Back at newspaper work, I followed news headlines with great interest:

Women Get Right to Vote

Plenty of shaking of heads (male heads, of course) about how the "republic was going to hell in a handbasket, the next thing you'd know they'll put women in charge of things, they'll go to medical schools, become lawyers, run for Congress, all very dangerous for this country" (of white men).

18th Amendment Implemented
Volstead Act Now Active in All States

Jack didn't like this one. He'd acquired a taste for wine and brandy in France. It wasn't until later that prohibition gave birth to a new brand of gangsterism: rum-running and bootlegging. Stills in backwoods became a cottage industry and sites of conflict between the feds and those who ran these little factories for alcohol.

War To End All Wars Officially Over

The Treaty of Versailles in June 1919 officially ended the World War. The treaty assigned blame for all losses and damages incurred in the war to Germany and ordered it to pay huge reparations.

President Wilson Suffers Major Stroke
Massive stroke leaves him paralyzed.

Wilson's illness left the League of Nations issue in limbo.

In sports, the Chicago "Black Sox" scandal left baseball fans disgusted, and finally, just after Christmas, the sale of Babe Ruth to the New York Yankees was the unkindest cut of all for Boston Red Sox fans.

About then, right in the middle of all that bad news, was when Jack finally heard back from Goodyear. He got his old job back, that was the good news. It would also allow him to marry Sarah. The not so good news came in the form of Goodyear's dispatching him to develop a new territory in Warsaw, Indiana.

"Well, this is providential for you," I told him, trying to put the best face on this development. "Now you can marry the woman you love, move to Warsaw as newlyweds, start a new life, say goodbye forever to drugstore life, and get rich with a big tire company."

My real feeling about his move was that I'd miss him a lot. Sure, his getting married would have changed our lives anyhow, but their living in a different town would return me to World War loneliness. It drove my decision to enroll in the IU journalism school. Tuition was minimal for in-state residents. Since I'd saved some money and had taken several courses at IU already, I could live in the dorm, take accelerated courses and graduate in a couple of years.

Before Jack went to Warsaw, a group of our new-found friends ushered in the "roaring twenties" at a New Year's Eve party. Sarah got permission from her landlords, who were away on vacation, to have a party in the house where she lived. We'd promised to be responsible and not tear up the house. Since prohibition was now in effect, Jack found some bootlegged booze (called "bathtub gin") and rationed it out to the assembled guests, most of whom were friends of Sarah.

Right after midnight, Jack rose to offer a toast.

"Here's to a glorious new year."

The small crowd of twenty howled approval.

"And here's to my fiancé, Sarah Griffiths."

The crowd sent up an even louder cheer. Sarah blushed, I choked up and joined everyone hugging them.

To Sarah's relief, we didn't trash the house, but neighbors probably thought we had, considering the noise spilling out. That New Year's Eve in Bloomington Indiana would remain a treasured memory for years to come.

~~~

Jack and Sarah's wedding took place in the First Presbyterian Church in Oakland City, where Sarah had been baptized twenty-two years earlier. She was being married by that same minister. The service seemed to take forever, cementing my resolution not to have a church service if I ever got married. This resolve was embedded in male misperception that a groom had any say at all in that decision.

The service and reception were obsessively choreographed by Minnie, Sarah's mother, who ran the show from beginning to end. What Jack told me about her not approving of him clicked into focus as I watched this pageant. She barely spoke to either of us throughout the ceremonies, as cold as the tip of Patagonia.

I was best man, and for ushers we rounded up a ragged crew of young toughs from the boarding house, dressed in the only clothes they owned, not exactly part of Minnie's grand design. It must have given her fits to watch. What she wanted was a royal wedding and what she got was a peasant frolic. It's hard to be a
~~~

snob in a town like Oakland City, Indiana, population 2300, but she did a good imitation of one.

I was glad to leave the church basement reception early for work and felt bad that Jack got a mother-in-law who personified all the stereotypical mother-in-law cliches. Sarah was so pleasant and warm herself that I wondered where that charm came from after being raised by such a wombat. Her sister Rachel was also lovely, so their late father must have provided enough nurturing to make up for her mother's haughtiness. Minnie was to fade away in Jack's and Sarah's lives by mutual alienation.

Jack and Sarah left the next day for Warsaw and planned to have their short honeymoon at the nearby Lake Winona Inn since Jack had to start work in a week. I bade them farewell with mixed feelings-thoughts of impending loneliness but with happiness for them. Jack quoted Milton to me as we parted:

"Hail, wedded love, mysterious law, true source of human offspring."

Chapter Eleven

I've Been Working on The Railroad

1920

March 27, 1920

Dear Cyrus,

We're settled in a tiny rental house in Warsaw, a nice little town with a lake right in the middle of downtown and another smaller pond close by. It's too cold now for anything other than an occasional stroll at the lake, but we're looking forward to summer when we'll be able to swim. We've already made friends here and Sarah sings in a local church choir. She's made quite an impression with her wonderful voice and pleasant personality.

When can you come see us? I miss your company and our talks. We don't have much room, but we can sleep you on our couch. Catering service is great!

Let us know when we can expect you.

Love,

Jack and Sarah

<div style="text-align: center">~~~</div>

April 2, 1920

Dear Jack and Sarah,
*   How about this weekend?*
Love,
*   Cyrus*

~~~

April 6, 1920

Dear Cyrus,
*   Great. When? Are you coming by bus? If so, I can pick you up at the bus station. Just let me know when to fetch you. I have a car again (courtesy of Goodyear Tire and Rubber Company).*
Love,
*   Jack*

I was heartened by Jack's upbeat letter. He'd seemed so out of sorts before he left for Warsaw. I'm sure his mother-in-law's condescending attitude had worked its way under his skin.

I arrived late Friday afternoon and Jack and Sarah met me. The run-down Greyhound terminal smelled like an actual Greyhound dog, mixed in with mice and urine. The bus had been deep-freeze-cold. The driver apologized before we set out and offered to let us off the bus before we left the terminal, but everyone stayed on, wanting to get to their destinations. The cold of the upper Midwest in March must be colder than Alaska, I was sure. I had a good topcoat with a
~~~

thick sweater underneath, so I wasn't shivering, but still I was glad when the trip was over.

"Welcome to beautiful Warsaw!" Jack cried as I stepped down from the bus. "How was the ride?"

"Not bad." I said, not wanting to start our visit with a complaint. "How are you?"

Sarah gave me a hug and we all piled into Jack's Model-A Ford.

He'd described his house accurately. It was tiny but on a quiet street in an attractive neighborhood. And it was warm! After dinner, we relaxed in front of a wood fire in a beautiful living room stone fireplace.

"Look at this," Jack said, showing me a cherry wooden upright piano in the corner. "This was Sarah's, and she lets me play it," he grinned. He sat down and played "Wabash Moon" and "Dear Old Girl," with a flourish. Sarah came over and the three of us sang a few favorite old songs together, like those days in Vincennes before Papa died. It felt so good.

After we sang Jack pulled out his cigarettes, offered me one. By now I'd adopted smoking too, but not nearly like Jack's two-pack-a-day habit. Jack lit them. I noticed Sarah still didn't smoke.

"It's good that you don't do this filthy thing," I said with a smile.

"Bad for my cords," she said, pointing to her neck. "Besides, I tried it once and nearly turned green. How do you guys do it? And more to the point, why?"

"We started years ago smoking corn silk behind the barn. I gave it up soon after I started, then in Washington I started smoking again. The Army gave us free cigarettes and I was bored. It killed time. Besides, people all around me were smoking constantly, so it seemed the thing to do."

Jack left the room to go to the bathroom and Sarah said in a whisper, "Jack coughs a lot first thing in the morning, so if you hear him in the morning, don't worry. He gets over it as soon as he gets his first cigarette of the day."

"Does my brother have any other bad habits?" I asked, in a joking way, not really expecting her to respond.

"He's nearly perfect," she laughed "except for smoking and sometimes when he's had too much to drink. But most of the time he's full of fun, has a laugh that lights up the room. He also has a good voice, and we do duets with him playing the piano. Mostly old folk and pop songs."

"Does he drink too much very often?" I asked, a little concerned and also surprised that she would confide in me, Jack's brother, this much.

"No, not too often. Only does it on the weekends, never during the week." She brushed her hair from her eyes and looked straight at me. "I think work gets him down. The company seems to think they own him."

"How so?"

"Well, his boss calls him day and night, like everything's an emergency. But it's only a tire business, you know. There aren't lives at stake, or anything like that. He doesn't like this guy, his boss, who luckily lives in Indianapolis. But his incessant calls are very disruptive."

Jack returned and noticed we were in serious conversation.

"Okay, you two, what're you talking about? Is Sarah telling you what a terrible husband I am? If you asked her mother, I'm the worst ever. She once called me a dirty dog."

"Oh Jack, never mind Mother. She never approved of any of my suitors. Or anybody else, for that matter. Besides, we hardly ever see her and I'm all right with that. She's always been difficult.

"We were just talking about your boss – you know, the man you love so much."

"That sonofabitch. Name's Walter McKenzie. Cyrus, you should hear his dumb phone calls. Criticizes me for every least little thing. Diminishes me. I'm doing a damn good job here. I've increased sales of tire and fan belts every month since I got here. He gives me no credit. It's always 'more, more, more sales.' He doesn't realize there are only about 1,000 cars in Warsaw and people don't have reasons to drive around and wear out their tires. He's such a pain in the ass.

"The one big account I landed is the Little Crow Milling Company. They make Coco-Wheats, a very popular hot breakfast cereal, sort of a combination of cream of wheat and chocolate. They have a lot of trucks, and they do wear down tire treads. I'm good friends with the owner, guy nicknamed Red. Sarah and I get together with Red and Peg, his wife, every couple of weeks. He's the only guy in town with a Cadillac. We get along great."

"Have you said anything to others in the company about this boss of yours?"

"Who could I talk to? I'd be seen as a disgruntled employee, and they'd use this as excuse to get rid of me. I'm stuck in this corner."

Sarah sensed this was a discussion between brothers and discretely slipped out of the room, saying she was going to fix dinner.

Jack got up and went to the liquor cabinet. "Wanna drink? It calms me down when I think about that S.O.B. Join me?"

"Thanks, I don't often take whiskey, or any alcohol. Makes me sleepy."

I watched Jack's hand trembling as he poured himself a generous tumbler of bourbon. I didn't know what to say or do. I haven't had much contact with him since he's been back from Europe. But he seems to have an increasing problem with authority. He complained repeatedly in his war diary about officers in the military. He's hyper- sensitive to criticism. His mother-in-law's rude comment must have hurt him deeply. I suspect Sarah worries about these reactions. As his brother, I wondered what I could do to help.

"Is there anyone you can talk to?" I asked him. "You know, maybe a minister, a doctor. You've made friends here. Maybe meet a friend for coffee and run this by them. You mentioned your buddy, Red."

"Our minister would tell me to pray. Not any help at all. I've thought of talking to him, but I think he's out of touch with the real world. Ministers have plenty of platitudes. Who was it who said, 'nothing is given so profusely as advice?'

"I'd hate to ask Red. Probably be the end of our friendship if he found out I'm a weakling. And I don't like to discuss these things with Sarah. She's sympathetic and tries to help, but she gets down when I tell her my troubles. So, no, I don't talk to anyone about it."

Growing up, Jack was always stoic, accepted whatever fate laid at his feet, simply worked harder to get past setbacks. Papa's death, his forced departure from school, followed by the series of unpleasant experiences in the Marines, seemed to be pushing him past his tolerance for frustration and disappointment. He'd given up all hope of being a doctor like Papa. His war journal showed an increasingly gloomy downward trend in his world view. I remembered the old days, how he sang with so much joy when we were around our grand piano in Vincennes, before Papa died. Mother sold the piano, and the house and those happy days ended abruptly.

I always believed his success in sales was because of his built-in extroversion. He was an affable, handsome man, but now what I was seeing was a man with a bleak outlook, a world weariness. I guess those attributes can be fellow travelers with a salesman's gregarious personality. He was lucky to have Sarah, who was devoted to him, seeing the cheerful and decent Jack underneath layers of defenses he built around himself.

I knew I'd been the lucky one, having the advantage, not available to Jack, of finishing high school, getting a cushy assignment in military service, out of harm's way during the war. Jack had repeatedly drawn the losing hand, and I saw it pressing him down, as mindless optimism of adolescence dissolved in the cold realities of adulthood.

"Okay, you guys, come and get it!" Sarah called out from the kitchen.

Sarah was not only a great singer, but she was also a helluva good cook. Her spaghetti and meatballs were the best. She served spumoni ice cream for dessert, home-made in the only Italian grocery store in Warsaw, keeping the meal's Italian theme. Sarah had to sing the next morning at church, so after she cleaned up the kitchen, she excused herself, allowing Jack and me a chance to keep talking.

"I see why you love Sarah so much. I'd like to go with you tomorrow to hear her sing," I said.

"She's wonderful. Only thing about her singing career worries me is all those guys who surround her after her solos, gushing over her, flirting with her. I admit it, I get jealous. Since she loves to sing so much, I try not to let it show."

"Want my advice? Don't mention those feelings to her. She loves you, no one else. Singing is her passion. Let her have that and try not to worry about those other guys. They're nothing to her."

We talked about old times for a while, and then Jack said goodnight and showed me where to sleep. I was glad he didn't want to talk any more. I was tired and a little sad.

The next morning, we all went to church, with Sarah getting there ahead of everyone to practice her solos. While we were getting dressed, I heard Jack coughing in the bathroom and when he came out, he was puffing on his Camel. He looked at me like a whipped dog.

"I shouldn't have had that extra whiskey last night. My head's the size of a jack-o-lantern and if it explodes there'll be a big mess." He looked at me through swollen and bloodshot eyes, tossing a couple of aspirins into his mouth. "I'm sorry, how are you this morning?"

"Fine. Are you gonna be okay for church?"

"Oh yeah, I'll be fine. Some bacon and eggs and I'll pull through. After I eat, since Sarah needs to be there early, I'll run her over, come back for you in a half an hour. Help yourself to coffee in the pot. I can make you some eggs before we go if you want."

"I can whip up some eggs. You go on and take Sarah. How far is the church? Can I just walk there?"

"It's four blocks. If you don't mind walking, it's easy. Just turn right out the door and stay on this street and you'll see the church. It's the First Presbyterian, old stone church on the corner. I'll meet you in the narthex."

I said a hurried good morning to Sarah as they scurried out to the car and were off. Jack had left some nice crispy bacon on a plate, and the eggs were in a bowl next to the frying pan. The aroma of the bacon filled the kitchen and got my salivary juices flowing. I tossed a couple of eggs into the frying pan, found some bread to toast, and had breakfast.

Walking toward church, I admired the small-town beauty of Warsaw. Pleasantville USA. Several people were headed in my direction, and they waved to me as we converged towards the church. Small town America, there's no place like it.

I'm not a church-going man, but the smell of furniture polish and burning candles as I entered the vestibule made me remember attending church in my youth. Jack soon appeared and we found a pew close to the altar, both waiting patiently through the service for Sarah's singing.

And sing she did. Her rich lovely soprano filled the church with "When Our Heart Is in a Holy Place." The audience did its best not to burst into applause, but the natural modesty inherent in midwestern America kept them in check. After the service there was a coffee hour in the church basement. Sarah was the center of attention, apparently the rule each Sunday, and I understood Jack's feeling of jealousy. But I felt he should feel pride instead.

Chapter Twelve

Wabash Blues

June 1920

I GOT BACK TO BLOOMINGTON, feeling I knew Jack and Sarah better, but also feeling blue by what I'd seen and heard. Jack's smoking and drinking were disquieting, as was his oppositional relationship with his boss. My powerlessness to change anything in his life put me in the doldrums. I hoped that it wouldn't jeopardize his marriage. Sarah was such a splendid human being.

My life, however, was on the upswing as I became absorbed with journalism. Writing looked like a good fit for me. I got promoted at the *Herald* with a small raise. That recognition and approval raised my spirits. I'd not heard from Jack and Sarah since my visit, but neither had I written to them.

Then a letter came.

June 20, 1920

Dear Cyrus,

    Sorry to be the bearer of bad news. I got a letter from Mother, written a week ago, telling me about Andrew's passing. I was astounded. Have you heard anything from her since we got back from the war? I haven't. Not surprising, though. She never gave a damn about us. She idolized Andrew, so this must be terrible for her.

    Apparently, he was driving home from a party and crashed into a tree. Nobody else in the car, so that's the only good thing. Alcohol was thought to be involved according to a news account she sent, but she said nothing about that. Always hard to know what she is thinking. I feel guilty I haven't been a better big brother. I never inquired about him since we left. On the other hand, Mother hasn't written to me either, even during the war. Have you ever heard from her?

    The funeral has been held already. Mother didn't even tell us so we could go to the funeral! What did we do to deserve her wrath? I had to quit school to help with money, and this is the thanks I get?

    Anyhow, write or call and we can talk.
Love,
    Jack

I was incredulous. I'd also lost touch with Mother and Andrew, but he and I had never been close. I always thought he was a stereotypical little brother, an annoyance, barely tolerated and endured rather than attended to. But like Jack, I felt embarrassed and ashamed that we'd been so neglectful. We both fell easily into blaming Mother for her overprotectiveness of Andrew and her hovering over him, but still.

I had always worried about Andrew being so different. He appeared to be a momma's boy, never relating to either Jack or me. We dismissed him as a spoiled brat, sissy and soft. But inside that kid there must have been a real person we never tried to know. And now, well, it was obviously too late. I wonder who he was.

Was he one of those odd kids who never made friends with anyone? Was he retarded? I wondered if he was hooked on alcohol, but during prohibition that would mean he had to have some imagination or friends to get alcohol. Maybe some mean kids in the neighborhood were feeding him booze to watch what happened. This thought led me back to worrying about Jack and what Sarah had told me about his drinking. It was definitely time to visit Jack and Sarah again to get a better understanding of what was going on in their lives.

June 25, 1920

Dear Jack,

Such sad news. I think you and I ought to talk and strategize about expressing our feelings to Mother. When are you free?
Love,
Cyrus

<div style="text-align: center">~~~</div>

July 1, 1920

Dear Cyrus
We're free this weekend. C'mon up!
Love,
Jack

I caught the late afternoon bus and by seven o'clock was sitting in Jack and Sarah's living room, chatting about trivia in our daily lives, of which there was plenty. We spoke briefly about my journalism courses and my work at the *Herald*.

I saw a grin stealing across Jack's face.

"What is it? I see that familiar sly smile that means you have news."

He burst out laughing in that infectious way that fills the room with mirth.

"You know that guy McKenzie in Indianapolis? He got fired! Couldn't have happened to a nicer guy. Turns out I wasn't the only one he was harassing. Several development men like me complained to the higher-ups and they kicked him out. I have a new boss who's a peach of a guy. I'm a new man!" he crowed.

Sarah was beaming as she looked at the man she loved and married.

"Jack's back!" she said. "We've even been singing together at the piano. You know, he's got a great baritone. With some training he could make a career out of singing," Sarah said.

"Not a chance of that!" Jack broke in. "I see how hard you work, what anxiety you go through to prepare for concerts, or for just singing in church. But it's not for me. I love just singing with you and Cyrus and anyone else who wants to join us around the piano."

"Back to your job and your new boss. How's it going?" I asked.

"Well, we've raised our sales by seventy-five percent, have expanded the store, and have built a real following. Goodyear is number one in Warsaw!"

I smiled at Jack and saw that he was very proud of what he'd accomplished. So different from the last time I was here.

"Well, turning to the less pleasant reason for my visit. What should we do about Mother?"

Jack admitted that he'd lain awake worrying about her. "I think we ought to write a letter to her expressing our sorrow about Andrew's passing, ask if there's anything we can do and leave it at that," he said. "After all, she didn't have the decency to let us know about the funeral, so I doubt she has any desire to see us. So maybe a letter will suffice."

"She always saw you as the more reliable son, so if that's what you think, I'm fine with it," I said. "Remember, she told me that I didn't know how to do anything, and you did, so you had to quit school and get a job. I protested, but it didn't matter. She'd made up her mind, just as she did about everything."

We paused in our conversation, weighing our options.

"I often wonder how she supports herself. She hasn't asked me for any help. You?"

"Nope, not a word. Maybe Papa had more money stashed away than she told us."

"I think it would be nice if the two of you went to see her, find out how she's doing," Sarah said, in a near whisper. "After all, she's your mother. If she came to some harm, you'd both feel horrible that you hadn't been there for her,"

We looked at each other, then both looked down, sort of ashamed.

"When could you go?" Jack asked.

"A weekend would be best."

We decided on a date and Jack said he would contact Mother to settle on a date that was okay for us to come.

~~~
~~~

Even though we never heard back from her, Jack and I decided to set out the first weekend in August anyway. We had no real plan about how we'd relate to our estranged mother.

"What do you expect?" I asked Jack as we got underway.

"Anger. My guess is that she'd rather we not come at all. But we're on our way and need to follow through. What's past is past. We can only try."

We pulled up in front of the house, parked and went to the porch. The place looked no different from when we moved there after Papa died, except it was even more shabby, with rotting wood cornices and in dire need of paint. A skinny dog crept around the corner of the house and stared at us, but he didn't bark or seem aggressive.

We stood at the front door. There were no signs of life, but we knocked anyway and waited. Nothing. We knocked again, but still nothing. We went to the back of the house and rapped hard on the door there. The dog had followed us, whining all the way. We looked at him and could tell he was a stray and hungry. After getting no response to our knocks, we went back around to the front.

"Let's go next door and find out if someone there can tell us anything," Jack said.

The house next door was scruffy and in disrepair. We climbed some rickety porch stairs and knocked. After a few minutes there was stirring in the house and then an old woman pulled the door open, a cigarette dangling from her lips.

"If yer sellin' somethin,' go 'way. I got no money. And if you're trying to convert me to some hare-brained religion, don't bother."

She was gaunt, must have weighed about 90 pounds, appeared to be 75- 80 years old. Her yellowing face showed creases and wear from years of hard living. Her dress looked like it was home-made from flour sacks.

"Sorry to bother you. We're not selling anything. We're Jack and Cyrus Lewellyn, the sons of Esther Lewellyn who lives next door," Jack said, pointing to the house.

"Ain't no one livin' there. Hasn't been for some time. She moved out when she got married, 'bout a year ago." She looked us up and down. "You're her sons, and didn't know that? Sounds fishy to me."

"Do you know where she moved to?" we said nearly in unison.

"Cross town, to a better part of town. Don't know the address. Check with town hall."

"Much obliged for your help. Best wishes," Jack said. She said nothing in response, closed the door and went inside her decrepit house. We went to Jack's car to plan our next move.

"You know, we could check with funeral homes. One of them might have a record if they had Andrew's funeral," I said.

"Good idea. Let's find a telephone booth with a directory. There can't be that many funeral homes in this town."

After several calls we found the one where Andrew's funeral had been, and they had Mother's address. That old cantankerous woman was right, Mother's new home was in a better part of town, near where we lived with Papa in better days. We found the house, a red brick, Georgian house, ivy growing up the sides, well landscaped and maintained. We looked at each other both clearly wondering who she'd tricked into marrying her so she could live in this nice house.

Jack knocked. Heavy footsteps got louder as they approached the door. A large man with white hair in a black suit, white shirt and plaid necktie opened the door and stared at us.

"What can I do for you?" he said in a tenor voice, surprising us with his high-pitched voice when we looked at this guy's size.

"I'm Jack Lewellyn and this is my brother Cyrus. We were told Mrs. Lewellyn, our mother, lives here. We've come to see her."

"I'm Ed Lindemann, her husband. She's no longer Mrs. Lewellyn, she's Mrs. Lindemann. I know who you fellas are, she's told me about you. Come in and I'll call her."

"Much obliged," said Jack.

His demeanor was neutral, civil but not welcoming. He ushered us into the parlor and pointed to two wingback chairs. We followed his directions meekly. We didn't know what to expect.

In about ten minutes Mother walked into the room, her face impassive. She took a seat opposite us. Ed left the room.

"Well, I can't say I'm glad to see you," she began, in that familiar tone of disdain. "You haven't been in touch for so long that frankly, I lost track of where you were," she said, and turned to Jack. "I heard you were in the Marines in Europe. Maybelle told me. Cyrus, I didn't know where you were. You both look like you survived the great war without damage. Is that so?"

"Yes, we both survived. I'm living in Warsaw and Cyrus lives in Bloomington. I'm married and working for Goodyear. Cyrus is in Indiana University studying journalism."

"Why did you come to see me?" she asked in her typical *get to the point* way.

"Your letter came, and we were both shocked to hear about Andrew. We're so sorry," Jack said, stopping there, not mentioning that we'd not heard about his funeral.

"Yes, it was a terrible blow. Andrew was my lamb. He never was a regular boy like you two. I had to take more care of him than I ever did with either of you. He had peculiar ways about him. Other boys never made friends with him. He couldn't tolerate school, so I taught him at home. But he learned about alcohol, somewhere, I'm not sure where. That's what happened to him. He was drunk when he hit that tree. You probably figured that out, right?"

This was the first time she was ever this straightforward with us. She was still distant, cold and behind a virtual veil. But at least she gave us the facts.

"It crossed our minds," Jack said.

Silence settled in the room. No one wanted to raise a ruckus. Finally, I said,

"Ed seems like a nice fellow. Where did you meet him?"

"At church. He's a widower and we got acquainted and we both were lonely, so we started seeing each other, one thing led to another and here we are. He's a good man and he treats me well. He also was good with Andrew."

It was sort of an unwritten script with Jack and me from there on. We hadn't discussed it in advance because we had no idea how this meeting would go. But no one got into recriminations. That wouldn't have helped anything. But we felt we'd accomplished what we set out to do.

"Let's try and stay in touch better. If Sarah and I have children, I'd like to think they could get to know their grandmother."

"Yes, I'd like to stay in touch too. Let's turn the page." This came as a surprise. We'd have to wait and see how that turns out.

We left, not feeling warm and fuzzy, but at least not hostile. Our trip home was quiet with both of us feeling that our visit went as well as could be expected.

Chapter Thirteen

Yessir, That's My Baby

1922, Two Years Later

DAYS TURNED INTO WEEKS, then months. Two years streaked by while Jack, Sarah and I were immersed in our own affairs. I was finishing my journalism courses and would soon graduate. Jack had prospered in Warsaw, but he was about to be promoted and moved, again, to Indianapolis. He was a little disgruntled, because he and Sarah loved Warsaw, and they'd made good friends there. But he couldn't turn down this opportunity. The other big news was that Sarah was pregnant! I was going to be an uncle in a few months.

Where to live? Jack could never anticipate when the next job move would be forced on them. Loans were parsed out grudgingly by parsimonious bankers, who apparently thought they were doing the borrowers a big favor to take their interest payments. Banks wanted prospective home buyers, especially young ones, to show they had fifty percent of the purchase price in hand. Jack hadn't saved enough to qualify for that high bar, so he and Sarah rented a small house.

~~~

I graduated from journalism school in June and applied for jobs at several newspapers, including the Indianapolis Star, a plum I didn't expect to get. But I did! Not only was this a great job, but it would put me in the same city as Jack and Sarah. I couldn't wait to move and watch Sarah and Jack become parents. I knew from watching friends that the first baby always makes neophyte parents exceedingly nervous.

By August, Jack, Sarah, and I were all settled in "Naptown," the nickname for Indianapolis that the younger generation had invented, believing that nothing ever happens here. As a newspaper reporter, though, I found the "roaring twenties" going full blast. Indianapolis was not as hot as New York or Chicago, but it wasn't asleep by any means.

I occupied the lowest rung of newspaper reporting, the police beat, but yearned to cover world affairs. And I'm here to tell you, there's plenty of crime in good ol' sleepy Naptown. International events still captivate my interest more than local burglaries, stabbings, and domestic violence, but I'll have to wait to get those assignments.

Sarah delivered John Clifford Lewellyn on November 13, with both Jack and Sarah laughing off
~~~

the idea that thirteen was an unlucky number. "Pure superstition," Jack scoffed.

At birth, John had a full head of black hair, which soon fell out to be replaced by flaming red hair. He was deemed "robust and strong" in the delivery room by both nurses and doctors. Sarah went home with him after five days, an inordinately long time by later standards, but resting newly delivered mothers was routine operating procedure in the early twenties. I peered through the nursery window and he looked like, well, a baby. Eleven other babies were in there and they all looked alike to me. But what did I know about babies?

Jack wrote the birth announcement:

"A mother's pride, a father's joy."
-Sir Walter Scott
Announcing the birth of
John Clifford Lewellyn
Born November 13, 1922
6 pounds 9 ounces.
With a lusty cry, he greets the world!
Mother and child doing well.
Not sure about the father!
-Jack and Sarah Lewellyn

When they came home, we had a quiet celebration. Sarah was told not to have any alcohol, but Jack was not to be denied a few swigs of moonshine whiskey.

After I held John and his eyes opened and regarded me, I changed my appraisal. He was a beautiful baby.

"You moved into your apartment, Cyrus?" Jack asked.

"More or less. Don't have much furniture. A bed, a kitchen table and chairs, odds and ends for dinner ware. I bought a new refrigerator, you know, the kind with the big coil on top. The newest thing. It's a little noisy, but I'll get used to it.

"How's the new job, Jack?"

"I think it's gonna be okay. I'm getting acquainted with the other men, but so far, it's looking fine. I'm the new guy, but that's a familiar role. And, I might add, the only one without a high school diploma."

This always ate at him, making him feel inferior. I believed his fellow workers didn't give this a thought, but Jack carried this heavy worry throughout his life. He was extraordinarily bright, a voracious reader, probably having more knowledge than his high school graduate coworkers, or even many college boys. What he couldn't do was talk about the once-in-a-lifetime social connections and networks that came with high school and college. Nothing he could do now could replace those.

Sarah excused herself to feed John and take a nap with him. I looked at Jack to gauge his mood. He seemed in good spirits, but if he kept drinking, I worried that would change.

"So, how's being a father feel?"

"Scary, actually. I recall how much I learned from Papa and how I need to teach John a lot of stuff. I don't know much about babies, though, and so teaching him anything will have to wait 'til he's a little older.

"I'm a little jealous, though. Sarah's in love with him. I'm feeling a little left out. I hold him every once in a while, and it feels unnatural, kind of strange to me. I guess I'll get used to it. You know, you and I never had much to do with Andrew, so we have no training for papahood. That reminds me, I need to write to Mother and let her know about the baby."

"Yeah, you should do that first thing tomorrow. She may already feel ignored by both of us, again, but then she may not give a damn. I've written to her three times since that visit of ours a couple of years ago. Course, she never wrote back. Have you gotten any letters? Sent any?"

"Well, I sent a couple, but no, I haven't gotten any back. I can only assume she's okay. You know, we said we'd try to stay in touch." Jack's face flushed with anger. "But, Jesus, she could have answered our letters. I shouldn't feel guilty, I held up my end of the agreement. But you're right, the new baby changes things. I'll write her tomorrow."

"About your jealousy," I said. "Other guys working at the newspaper whose wives had babies say the same thing. After you've been number one in your wife's life, it's hard to give that up."

"I'm well aware of my jealous streak," Jack said, pulling at his ear. "But I get plenty annoyed when Sarah gets a flood of attention when she sings, and now I'm jealous of the baby, for crissake. I don't know how to counteract that feeling. It creeps up on me and jumps me from behind. It always makes me want to have a drink. You have any advice, brother?"

"Only one piece of advice: don't turn to alcohol when that feeling comes. That'll only make it worse. I guess the other thing I'd say is talk to Sarah and let her know you get jealous. Maybe she can reassure you that your fears are groundless."

"I dunno. She's already having to deal with so many things, so that's gonna be hard to do. Her breastfeeding isn't going well. She worries about that. I told her she should just give it up and give the baby carnation. But she's determined, says it's a measure of her motherhood. I told her she's a damned good mother whether she breastfeeds or not. I don't know how it goes with other mothers. She may be experiencing the same thing as other new mothers when they try to breastfeed, but you know how women are."

"Well, no, actually I don't. I've been so busy with my job I don't even think about women. Think something's wrong with me?"

"Well, to be honest, I've often wondered why you never date or talk about girls. I don't necessarily think there's anything wrong with you. Maybe you're just undersexed."

"Boy, that sounds like something wrong to me!"

"I don't mean it that way. Some people are simply disinterested in sex, for all kinds of reasons. Do you ever dream about girls? You know, ever have wet dreams?"

"I've had wet dreams, but I don't recall whether they involved girls."

"Do they involve boys?" Jack asked me with caution in his voice.

"I don't recall," I answered, sort of embarrassed. "I can't really remember my dreams after I wake up. They dissolve soon as I open my eyes."

"Dreams are like that. The only dreams I remember have to do with scary stuff, the ones that wake me up. War scenes are my usual theme. Then I have to take time to look around the room, re-orient myself to where I'm at. Sometimes I need to get up and turn on a light to come fully awake."

"I do sometimes wonder if I'm queer," I said, finally acknowledging a fear I've had for some time. "How can you tell?"

"I don't know, really. I suppose the obvious thing is if you feel sexually attracted to guys. But most men are terrified to admit, even to themselves, that they're attracted to men. I had a friend once, who got married and couldn't perform on his wedding night. He continued to try but was never able. He'd never had sex before he got married but he went ahead, tied the knot. because he thought that was what men were supposed to do. Got very melancholy about his inability to get it up. One day I was astounded when I heard he'd blown his brains out. What a waste of a life! Actually, two lives. I wonder how a woman gets over that experience. Can you even begin to imagine how devastated his wife must have been? Could be that she felt guilty she wasn't attractive enough and that was why he never got aroused by her.

"You know, the expectation is that boys and girls grow up, they get married, have children, live in nice homes and so on. When someone doesn't follow that script, they may feel they're defective or something. Now, I'm not suggesting you're queer or anything, but I care about you, and don't want you feeling that way."

"Well, you don't have to worry about my shooting myself. I love living too much for that. My life has never revolved around sex. Maybe you're right. I'm just undersexed, whatever that means."

"Maybe you could talk to your doctor about this."

"If I had one. I never get sick, so I don't have a doctor who knows anything about me.

"You know, ancient Greeks described homosexuality, and people accepted it as part of regular life. So, it's been around forever," I said. "The trouble is, it's hard to get facts about this in our society since homosexuality is so misunderstood and frowned upon. We put such an emphasis on *manhood*, usually defined in terms of derring-do, heroism, physical feats, the size of your penis, athletic sex. Hard to know how to find out about this. Maybe I should do an article about it. Dig into this, get some factual information about it."

Jack circled back to my confession about not having a doctor.

"As the son of a physician, I'm surprised you have no family doctor. You ought to have one. As for the other idea, writing about homos in the newspaper might not garner you a Pulitzer Prize. Not exactly today's popular human-interest story."

"Journalism, though, tries to open people's eyes to problems they might not otherwise think of. I think I'll follow through on this idea. I'm intrigued, not only for personal reasons, but as a general interest issue.

"But back to your issue, Jack. You do have a family doctor, and you could bring up your jealousy problem. You might also talk to him about your drinking."

"Knowing my doctor, though, makes me guess he'll brush off the jealousy thing, saying all husbands feel that way. And the alcohol thing. He'll just say 'get ahold of yourself. Just don't take a drink when you feel stressed.' I'll bet that's what he'll say."

We left it at that. Jack was probably right about his doctor's response. Most doctors nowadays are focused on the latest and greatest scientific research, not so much on patient's feelings. Even if I had a doctor, broaching the subject of homosexuality with him might be dangerous territory. From what I'd heard, homosexuality these days is considered a mental disorder to be corrected by treatment. I wasn't about to get treatment for something that I didn't even think I had.

Chapter Fourteen

Why Can't You Behave?

1925

WE HAVE THE MOST unexciting president in history. Silent Cal. Such a gray eminence supposedly running the country in the roaring twenties is pure irony. But, on the other hand, maybe a calm demeanor in the nation's "leader" is needed to slow this runaway train.

Prohibition's a cruel joke. Anyone wanting a drink can find as many as they want, making the Women's Christian Temperance Union a laughingstock. Crime has open season with bootlegging and backwoods stills turning out thousands of gallons of homemade hooch.

A guy named Al Capone seems to be running the gangster show in Chicago. And it's rumored that Joseph Kennedy of Massachusetts has a bunch of boats in Newport bringing in Scotch for those with money. Those without money are buying booze in speakeasies, clubs, and back rooms. Some of it is rotgut whiskey, and some even kills people, either because it's so impure or they overdose.

The good news in family Lewellyn is that Sarah's going to have another baby! Due in September. Of course, she and Jack want a girl this time. John is three and he's a character, charming and full of himself, good looks, smart as hell. Sarah spoils him, Jack tries to discipline him, but it doesn't do much good since he's a force of nature. Jack loves teaching him to sing and he's a willing and receptive pupil. Carries a tune with ease and has a sweet soprano voice. Sarah coaches him too, so we now have a quartet and sing together when I visit. Jack still plays a mean piano. It's like the old days in Vincennes when we get going.

In this family portrait, the only blemish is Jack's drinking. Lost weekends, but he goes about business during the week. It puzzles me that he's able to curb his drinking during the week when he needs to be sharp at his job, and then he disappears in a cloud, starting Friday night. I've read about this, and the experts call what he has "functional alcoholism," meaning he can execute the necessities of his job while getting smashed on weekends.

Sarah has found some refuge in singing in church on Sunday and rehearsals on Saturday. Liz, a neighborhood teenager, now comes and watches John when Sarah goes to rehearsals or performances, but Jack has occasionally scared this poor girl when he's drunk. If she gets too frightened and quits, that would be the end of Sarah's singing. It would be hard to find another girl to babysit once word got around that the child's father is a drunk.

On a recent visit I tried, in a most low-key way, mentioning this to Jack.

"As your brother, I have something to say to you," I said quietly. I hesitated and looked at Jack to be sure he was paying attention. He was.

"I think your drinking is becoming a problem."

Jack looked at me in disbelief.

"What are you talking about? I only have a few drinks over the weekend. I never drink during the week, and I never get drunk."

As I expected, this was going to be tricky. I didn't dare reveal that Sarah told me how worried she was. That would seriously complicate things. But I didn't expect Jack to deny it completely.

"Well, just think about it," I said. "I'm not here to judge you. You know what Papa said: 'judge not lest ye be judged.' I have faults too and understand that sometimes it's hard to see yourself as others see you."

"Has someone told you this? Has Sarah been complaining to you?"

I couldn't lie. He'd figure out this had to come from Sarah, who else?

"Complaining is the wrong term. Sarah told me she's worried about leaving John with a babysitter while you're a little tipsy. She doesn't want to lose her as a babysitter. She wants John to be properly cared for while she goes to rehearsal. She cherishes her time practicing and singing in the choir."

"Well, she needn't worry. I'm perfectly okay when she goes to choir practice," Jack scoffed. "If she's so worried, she should stay home. I'm not a big fan of her singing in the choir anyhow. I told you how much she enjoys the attention from all those guys at church."

That thing again. Where did such insecurity come from? I know losing Papa made our world unpredictable and threatening. If our wonderful father could be snatched away, anything could happen in this world. Our abnormal relationship with Mother, his having to quit school at 13, all these things damaged him, poking holes in his self-worth. I'm seeing him now again as a frightened little boy, now terrified of losing his best friend, lover, wife, and mother of his children. He loves Sarah utterly, and I know she's devoted to him. This jealousy about Sarah is rooted deep in Jack's history.

I looked at him. He was staring into space, lost in rumination. I tried a different tack.

"To change the subject, have you heard from Mother?" I asked.

"No, I haven't," he said, shaking off his gloom. "I'm getting a bit concerned." Despite her lack of interest in us, Jack's innate decency still made him worry about her welfare. "Sarah's also worried. Can you understand why our own mother doesn't respond to us, ever? Unless she's sick. But you'd think that Ed would let us know. Think Ed might have something wrong with him too? He's no spring chicken himself." He pulled on his ear. "Maybe one of us should visit," looking my way.

"Well, with all that's going on with you, Sarah, and John, that should be me. I'll look into it," I said. "My schedule is not too bad right now and it would only take a couple of days to spin down there."

So, ten days later, I was on my way to Vincennes. It was a pleasant day, and driving was easy as I watched cornfields drift by. When I got there, a flood of memories overwhelmed me. What ever happened to that Wainwright kid? What did our old house look like now? Did the new owners maintain it, or improve it or let it go to seed? It's funny how when you live in a house, especially as a youngster, you think it will always be yours, and it *should* be yours, forever. It should stay the same. No one should be allowed to tamper with memories of your house, your homestead. I wasn't sure I wanted to go by the old place, but I did. Wait 'til I tell Jack that our house survived our leaving, and the new owners hadn't screwed it up.

I drove to Ed Lindemann's house, parked at the curb. There was a battered old Ford in the driveway. I walked to the door, knocked, and waited.

"May I help you sir?" a colored woman in a nurse's uniform said as she opened the door a few inches, peering out at me suspiciously. She looked to be in her forties, slender, and spry in her movements, her head nearly touching the top of the door jamb.

"Pardon me, but I'm Cyrus Lewellyn, Mrs. Lindemann's son. I've been trying to get in touch with her, but my letters are unanswered. Can you tell me anything?"

"What'd you say your name was?" she asked civilly, but with more than a little edge of suspicion.

"Cyrus Lewellyn. I'm Mrs. Lindemann's son," I said again, hoping she'd believe me.

"Can you wait there a minute?"

I waited, wondering who this woman was. Because of her uniform, I guessed she was taking care of someone in this house, but I was uneasy. Who could she be caring for? And why? She closed the door and in a little while, she returned and invited me to sit in the parlor.

"My name is Iris, and I take care of your mother," she said as I sank into a wing chair. "I had to call my employer to see if it was all right to allow you in. He said he knew that Mrs. Lindeman had a son named Cyrus, and it was all right that I talk to you. Sorry, but these days, you never know."

Iris sat across from me, leaned forward and locked her eyes on mine.

"Mr. Lewellyn, lots has happened to your mother," she said with concern. "No wonder you haven't heard from her. She had a stroke about a year ago, left her paralyzed. She can't talk or take care of herself. I live here with her because she needs someone to look after her. Mr. Lindemann passed last year, but he left money with the bank in some sorta legal account. The lawyer in charge of that hired me to mind her."

She looked at me and I thought she must wonder why it had taken me so long to find out about my mother. My stomach turned and I flushed as I pondered about what uncaring sons Jack and I were. Iris had no way of knowing about our long-standing alienation from Mother. No way to explain this to her.

"Did you know my mother before the stroke?" I asked her, wondering if she knew anything about Jack and me.

"No sir, I only met her after she got sick."

"Did anyone tell you anything about us?"

"No sir, no one never mentioned that she had children."

"Well. It's a long story." I sighed. "I doubt you can understand how my brother Jack and I got so disconnected to Mother. We're not ideal sons.

"But she wasn't the best of mothers either," I said defensively. "The three of us drifted away from one another when the war came. Jack and I both went into military service. She never once wrote to either of us during the war. When we got home, she never contacted us then either. When our younger brother Andrew died, she didn't even let us know about his passing. We missed his funeral because she never told us." Realizing that I was whining to this woman whom

I'd never seen before in my life, I told myself to straighten up and try to stay on story.

"We visited her when we heard about Andrew's death. During that meeting Mother, Jack and I vowed to stay in touch better, but it simply never happened. Jack and I wrote lots of letters to her but never heard back. Jack and I thought we had to make a better effort. Perhaps we should have come sooner. But that's history now. No matter what's transpired, she's still our mother."

Iris sat there, almost catatonic. When I finished, she shifted in her seat, cleared her throat.

"I'm so sorry. I had no idea she had family. If I'd known, I would've tried to let you know 'bout her troubles.

"Would you like to see her?" Iris asked with a degree of unease in her voice. "She won't recognize you, 'cause she doesn't even recognize me. I jes take care of her. She's no trouble, but she can't feed herself, and of course I take care of everything else. She's like a baby."

"How are you getting paid?" I asked, as the reality of taking care of her sank in. "And is it satisfactory?"

"Yeah, it's okay. My pay comes from that bank account I tole' you about. I live here during the week, get groceries delivered 'cause I can't leave her to go shopping. I listen to the radio a lot. We get along."

"Does someone spell you? You get time off?"

"Yessir, there a weekend girl who gives me a break."

"Pardon me for prying, you don't have to answer this, but do you have family? A place to live?"

"Yessir, I have a man and some nearly grownup kids. I live with them when I'm not here."

I marveled at this woman. She was clearly dedicated to looking after my mother's every need. I wondered where such stamina and inspiration came from. Where--how-- does a caring person like this learn such empathy?

"I want to thank you from the bottom of my heart for doing this. You're so..." I searched for the right word and only could come up with an uninspired one. "...*good* to do this." I asked her for some paper and on it I wrote my name and Jack's with our addresses and phone numbers.

"If you need anything, ever, call us or write us. We'll respond, I promise."

We went into the room where Mother was. I didn't recognize the emaciated, pale body curled up towards the foot of her bed, staring straight ahead with vacant eyes. At what? The odor of urine and feces were faint because Iris attended to that, but I still got a whiff of it.

I wondered, what do people in this state absorb from their surroundings? Do they have any mental abilities left? Can they think, and if so, what can they possibly be thinking about? But if they do have thoughts, that would be worse, their frustration with endless days of nothingness would be excruciating. I hope people in this condition have no awareness. That would be a terrible purgatory to endure.

I came out of that room profoundly moved, both by the futility of Mother's situation, but also by Iris's commitment to her. I wanted to hug her but knew that would be inappropriate and awkward for her. There has to be reward for such people. I hope so.

On my trip back to Naptown I tried to make meaning of this last twenty-four hours: Jack's drinking and jealousy, Sarah's innocent pleasure of being praised for her singing, Mother suspended in an unworldly absence of consciousness, neither here nor there. I grew melancholy as I neared home. What would I be able to convey to Jack without upsetting him more, contributing to his tentative grasp on normalcy?

I called Jack and saw him the next day at a restaurant near his office. I told him about Mother's stroke and how Ed Lindemann had provided for her before he died. I described Iris, how she seemed a saint in my view. He, like me, didn't shed a tear.

Chapter Fifteen

Ain't She Sweet

March 1926

MARTHA WAS BORN IN September 1925, right on time according to her doctor. Another redhead! She's now six months old and John must think she's a curious creature. Will he give her a chance to justify herself in his eyes? Is he unsure what she's good for? She certainly pulls attention away from him, and in some ways, that's good.

When I visit, three-year-old John is a lot more interested in me than before, I think to curry my favor. Everyone else is focused on this little girl. And she's adorable. So, John has cause to worry that his being the center of the universe is no longer the natural order of things.

But that's all the good news from Jack and his family. Other developments in the Lewellyn family's ever-changing experience, is that Jack has been transferred, again, this time to Terre Haute. Luckily, it's in Indiana and I can visit them regularly, but popping in for dinner or an evening of singing is no longer easy to do. Now I'll have to plan my visits. Dinner is with them tonight when I'll get the whole story.

"We don't move until June, gives us summertime to get settled. Moving is such a bother," Sarah said as she put the chicken in the oven to roast. "Jack was blindsided by this. He's had a good relationship with his boss, and he's been their top salesman. The customers all ask for him when they come in. The irony in all this is that his good sales record is the main reason he's being transferred. For Jack it's like 'no good deed goes unpunished.' They need him to go to Terre Haute and rescue their outlet there from folding. The manager there got caught with his hand in the till and they fired him in a flash."

Sarah was close to tears as she said this. "The other thing, we've really grown to like Indianapolis. Where else can you have Hoagy Carmichael walk into your living room and play on your piano?"

"What in the world are you talking about?" I said, confused, thinking maybe I'd missed part of the conversation.

"Well, here's that story. One Sunday, we'd gone to church," Sarah said. "When we came home, we were surprised to hear someone playing our piano. We never lock the house, no one does around here. We walked in, and there was this guy sitting on our piano bench, lovingly running his fingers over the keys. He looked up and I recognized him immediately as Hoagy Carmichael.

"I hope you'll forgive me," he said. "I was out for a stroll and saw this beautiful grand piano through your window. I couldn't resist coming in to see how it sounded. It's a wonderful instrument. Which one of you plays?"

"I was so flustered I could hardly talk," Sarah said. "I told him I played, but not as well as he did."

"Sit down, and let me hear you," he said.

"I was very nervous, but I sat down and played a couple of easy pieces. Hoagy grinned, said he liked my playing, and then he was gone. He's basically very shy."

Jack came from the living room with the kids ambling into the kitchen, cradling Martha in one arm. John trailed behind them.

"Sarah fill you in on the move?" Jack said.

"A little. When are you going looking for a house?"

"Next weekend. Sarah thinks I can do detective work, narrow the options down, then she can come help decide."

"Want some company?" I asked.

"Sure, wanna come? Love to have you along."

"I'm game, if Sarah doesn't mind my nosiness," I laughed.

"Jack needs someone to ride shotgun, so you should go to make sure he doesn't get into trouble." Sarah's mood brightened as she said this.

We dove into dinner and afterwards, without any cue, we all gathered around the piano.

"Martha doesn't know how to sing, you know," John chirped with a trace of big brother condescension.

"This is your chance to show her how. You sing alto, Cyrus will sing bass, mother will sing soprano, and I'll sing lead," Jack said as he began to chord on the piano. We ran through Sweet Adeline, Dear Old Girl, Lida Rose, Mister Moon, and Swing Low Sweet Chariot. We agreed that we sounded damned good. John sang better than I'd expected, being as young as he was. My bass was okay, but I'm out of practice. Sarah, of course, has the best voice. Martha made some chirping noises, as she sensed this was a family endeavor and wanted to be a part of it. After we sang, John tried to get the hang of the piano as he followed Jack in pressing out some chords.

On Saturday morning, Jack and I drove to Terre Haute in his company car. We picked up a map at a filling station and plotted our route. After usual small talk, Jack talked about more serious matters.

"I hate leaving Indy. Our house here has been so comfortable. I hope we find something comparable in Terre Haute." He used the name we found funny growing up in Vincennes. "You ever been to Terre Haute before?"

"Not that I remember. You?"

"Yeah, a couple of times. Business trips. Never stayed overnight but I know of a hotel downtown where we can stay. Not too pricey, standard rooms, twin beds. There are places to eat near the hotel."

I wondered how his drinking was going, but I hesitated to bring it up. Sometime on this trip I would. Sarah hadn't told me anything more about Jack's weekend blackouts, but I couldn't help being worried.

We lit up soon after we left Naptown, and the car filled up with smoke. Magazine and newspaper ads touted the "health benefits" of smoking and we felt it was perfectly healthy to smoke. These ads were very convincing with pictures of white-coated actors playing doctors, contentedly blowing smoke and advocating that their patients do likewise.

Practically everyone smoked now, even women, especially the flappers. Smoke filled the room at parties and if you didn't smoke and drink, you were not one of the "in" crowd. In my newsroom you needed a machete to cut through the thick smoke. Everyone, it seemed, smelled like an ashtray. Cigarette butts were scattered on sidewalks, and car ashtrays overflowed with remnants of cigarettes, ashes, and paper wrappings. Tobacco companies handed out cigarette samples to all comers on street corners and at every business convention, including those sponsored by professional medical associations.

I was shaken out of my reverie when Jack said, "Whaddya think about that little Martha? Isn't she a cutie? John's jealous as hell. He tries to ignore her, but it's hard since even he is drawn to her. I think he kinda likes her even though he wanted a brother. Getting a sister was his first disappointment. Then when everyone was ooing and aahing about how cute Martha was, he got plenty jealous, started banging things around, had a couple of temper tantrums. I came down hard on him for those. Sarah also cautioned him about it. He probably listened more to her than to me. He finally stopped.

"I never spanked him, though. I think that's not the proper way to raise kids. Papa never once raised his hand against us, remember? And I know he told his patients not to spank their kids.

"We were lucky to have such a caring father," Jack said. "I still get choked up thinking about him. I even dream about him. He walks in the door and goes to his favorite chair, fills his pipe, and picks up the afternoon paper. Do you ever dream like that?"

"Sure do. I've talked to some guys about that, and I've read that many people have dreams about passed-on loved ones," I said.

We went silent. Talking about Papa always made both of us pensive, withdrawing into our own personal boxes.

"How are you finding fatherhood by now?" I said after riding a few miles.

"Confusing. One minute my heart melts with love, the next I get mad as hell at John, who demands attention whenever he's in the room, jumping around, yelling like a banshee. He talks all the time, interrupts you when you're talking to someone, takes hold of your arm to get your attention to whatever he has to say. Martha's still so new it's hard to tell who she is just yet. One thing's for sure, she's much mellower than John was at that age. Hardly ever cries, smiles a lot. Could be girls are just a different species, or maybe second kids are just easier. I've heard that. I think that's maybe because parents use their first kid as a practice model."

We lit another couple of cigarettes, watching cornfields fly by our windows as we drove over the flat terrain that is Indiana. I thought this might be a good time to bring up his drinking issue.

"Any more trouble about the babysitter?"

"No. Main reason is I quit drinking." I was floored when I heard that and waited to hear more. "I decided I got too many responsibilities to get lost in booze. You know, it's easy to fall into that trap. Everyone's drinking, despite prohibition, and it's become a way of life for some people. I felt myself sliding down that slippery slope and just made up my mind to quit."

"That's such good news, Jack. Frankly, I was worried. I never took to drinking very much. I never liked the feeling of loss of control, and besides, if I took too much alcohol into my body, the next morning was horrible. So, I never got very far into it."

We got to Terre Haute and stopped for gasoline. I spread out a map on the hood of the car. "What's the address of this house?"

Jack pulled out the real estate ads from the local newspaper. "2933 West Telford Street. See that on the map?"

"Just a sec. Here it is." I told him how to proceed and we pulled up in front of the house. Not bad, but not as nice as houses in Naptown.

"Well, we're here. Let's go take a look."

By the end of the day, we'd looked at four more houses and Jack had narrowed it down to two for Sarah to look at next weekend. We spent the night at the hotel, checked out the exteriors of a couple more houses the next morning, then headed back to Indianapolis.

"How're you feeling about Goodyear now that they're moving you again?"

"Overall, good. But since I've done so well, they've put me in charge of a store where they fired their last manager. Pilfering funds. That's so dumb. I got a raise too. But continual moving exhausts both of us. We like Indianapolis and love our house. We've made friends and hate to say goodbye to them. Sarah's so good at connecting to people. They seem to like me, too. I'm usually easy to get along with. Part of my salesman role," he laughed.

"Terre Haute isn't that far from Naptown," Jack went on, "but it's hard to keep current with friends, and once you're not around them every day, it's easy for them to forget about you. I think there'll come a day when I say to hell with my employer and strike out on my own, find a place we can put down some real strong roots."

We walked into Jack's house and Sarah came out of the living room looking drawn. Jack noticed immediately.

"What's wrong, sweetheart?"

"Iris called. You mother passed during the night. Iris was sobbing on the phone, almost like she lost her own mother. She wanted to talk with you or Cyrus to get some idea of what she should do."

"I'll call her right away," I said. I'd met Iris and felt she'd be more reassured if someone she knew from the family talked to her. I went into the kitchen where the phone hung on the wall and dialed the operator, gave her the number Iris had left with Sarah, and waited.

"This is Iris. Who's callin'?"

I told her it was me, Cyrus, and she began crying. Once she'd settled down, she told me the whole story.

"I jes gone to bed when I heard a big thump from her room. I jumped outa bed, ran like lightnin' to her, found her on the floor next the bed. Honestly, Mr. Cyrus, I'd tucked her in 'fore I left her, you gotta believe me. I dunno how she coulda fallen out."

"I'm sure you did, Iris, don't worry, it's not your fault."

"But that's sposed to be my job, takin' care of your mama. And I failed her." She began sobbing again. When she gathered herself, I said, "Listen Iris, to me, very carefully. We know you did your job. You were always wonderful to Mother. No one will ever blame you, and if anyone even hints at blaming you, tell them to see me and I'll straighten them out. So, don't you worry one bit.

"Have you called a doctor?"

"No, I called and got your brother's wife on the phone soon as I found her on the floor."

"Okay, now listen, Iris. First thing to do is call her doctor. Do you know the doctor's number?"

"Yessir, I know it. I'll call him right away. Can you come? Soon? I'm scared someone will blame me and I need you to be here for me."

"I'll be there later tonight. In the meantime, don't move Mother. And after you've called the doctor, tell him to call Jack here at this number. I'll be on my way."

I huddled with Jack, and we planned our next move.

"I'll go over there and get a sense of what needs to be done and call you, okay?" I said.

"Sure, I'll join you soon as we know what's goin' on," Jack said. "Glad you're here and can go." He paced around as he tried to sort out his thoughts, running his fingers through his hair. "I'll take a few days off work. Think we should have a funeral? We don't know what friends she has. Iris might be able to help with that," he rambled on. "I think she was a solitary soul since Ed died. He seemed to be the only person, besides Andrew, that she was at all close to in her life. We sure weren't."

I called my editor and headed for Vincennes. I couldn't answer Jack's question about the funeral. We were operating in a fog of indecision.

Chapter Sixteen

Sometimes I Feel Like a Motherless Child

IRIS WAS STILL UPSET when I got there. Dr. Whitnauer had come, pronounced Esther dead, and arranged for the funeral home to come and remove her body.

"Those men from the funeral company looked at me funny when they came and got her. I know they think I didn't take care of her, but I did!" Iris sobbed.

"Iris," I said firmly. "Let me tell you once more. You did everything anyone could have done. You've got to stop feeling so guilty. She was an old lady who had a stroke and dementia. She had nothing to look forward to."

I sighed and recognized the futility in my reassurance, at least for now. We sat quietly for a few minutes until she had dried her tears and regained some composure.

"What I need to find out from you is, do you know if she had any friends?" I asked.

"No one ever came to see her, pitiful thing, don't know why. I never once met anyone come see her."

My mind raced as I considered what needed to be done next. I realized how little I knew of the arrangements made for Mother's care and now for her burial. Perhaps Iris could help sort this out.

"Iris, do you know where your pay comes from?"

"There's the man at the bank who knows."

"Do you know which bank? Name of the man there?"

"First National Bank of Vincennes is what's on the checks. Think the name's Jenkins who signs them."

"Thanks Iris. Mind if I leave you for a while to go to the bank? I need to find out what to do next."

"No sir, all is calmer since you're here."

I found the bank's address in a phone book before I left Iris. After explaining to one of the tellers why I was there, I was shown into Mr. Jenkins' office. I told him that Esther was my mother, and that Jack and I, despite many attempts, hadn't had any contact for some time.

He understood, which was reassuring. and made me think the people who managed the trust fund knew she had no friends or relatives involved with her care. Mr. Jenkins told me about the trust fund Ed Lindemann had set up. Jenkins hadn't heard she'd died, so he thanked me for coming to see him.

"Ed Lindemann banked here for years and set this trust up for Esther before he passed. It will also take care of all funeral expenses. He wanted whatever's left after expenses to go to the Lion's Club," Jenkins said, looking up to see if that caused any response of disappointment or anger. It didn't.

"Do you know of any friends Esther had? Anyone we should notify of her death?"

"I don't know about friends. Her death notice will be in the paper and if there's any service, that will be posted as well," Jenkins said. "May I speak frankly to you, Mr. Lewellyn?

"Please do, Mr. Jenkins."

"Esther was seriously demented, for a long time. It's no surprise you hadn't heard from her. She had no capacity for relationships."

"Well, my brother Jack and I, we both live in Indianapolis but lost touch with her when we went to the war. Neither of us got mail from her the whole time we were in the military. When we returned, we tried writing several times, got no response. She'd always been distant, even when we were kids, so this wasn't new. We figured she didn't really want to see or talk to us, so we stopped trying.

"Do you know when she had the stroke?" I asked.

"March of 1923. But even before that she was sort of incommunicado. In my distinctly non-medical opinion, she had some psychological problem affecting her ability to form relationships. What you tell me of her attitude to you and your brother is consistent with that. It's too bad when your own mother is that way."

"We survived. My brother Jack and I are very close – we're twins, by the way-- and that may be one of the reasons we've been able to tough it out.

"Do you know Dr. Whitnauer? I'd like to talk to him. Jack and I are trying to decide about a funeral. With few or no friends, it's hard to see the point. I'd like to get his take on a funeral."

Jenkins gave me his phone number. When I told his receptionist who I was, she told me that he would want to speak to me. In a few minutes he came on the line.

"Dr. Whitnauer here. Thanks for calling. Your mother is at Cummings Funeral Home. They're waiting for instructions from you. Here's what I know. Your mother was going downhill for several months. Not sure how she fell out of bed nor what killed her. She may have had another stroke, could have had a seizure that moved her over the edge of the bed, all very hard to say. Don't think we need an autopsy. I'll sign the death certificate, call it a natural death.

"Any other questions?"

"Do your services get paid out of the trust?"

"Oh yes, don't concern yourself with my bill. There'll be no bill from me."

"Thanks. One other thing. Iris is all perturbed that she'll be blamed for not taking good care of her. What should I tell her?"

"Oh, Iris is a lovely person but such a worrier. Tell her I think her care of Esther was perfect and I'll be happy to recommend her to other families who need a caretaker. Tell her to let me know how I can get in touch with her and a little about her nursing skills. Nothing fancy, just a half page of information. I'm sure we can find her another patient who needs care." He paused. "You know, Iris knows what's goin' on in this community and that's one of the reasons she's so scared."

"What do you mean?" I was confused.

"There's been a lot of racial tensions here. A recent Ku Klux Klan lynching has colored people both scared and angry. It has the makings of a race war. I don't like it at all. No reason for people to act like those crazy Klansmen. It's very upsetting to most of us. We take pride in being a caring community, but when something like that happens, well..." he trailed off, shaking his head.

Right here in Vincennes? I had no idea that was going on. I knew of incidents in the South but didn't know the KKK was active here. Live and learn.

When I told Iris what the doctor said about his confidence in her, it was the first time I'd seen her smile. Her eyes crinkled up almost shut and her smile gleamed. She looked at me with a tear streaking down her cheek. I wanted to hug her but feared that would be misunderstood. Human relationships are hard to figure out.

I called Cummings Funeral Home and told them to skip a viewing and funeral procession and arrange to inter her body next to Ed Lindemann's grave in a simple wood casket as his will had suggested.

Driving home, my mind spun back to childhood, to Papa and Mother, and to our barely known brother Andrew. Who was he? What was his relationship with Mother? I always tried to remember my childhood as a happy one, but these memories distorted that fantasy. Unanswered questions abounded: why did Papa choose such an austere woman for a wife? Why was Mother so attached to Andrew and not to us? This kept nagging me. As I drove by meadows and cornfields, I feared these questions would haunt me and disturb my sleep for a very long time.

My personal sadness was soon to be crowded out by widespread misery of a different sort.

Chapter Seventeen

As Time Goes By

1931

RUMBLINGS OF COMING bad economic times aired nightly for weeks on WLW radio, the "clear channel station," before the stock market crashed. When that happened, the "Great Depression" was on. Stocks lost something like $30 billion. I'm no economist, so I don't understand why this happened.

Some economists called it a "banking crisis" and "deflation." But why? Some blamed the Federal Reserve for not lowering interest rates to allow businesses to borrow more needed money. Investors "bought on margin," meaning they borrowed money to buy stocks and then couldn't borrow more to cover their huge losses.

Whatever the reasons, the country is now in an economic tailspin, people losing jobs across the country, a third of US banks failing, and economic depression is spreading worldwide. People are leaping out of tall buildings, or killing themselves with pills, guns, or knives.

In the midst of this, President Hoover says prosperity is just around the corner. I don't know what corner he's looking around, but with 30% unemployment I doubt folks without jobs would agree. Being president is a horrible job. Why would anyone think they could save the world these days?

Well, at least there's no war. Yet. Fascism is gaining a strong grip in Germany. In Russia, Stalin keeps killing off his rivals. He sent Trotsky into exile, probably never to be heard of again. What strange countries. Jack always said we should stay out of foreign disputes and war.

~~~

March 30, 1931

Dear Jack,

Sorry I haven't written for a while, but economics have muddled my brain. I'm not personally in money trouble yet, but we've had a host of layoffs at the paper. Those of us remaining wonder if we're next. It's like the sword of Damocles hanging by a horsehair over your head. So far, so good, but I'm not sure why.

Some of those people laid off were damn good reporters, and my friends. So, it's not about poor job performance or personal animus. Ever heard of survivor guilt? Well, I'm having it, mixed with anxiety.
~~~

How are you and family? Give Sarah and Martha hugs and say hello to John. Tell him I'll catch up with him at Easter.

Love,

Cyrus

~~~

April 10, 1931

Dear Cyrus,

We're looking forward to your Easter visit. I told John and he's very excited to see you. You two have such a great relationship. I wish mine were as good. Your advantage is not living day to day with a young stallion.

Sarah says hi. She's singing in a big oratorio on Easter Sunday afternoon, after her morning church choir performance. It's in our downtown auditorium where there's more seating. She's a nervous wreck, but that always happens before concerts, even to famous performers, I'm told.

Did you see that Al Capone got convicted of tax evasion? With all the criminal activity and murders he's been involved in, I think it's ironic they got him for cheating on his taxes. His stable of lawyers failed to get him off this time, and now he's going to the clink. They say he's sick, so he could die in jail.

We'll get our piano tuned up for quartets (or quintets if Martha keeps progressing in her singing).
~~~

I got some new sheet music, like "Stardust" by our old friend Hoagy, and a tune called "On the Sunny Side of the Street." That's sure what we need most-- hope.

See you soon!
Love,
Jack

~~~

It was twilight on Friday when I left Indianapolis for Terre Haute. I wondered in what wonderful ways the kids had changed since I last saw them. John is now eight and Martha five. It's been two years since I've seen them. Some uncle I am!

My arrival caused pandemonium, and our exuberant reunion led rapidly to exhaustion. Jack took his bleary-eyed kids to bed, and since Sarah had rehearsal next morning for Easter Sunday Service, we all collapsed into bed. She was going to sing some old chestnuts, "Christ the Lord is Risen Today" and Malotte's "Lord's Prayer," so rehearsing these was primarily for choral and organ accompaniment. Her more important concert was in the afternoon.

We dropped her at church early, and a glorious spring day beckoned us to a park where we killed time before the church service began. The kids joined a swarm of arms and legs on swings and slides while Jack and I leaned against a couple of early leafing trees,
~~~

smoked, and talked. When we'd caught up on each other's lives, Jack casually said,

"What do you know about Freemasonry?"

"Heard of it, but really don't know much about it. I thought it was some sort of a cult until I found out that some prominent people, including George Washington and Benjamin Franklin, had been Masons, so that seemed to indicate something valuable in it."

"No, no, it's not a cult. It started as small trade organizations for stone masons, way back in the 1400's. It evolved over the centuries, adding oaths of fidelity, then symbolism and secrecy. To be accepted for membership in a lodge now, an applicant just has to show he is independent and has a good reputation."

"How'd you get interested?" I asked.

"Some fellows at the store are Masons, and I heard them talking about their meetings and lodge hall, so I asked some questions. I wondered, was it a religious thing or what? They said that it's not a religion, though candidates are required to believe in a Supreme Being. That seems to be defined in lots of ways, depending on the Lodge. There are many variations about requirements. For example, in some countries, only Christians are accepted for membership, but in others, atheists are allowed in. It's all local."

"Seems sort of loose to me."

"Far from it. Very serious stuff. And once you enter into it you can count on fellow Masons to help you out if you run into any trouble. And Masons and Shriners do all kinds of important community service."

"What do organized religions think about Masonry?"

"The Catholic Church doesn't like it, and some Protestant churches don't either. The Church of England used to have Bishops as Masons, but lately that's been discouraged by the higher-ups. Members of Masonic Lodges insist it's not a religion, so, they argue, churches shouldn't discriminate against Freemasonry. In most Lodges Jews aren't allowed in. Don't ask me why. But you know how touchy mainline religions are about their firmly held beliefs and their domains. One of the attractions Freemasonry has for me is its seeming independence from all religions."

"If they are so independent from religions, how come some Lodges don't have Jews as members? Are there colored Masons? This is all very interesting. Maybe I should write an article for the paper about it."

"Well, I don't know the answers to all your questions. But I can tell you that many articles have been written about Freemasonry. Some articles only create controversy, stirring up feelings. Many people look at Freemasonry with suspicion, with its secrecy and rituals. I'll tell you more about it after I join a Lodge. At least, I'll tell you what I'm allowed to."

"Sounds a little spooky to me," I laughed.

"Oh, now, Cyrus, don't be judgmental before you know anything."

"Well how can I know anything if it's all secrets?"

"Join a Lodge and see for yourself!" he laughed.

We left it at that. It was time to attend Easter Sunday service. It seemed incongruous to have this discussion right before we went to one of the largest and most important of Christian celebrations. We managed to convince the children to leave the playground to listen to their mother sing. What a lovely voice she has, her phrasing so sensitive.

After the service she was mobbed by admirers. I noticed Jack shrink back a little when this took place, his little green monster of jealousy spoiling, for him, the enjoyment of Sarah's success. But he seemed to be getting a little better at these moments, so that was progress.

We hurried home for a quick bite, welcomed a babysitter to look after the kids, then were off to hear the oratorio, the main event of the afternoon, at two o'clock. Sarah ate nothing at lunch and drank gallons of water to "keep my vocal cords moist." Not sure what she'd do if nature's strong voice called during her performance. She changed into a full-length maroon gown, looking lovely as she scrambled through the stage door, clutching her score to her chest. Which, as it turns out, she never looked at during her performance, having committed her part to memory.

The auditorium was a Gothic structure, gray on the outside, with rococo interior design. Huge balustrades separated the first floor from the U-shaped balconies.

Vertical golden columns of organ pipes at the rear of the stage gave the auditorium a majestic feel.

After planting ourselves in front row seats, we waited only a short time until the singers filed onto risers. Boys would sing the upper voice parts. The men, except for the soloists, were young, in their twenties. Sarah told me later that several of the men were music students from Bloomington, which reminded me how close to Indiana University's Music School we were. I know that scores of musicians were turned out of that famous school every year. Plus, in Indiana choral singing was second only to basketball as the most popular activity.

Men wore black tuxedoes, and the boys wore choir robes with white collars. Each singer carried a black music folder. There were instrumentalists in front of and to the sides of the chorus, leaving room for the soloists on separate podiums, flanking the orchestra. We were so close, I could almost smell resin from the string instruments' bows.

I opened the program to see what we were going to hear: St. Matthew's Passion by Johann Sebastian Bach. I'd never heard this performed, so this was going to be a huge treat. Sarah sang a recitative, celebrating all Jesus' good works. It was ethereal. The entire performance was superbly done, and many in the audience were dabbing their eyes before it was over.

When the concert ended, the audience was still in a somber and contemplative mood, reflecting the profound sense of grief the music portrayed. This was the genius of Bach. His music was considered transformative at the time it was first presented and is still considered the holy grail of serious music. Mozart and Beethoven followed with their own brilliance, but Bach has remained, for many, the ultimate maestro.

We found Sarah talking with some fellow singers, laughing and relieved that the concert had gone so well. It was long, no doubt too long for some, but so perfect. When I gave her a hug, she was ebullient, on a high after virtuoso performances by all. Jack looked at her with glistening eyes of admiration.

"Did you know this music?" I asked Jack.

"I'd heard Sarah practicing her part, but no, I didn't know the whole thing. Very moving, even to me."

"What do you mean, even to me?"

"Well, I'm not exactly a believer in the whole Jesus myth. I think he was a great prophet and philosopher, but really, the Son of God? Can't quite accept that part. His Sermon on the Mount was truly inspirational, but I can't believe the rest of it, you know, rising from the dead, and ascension into heaven to sit on the right hand of God, and all that. It's not rational. On the other hand, St. Matthew Passion is great music, enough to make a body wonder a bit."

"Faith is the foundation for religion, Jack. If you don't accept certain things on faith, then it's difficult to accept religion. I'm still on the fence, too, but not as skeptical as you."

"You weren't in Verdun or the Somme, in 1919. I saw things no human being should have to see. That's when I lost my faith that there is a God who would let such horrible things happen. I respect those who have faith and religion. I'm envious. I just can't believe like that."

"Well, of course you know that many things in the Bible shouldn't be taken literally. It's quite a lot of allegory."

This interesting conversation unfortunately had to end, as Jack pulled into the driveway. The kids were asleep when we finally got home. After Sarah checked on them, she came into the living room and plopped down on the couch. Jack left to take the babysitter home while Sarah and I had time to talk.

"That music was beyond belief," I said. "Your solo was so touching, the good works of Jesus. Are you religious?"

"Oh yes, very much so. Jack's not, but neither of us tries to influence each other. I pray every day, very comforting to me. It helps me during stressful times."

"Are these stressful times these days?" I asked cautiously.

"Well, relocating always is stressful. Getting the kids adjusted to a new home, new schools, meeting new friends. And then there's Jack's mood swings. Jack has these unhappy times when he grouses about. He seems to be either up or down. When he's up, he's way up, but when he's down, he's unreachable. That's when he starts drinking, making it all worse. He rants and raves, talks as though other people are in the room, cursing at them. It's almost like he's detached or in some sort of trance."

"Does he ever hurt you when he's like this?"

"Never touches me. Sometimes he yells at me, accuses me of being unfaithful. That hurts so much. I would never do that. When he gets it into his head that I'd leave him for someone else, his jealousy takes over. It's crazy thinking and it only gets alarming when he's drunk."

Her hand went to her forehead, and she flushed, close to tears.

"Cyrus, I'm at my wit's end. I've talked with my minister who tells me to carry on my marriage, not only because I took vows, but reminding me how difficult it is for women to survive in today's world without a man. That reality makes me mad as hell, but it's true."

She collected herself and continued.

"But I do love him for his inherent goodness. He's a considerate husband when he's sober. I just wish he'd stop drinking and be himself instead of this other person, his alter-ego."

She said this now in a dispassionate voice. She seemed resigned to his unruly behavior, excusing it and attributing it to drink muddling his mind. I think her religious faith must be what keeps her from falling during this delicate balance.

Am I getting too involved in their private lives, their marriage? Was I being a voyeur? I was, after all, a journalist, a reporter, always trying to get to the bottom of a story. Would my conversations with Sarah, if known by Jack, increase his paranoia, his jealousy, his anger and perhaps cause alienation from me? This nagged at me, but I worried Sarah had no one else to talk to that I knew of. It was hard to share confidences in a new place. She needed to be able to air her problems to someone she could trust. Was I trustworthy? I tried to convince myself these conversations wouldn't make the marriage more problematic.

"Jack told me he's joining a Masonic Lodge," I said, moving away from this discussion about his drinking and acting out. "Perhaps that will help put things into perspective, having some men around him he can confide in. Don't know much about Freemasonry, but it's been around a long time. Jack has always been motivated to do good for other people. He wanted to be like Papa, become a doctor. He has a need to help."

"Yes, I'm happy he's looking into that. I don't know much about it either, but I've heard the same thing, that they do a lot of good. I think Jack has transferred his dream of being a doctor himself to John. He often talks with him about medicine. I think he'd love it if John would get interested in going to medical school."

"I'm back!" Jack called from the kitchen. "That girl is nice, but boy is she a chatterbox. I couldn't get one word in on the way home. But she loves the kids. I think we got the right sitter."

"The kids like her, too," Sarah said. "Definitely a keeper."

"What have the two of you been up to?" Jack said.

"Talking about the concert. What marvelous music!" I said, relieved that we could shift the conversation.

"Wasn't Sarah great? I love to hear her sing, like an angel. Which of course is what she is. Aren't I one lucky son of a gun?"

"You are, for sure. The other thing I loved about the concert was watching and hearing those kids. They really knew their parts and sang with such feeling. When you see kids doing things like that, you can believe the world is gonna be all right."

Jack poured himself a whiskey.

"Want one?" he said to me.

"No thanks. Bothers my sleep."

"Are you staying the night?"

"Yeah, I'll get an early start in the morning. It's not a long drive. I'll sneak out before you all get up. I'm not a breakfast eater so I'll grab some coffee on the way."

"Thanks for coming, Cyrus. Glad you got to hear my sweetheart sing. Next time we'll do some of our patented barbershop singing right here in the living room. Not high culture, but lots of fun."

"Let's make it soon. Much too long between visits,"
I said as I climbed the stairs to bed.

152

Chapter Eighteen

Brother, Can You Spare a Dime?

1932-1933

WELL, JACK AND SARAH are back in Indy. Again. He's upbeat about it, glad, I think, because he knows he's lucky to have any job in this current fiscal turmoil.

On Sunday, we sat down to a sumptuous after-church meal, cooked by none other than the talented and beautiful Sarah. I should say, the *pregnant*, talented, and beautiful Sarah. I noticed the bulge but hesitated to say anything. I recall once asking a woman when she was due and she abruptly turned away from me, as I flushed red from embarrassment. All she was, was overweight.

John was tall for his age, a beautiful ten-year-old boy. His auburn hair was wavy, his face narrow with a strong chin, ready smile. You could already see an athlete's body forming. Martha was equally endowed with beauty, her hair much brighter red, falling down her shoulders, her blue eyes fixing on yours with an intensity unusual for a seven-year-old. She must have gotten that look from Jack.

"You know Mother's gonna have a baby?" Martha chirped.

"Well, no, I didn't know that!" I lied.

"Martha, that's impolite!" Jack barked in a mocking rebuke. "That's news your mother and I were going to tell Uncle Cyrus," he smiled. Martha continued to smile, signaling she knew her father was joking.

"So, when are you due?" I asked Sarah.

"Sometime in December the doctor said."

"Well, congratulations to both of you. And you two are going to have a new baby to take care of," I said to John and Martha. "What do you want, a brother or sister?" They answered with different answers, but in unison, "Brother, sister."

"Well, whichever it is, we'll love the baby," Sarah said.

"Your father tells me you're playing piano now," I said to John.

"Yes, I am. When I'm older I'm gonna start a band," he said, and I knew he would, because he was one determined fellow. "And be a star quarterback too."

"How's football going for you now?" I asked, knowing he was playing on the elementary school team.

"Great! They made me captain and I'm quarterback." Humility is not a strong suit for ten-year-old first-born boys.

"And Martha, how're you doing?"

"Fine."

"That's what she always says when you try to find out her thoughts," Sarah laughed. "Tell Uncle Cyrus about your singing."

"Well, I sang a solo for the school concert last week."

"Wonderful. Just like your mother, eh?"

She giggled and covered her face, clearly embarrassed by the attention.

I left after dinner, feeling this family was doing well. Jack's drinking had been under control since they'd been back in Indianapolis. I mentally crossed my fingers that this was a prelude to continued forbearance.

~~~

In late November, Jack called me.

"Hi Cyrus. I called because we had to rush Sarah to the hospital because of stomach cramps," he said, his voice more tenor than his usual baritone. "We thought she was in labor. Turns out she had appendicitis, and out came her appendix."

"She's okay now?"

"Yup, she's fine. But I'm a wreck. She's gonna stay in the hospital for a few days. I'm taking a few days off to take care of the kids."

"Your boss okay with that?"
~~~

"Well, if he isn't, he can go to hell," Jack spit out the words. I tried to judge his level of anger. Was his face scarlet, a frown creasing his forehead?

"You're not getting on with him?" I ventured to say.

"He's one of those pricks who think they can call all the shots. A college boy who looks down on anyone who doesn't have a degree. If he doesn't like my taking off some time to take care of my wife who just had a major operation, he can stuff it!"

I sighed to myself. This was not a good sign. But Jack took the time off and I didn't hear more about his boss, so I assumed Jack's reaction was uncalled for, another flare of his simmering anger.

Sarah recovered from her operation in time to go into true labor on December 13th, a snowy night when Jack nearly skidded off the road on their way to Methodist Hospital. She had an easy delivery of a nine-pound boy early the next morning, named James, a name which more fittingly became Jimmy.

Having a new baby during the worst economic depression ever was not part of their plan. Banks are failing everywhere, people panicking, unemployment at an all-time high. Bread lines abound, people are losing their homes, many living under bridges and other makeshift shelters called "Hoovervilles."

Ordinary people are desperate and discouraged. Women try to help by taking in wash or doing other menial work. Men stand all day in unemployment lines. The general mood is mean. Politicians are frothing, blaming the other party for the situation, and popular demand for help from government has never been greater. Calls for change in leadership are everywhere.

In November, that change came in with a bang. FDR won in a landslide, injecting hope with his confident attitude and style. If ever a country needed an optimistic chief of state, it was now. Things are no better in Europe. Fascism has gained acceptance owing to downward economic pressures, but also because of the Nazi stoking of long-simmering German resentment about the Versailles Treaty, its economic punishment of Germany and blaming them for everyone's losses in the war.

"How are things at the paper?" Jack asked. He and I had gotten together now that the early days of caring for a newborn baby was in the rearview mirror.

"Things have stabilized a little. No layoffs for a few months," I said. "The other paper, an evening daily, has been shuttered. Gives us all the willies. Our circulation has stayed steady, but we're printing about ten fewer pages a day now, the funnies have shrunken down to one page, and ads are practically non-existent. We've kept the price of each issue at a dime, which may catch up with us. We won't break even without more advertising and selling at ten cents a copy.

"My good news is that I have more responsibility for world news, always my greatest interest. The bad news is that what I report has been disastrous. But we reporters don't have a say in how the world behaves, just try to tell the story.

"How goes it with you?" I asked Jack.

"Tire sales are sagging as you would expect. People can't afford gasoline, so they don't drive much. Commercial accounts keep us afloat, things like city buses, trash trucks, utility vehicles. If it weren't for those, we'd be in big trouble.

"But it reminds me of those lines of Shakespeare: 'Our purses shall be proud, our garments poor: For 'tis the mind that makes the body rich.'"

How he remembers these things! But he comes up with these "words to live by" and they help get him through.

"Since you've moved back, have you found a Masonic Lodge?"

"Not yet. I'm casting about for one. Family life is fine, but I would like other guys to talk to, share experiences with, you know. Drinking buddies too."

"Can you drink in the Lodge?"

"Oh, no, the drinking goes on afterwards."

I wondered where that issue stood. I know Jack cut down a while back. His other worrisome vice continues. He still smokes a couple of packs a day. Sarah says Jack still spends the first ten minutes of each morning coughing. But he's not about to stop smoking.

Sarah joined us after she put the kids to bed.

"How's little Jimmy?"

"He's an angel," Sarah said. "Sleeps a lot, but Doctor Weinstein says that's normal. John never slept this much. But then John has never been exactly relaxed. You know he's playing piano? And football. I don't really like that sport, worry about injuries, especially of the head, but I can't keep him from doing what all the other kids are doing."

"I'm really proud of John," Jack said. "His piano playing is super. He's already passed me up when it comes to skill and improvisation. But I'm still in charge when we have the family quartet going. We'll have some fun next time you come. It'll be like old times!" Jack said.

I hadn't seen Jack is such a good frame of mind for some time. He didn't always approve of some of John's antics, so this was good to hear.

But I never know how to take Jack. Sometimes he's completely extroverted, cracking jokes, with his full-bodied laugh infecting everyone in the room. Like now. Other times, he's morose, railing against the world, his anger and resentment running over. His highs and his lows are extreme.

Was he like this as a child? It's hard to call up those memories, they're so embedded in my own youthful narcissism and the wondrous confusion of growing up. Are these moods determined by external events or do they come from deep within him, bearing no relationship to what's going on around him?

Chapter Nineteen

Pick Yourself Up

1936-1940

AS A REPORTER COVERING world events, I found the news dispiriting. In Germany, Fascism was emboldened. Hitler muscled his way up the political hierarchy to become "Fuhrer." Europe was in turmoil, with several countries signing the Balkan Pact, a mutual protection agreement, more symbolic than real, in response to Germany's threatening posture.

Austria became a Fascist state, assassinations occurred regularly in Germany as Nazis mercilessly purged political enemies. The world economy was reeling. Ordinary people in Europe were preoccupied with their own personal survival, turning a blind eye to dictators taking over their government's functions.

Back home, the Lewellyn family's determination and hope for better days took another hit. Goodyear's marketing department recognized Jack's past managerial success in developing new territories. His reward was still another transfer, this time to Defiance, Ohio.

"I have news," Jack said to me. "Moving to Ohio. Not happy about it, but I have no choice. It's either take this or go on relief. Although Sarah's developed admirable skills at moving, I don't know how long she can tolerate these repeated disruptions of everyone's lives, changing schools, losing friendships. To say nothing of thankless house-hunting and constantly reorganizing our stuff."

He sounded resigned to another uprooting of family, business associates, community relationships. This couldn't be good for the psychological health of anyone in the family. But poverty wasn't an option for Jack, with a wife and three kids. They moved in the summer, and I visited them in the fall.

"Nice neighborhood!" I said when I saw the classic middle American street they lived on.

"We got lucky when we were looking," Jack said. "An elderly woman lived here, and she passed. Her adult children didn't need another house and couldn't sell this one easily since no one is buying houses these days. They decided renting it out was their best option."

"And now we can finally get a dog!" John cried. "We're going to see one this afternoon!"

"Where? Can I go with you?" I asked.

"Sure, Uncle Cyrus, you can come and help us pick out the best dog at the dog pound."

Sarah told us she couldn't handle a big dog "so don't come home with anything over 20 pounds!" We picked out a black, tan, and white Fox Terrier, about 4 years old. Martha wanted to name him Danny and no one objected. So, Danny it was.

We all took Danny for a walk as soon as we got home. He'd been trained to a leash, following verbal cues while walking and he didn't bark much. From the beginning he took to Jack, who loved him unconditionally. When Jack sat down in his favorite chair, Danny would, unbidden, hop into Jack's lap. Jack would invariably give out with his patented laugh at this, give him a tummy rub and then Danny settled into Jack's lap. John and Martha each had to see to it that Danny got fed and had water. They took turns walking him come rain, snow, or sunshine. Jimmy had no regular chores yet, but loved having Danny lick his face.

Just before we sat down for supper that evening, Jimmy was chasing Danny around the dining room table just as Martha came from the kitchen carrying a bowl of hot lentil soup. Jimmy crashed into her, hot soup spilling onto Jimmy's face. He screamed, Martha started crying and Sarah, Jack and I all sprang up to help.

Sarah wiped Jimmy's face off with a dish cloth, looked at it and decided to call the doctor. Sarah was worried that the burned area may have included his right eye. While they waited for the doctor's call, Sarah put cool cloths on his face.

When Doctor Johnson called, Jimmy had stopped crying, but they whisked him off anyway to the doctor's office just down the street. He returned with a bandage on his right cheek with a V-shaped notch cut out for his eye. The doctor had applied ointment and reassured two shaken parents that the burn was only first degree and would heal without incident. We all finally sat down for dinner, relieved.

Defiance, a small town in Northern Ohio, was to be home to family Lewellyn for four years, a distinct change from their peripatetic life. John, at age sixteen, was back-up quarterback for Defiance High. Popular with everyone, teachers, coaches, classmates, his handsome appearance had only gotten better as adolescence took charge of his body. His ready smile and friendly demeanor made him a favorite in his class. His academic achievements matched his popularity, with straight A's in all subjects, including shop. By the time he was a senior, his class elected him president of student council and the football coach made him starting quarterback. His piano-playing skills prompted him to organize a six-piece band that played at school functions.

Jack was intent on getting John into a good college for the education he himself never had. He told me about spending many evenings writing letters to colleges asking for their catalogs, agonizing over choices, comparing facts not only about course offerings but also costs of tuition, living expenses and books. There were many colleges in Ohio and Indiana to choose from, but the allure of famous universities of the East caught Jack's attention. He wanted the best for John and knew that Harvard, Yale, and Johns Hopkins were the holy grails of colleges. When he scoured catalogs from those universities, he immediately saw that these prestigious institutions had tuition costs in the stratosphere, far above his means. Jack searched for a college that would prepare him for medical school and afford him the best opportunity for admission. Costs were discouraging and kept staying his hand. How could he afford this? He was determined he'd find some way to get John, Martha, and Jimmy educations he felt they must have. This had become the guiding force of his life. He'd often told me that if he failed at this task that his life would have no meaning. Plus, in his head he could hear Papa's voice of encouragement of this goal.

In late October I got a letter from Jack.

October 20, 1939

Dear Cyrus,

It's been too long since we've seen you. Sarah and the kids keep asking about you, wondering what you are doing, how you are.

Any chance you could visit soon? I'd like to pick your brain about colleges, among other things. Sarah is also anxious to have you come and I promise she'll spoil you for a few days.

Let me know. Soon, I hope.
Love,
Jack

Just before Halloween I jumped in my car and headed northeast to Defiance. I was glad to get away from the paper and depressing news from Europe. Hitler was running rampant over eastern Europe. Kristallnacht, the "night of broken glass" caused looting of Jewish businesses and the burning of nearly 300 synagogues. Twenty- five thousand Jewish men were arrested, all in reprisal for a young Jewish man assassinating a Nazi.

Franco's Spain recognized Nazi Germany. The bad guys were winning. There's so much misery in Europe, but the United States was still looking the other way. So, going to see my brother and his wonderful family was a welcome respite.

~~~

"Well, howdy, stranger!" Jack called to me from his front porch. Jimmy came running full blast towards me, jumping into my open arms. Danny's whole rear end was wagging furiously.
~~~

Sarah looked on from the porch, waving as I was assaulted. We all went inside, hugged and patted each other. So happy to be part of this family.

"What would you like to drink?" Jack asked as he poured himself a generous glass of bourbon followed by another, moments later.

"Have any coffee?" I asked.

"Freshly brewed!" Sarah said.

John and Martha were still at school, so I could look forward to another enthusiastic welcome later. Sarah handed me my cup and motioned toward the creamer and sugar bowl.

"How was the trip?" Jack asked. "Need any tires?"

"Actually, I do need tires. Does your place also change oil?"

"Anything you need for the car, we've got," Jack laughed, proving once more how good a salesman he was. "We aim to please!"

"Can you stay the weekend? John's going to play football on Saturday afternoon, and later his band is playing for the school dance," Sarah said.

"That's wonderful! Yes, I'm here to bother you until Sunday night. I'll head home after supper."

Sarah sat down beside me, her fragrance floating over me. She seemed not to have aged at all. Three babies hadn't changed her figure either and she still had her charming easy laugh.

"Singing much?" I asked.

"Every Sunday, at church. An occasional recital, but no big works like the last time you heard me. Defiance doesn't have as active a music scene as Terre Haute. But I'm busy enough taking care of this brood."

"And she does a fabulous job of taking care of all of us," Jack said, planting a kiss on her cheek. "She spreads love around like a painter."

Jimmy and Danny wandered off now that the excitement had died down. Jack and Sarah sat down for some adult conversation.

"My current worry is about college for John," Jack said. "I'm deep into research about where he should apply. You have any ideas?"

"Not much. But I'm a good sounding board. The only college I really know is IU, and that's not a bad one."

"Of course, Sarah went there, as you know," Jack said.

"I'd like him to go to a university where they have both pre-med and a medical school, so he wouldn't have to move between college and medical school. Also, it's more likely he would get into medical school at the same university where he took premed courses. You know, the professors there would know him, and their recommendations would have more weight.

"What I'm thinking now is to move the family to Cincinnati where the University of Cincinnati is. I've found their med school is one of the best in the country.

It's certainly one of the oldest, established in 1819. Has a good reputation. What do you think?"

"That sounds like a good choice. I've never been to Cincinnati, but I hear it's a great town. They have a fine symphony orchestra and a Conservatory of Music. Sarah would like that."

"The other advantage is that it's a city college and if you live in the city, tuition is cheap," Jack said. "Also, John could live at home, so room and board wouldn't cost anything. That may sound miserly, but in these times any way a guy can save a dime the better off he is. Then there's Martha coming along right behind John. Two in college at once ain't cheap!"

"Sounds like a good plan for the kids' education. I guess the other consideration is your job."

"That's another thing. To move there, I have to negotiate a job either with Goodyear or another company. That's a little tricky. But I'll work that out. I'm a good salesman, have a good track record with Goodyear. Other tire companies are out there if Goodyear doesn't do the right thing, and if none of that works, I'll figure something else out."

I turned to Sarah, who was quiet.

"What do you think?" I said.

"It all makes me nervous, truth be told. But Jack is right. College is right around the corner for both older kids, and then later, there's Jimmy. The job part is why I'm worried. Jack's been with Goodyear all this time, even during the depression, when a lot of good people are enduring terrible times. I don't know what Goodyear will think of all this."

"Well, I'm tired of worrying about what the great god Goodyear thinks," Jack blurted. "I've worked for them for, what, off and on for 18 years, time out for the war years. They owe me plenty for developing eight territories in six cities. There's gotta be an outlet in Cincinnati where they can find a place for me. If not, well fuck 'em, I say. I'll find something else, damn their souls."

He looked at Sarah, whose eyes were looking down, and said, "Pardon my French, Sarah."

This was my brother Jack ranting. The leaden weight of responsibility for educating three kids was stirring up a host of anxieties. He believed to his very core that his own lack of education had cost him dearly over the years; promotions he didn't get, all those transfers to back-water towns ostensibly to "open new territories," and a long list of other grievances I'd heard him complain about. His bitterness was usually hidden behind his "good guy" façade, until alcohol enabled his anger.

I watched Sarah wince as Jack spewed his rage.

"Jack, calm down. The kids will hear you going on."

"Don't tell me to calm down! You don't help a bit, with your holier than thou attitude, and I know coquettish behavior at church. I know what's goin' on, don't you think I don't."

"Oh, Jack, that's ridiculous. Stop it right now!"

This was a side of Jack I'd seen only on a few occasions when he'd been drinking, but not when he was sober. The storm passed as quickly as it rose. Jack took a deep breath.

"I'm sorry, I get upset when I look at all the things I gotta do," Jack said. "The world's a hostile place. I have to guard my family, so they don't get ground down by those bastards out there. These upcoming years are critically important, I don't want anything to screw them up."

I looked at Jack and saw my brother as a young boy of 13 when we lost Papa. He stood tall then, personally taking on responsibilities that Papa had carried before he died. Quitting school for Jack had been the ultimate sacrifice for an intelligent, hard-working boy his age, but he never complained about it, not then. All the repressed anger of the intervening years seemed to be erupting now as he was overwhelmed with primal protective instincts.

The afternoon sun was dipping behind the maple trees out back. Martha and John soon arrived home from school. If I was surprised about how much Jimmy had grown, when I saw the two of them, I was floored. Martha was nearly as tall as I was, her wavy red hair flowing over her shoulders, her freckled face smiling radiantly as she ran to me for a hug. She had bobby-sox atop her saddle shoes, and she wore a yellow patterned jumper over a blouse. John was this six-foot

Adonis. His auburn hair was in a stylish pompadour on top of his head and there was a hint of beard hair on his cheeks and chin. His movie-star good looks were striking. He was dressed in tan slacks, blue button-down shirt, and brown Harris tweed sport coat. Both greeted me boisterously, with big hugs and pats.

"How long you staying, Uncle Cyrus?" Martha asked.

"Through the weekend. But don't expect me to dress up for Halloween. Didn't bring any costume or mask."

"But you can come to my band show on Saturday night, right?" John asked.

"Oh, sure, that's a given. Wouldn't miss that. I'll probably be the oldest person there!"

"Oh, no, there's lots of parents who'll be coming. They're all much older than you!" John said.

"You seem to forget that Uncle Cyrus and I are twins, which makes us the same age," Jack laughed.

"Well, he seems much younger," Martha said, as Jack shot her a mock angry glance. "That just shows how much you kids made me age!" he said. After we all stopped laughing, as Martha, who realized her faux pas, blushed, her freckles lighting up. As we sat down to talk, Danny, who'd been a little shy when I first arrived, hopped up into my lap.

"He must trust you. He usually gets into Dad's lap as soon as he sits down," John said.

"We probably smell the same since we're brothers," I said. "You know dogs are all about smells."

"How come, if you're twins, you don't look alike?" Jimmy asked.

"Well, that's a complicated story, Jimmy. We come from different eggs. Some twins come from the same egg that splits in two. Those twins look exactly alike. We're what are called fraternal twins."

"Oh," was Jimmy's response to my explanation.

The next evening, we went to the concert at the high school and John's band of seven played several current pop tunes and jazz. They played them as well as any versions I'd heard on the radio. After they stopped playing, people crowded around John's piano, slapping him on the back, shaking his hand and praising the band. All the boys loved such attention.

The rest of the weekend sped by. As I drove back to Indianapolis, I realized how much I loved this family and wanted to be with them more often. If they moved to Cincinnati, as it seemed Jack was intent on doing, maybe I could find a job with the Enquirer, the main newspaper there. Then I could watch as a proud uncle as my niece and two nephews grew up. And be close to my brother and his wonderful Sarah. Was I dreaming? Do all bachelors dream like this?

Chapter Twenty

Can't Get Indiana Off My Mind

1938

JACK IS MOVING THE family to Cincinnati. He said the first order of business was to find a place to live near schools for all three kids. Clifton School for Jimmy was easy. High school for Martha was harder. She wanted to go to Walnut Hills High School, a public "test" school, meaning applicants had to pass an entrance exam. Jack thought the local public high school was perfectly adequate, but Martha, in her usual stubborn mode, was adamant. She'd done her research and insisted on going to Walnut Hills, a long way from Clifton. She'd have to transfer several times on public transportation to get there and back each day. She took and easily passed the entrance exam. Jack couldn't justify even to himself telling her she couldn't go. So, she won that one.

"Our apartment's a block away from Clifton School for Jimmy and right on the streetcar line that goes to UC. Martha, my intransigent redhead, held out for a school way the hell on the other side of town. Boy, when that girl makes up her mind to do something, nothing stands in her way."

But there were problems as the Lewellyns decided to strike out and do what Jack thought was best for the family.

"Those goddam sonsabitches at Goodyear told me they had no jobs for me in Cincinnati. All those years of building up a territory and then turning it over to a lower paid salaried guy, moving all over Hell's half acre to develop new territories, and this is what I get for it. The bastards! Now I'm jobless and we're scheduled to move to Cincy in two damn weeks. I'd naively hoped the company would see my value. But I covered my bets, because that little voice in my head told me not to trust those jerks. I saved some money, so we're not gonna starve, but that dough won't last more than a few months."

"You think there's some other tire company in Cincinnati that'll hire you?" I asked, knowing Jack's deep knowledge and success in the tire business would make him an attractive hire.

"I have some inquiries out. There's a small company, Dayton Tire and Rubber. Well, smaller than Goodyear, but then who isn't? Maybe that'll work out. Meanwhile, I got a night watchman's job at P and G, you know, Proctor and Gamble, the big- time soap company with headquarters in Cincy. That'll keep us afloat 'til I find a real job. Only thing is, I'll have to spruce up my gun-totin' skills as a night watchman. Haven't fired a gun since I left France.

"Cyrus, I'd love it if you moved to Cincy too. Have you talked to the Enquirer people?"

"Have an appointment next week. I sent my resume, so we'll see. How's Sarah doing?"

"She's right here. Wanna talk to her?"

"Sure." I heard the rustling of the phone being transferred.

"Hi Cyrus. How're you? As for me, I'm deep into packing up the house, getting to be an expert at moving. Seems like that's all I do! But I know this is going to be good. The new apartment's a little tight, but Jack says it's temporary until we find a real house. But we'll make it our home for as long as necessary."

So typical of Sarah, always making the best of things.

"Soon as I get settled there, I'll set up my sewing machine and put out word that I design and sew drapes and slipcovers," she said. "I've already made some contacts at the church we're going to join. With Jack in his temp job, we're going to need a little extra income.

"Jack said you're looking at a newspaper job in Cincy," she said, already picking up the nickname for Cincinnati. "Hope that comes through, so we see you more often."

"I'd like that too," I said, as one of the kids in the newsroom handed me a note. "Oh, gotta go, sorry, have a call to cover a story. Talk to you later."

The story I needed to cover was a big one: the Republican Party's nominating convention in Philadelphia. Some thought Wendell Willkie was their best candidate, but others thought Roosevelt would beat him handily. Willkie was an Indiana Hoosier, seen as a "nice guy." His opponent for the nomination was Senator Robert A. Taft of Cincinnati, whose appearance, demeanor, and dark three-piece suits were those of a stern private school headmaster.

It was serendipity for me to cover this political rivalry since I was currently working for the Indianapolis Star but thinking about a job with the Enquirer in Taft's hometown. Willkie headed up a private energy company in Tennessee and was a strong opponent of the Tennessee Valley Authority. The TVA was seen by many in the private business sector as a socialistic governmental takeover. Being opposed to TVA and his stance on non-intervention in the war could be critical issues in the general election.

I talked with Jack about Willkie. He knew of him in another context and told me that Willkie had once been President of Firestone Tire and Rubber in Akron, a head-to-head competitor of Goodyear.

"They're both run by bastards," Jack said disgustedly. "I had nothing but trouble with Firestone.

Their sales guys were squeezing into my Goodyear territories. So, a pox on both their houses, I say."

"So, what's your political inclination, Willkie or FDR?"

"Well, I suppose I'm a Republican. I think Roosevelt is an upper-class snob, and a first-class bullshitter."

He pulled on his ear as he considered saying more. "But I give him due credit for some good things he's done for regular people. Social Security, for instance. And he's tried hard to stop this damned depression, but nothing seems to work. I have trouble with all those WPA guys, leaning on their shovels, getting paid for doing nothing. That bothers me. So, I'll listen to these guys to see who gets my vote.

"One thing's for sure, though, if Willkie starts talking about getting into this stupid war, I'll vote against him and tell anyone who'll listen to do likewise. No one should have to go through another World War, and that's what it would become if the US got involved."

It was interesting to hear Jack's take on Roosevelt, who was very popular with men in the trades, despite his own patrician background. Jack was one of those in-between guys, sort of in the management sector but not in the upper echelons, but his attitude towards the "working man" was more Republican than Democrat. On the other hand, he felt grossly mistreated by

Goodyear, surely all run by Republicans. It'll be interesting to see how he votes.

John started at UC in the Fall and immediately became known for his intellect, his musical talents, and his best all-around persona. He was rushed by several fraternities, but because of initiation costs and dues, he didn't join any. This didn't stop him from being elected class president and becoming active in several extracurricular clubs.

He took the required pre-med courses, but his electives were in art, history, and literature. He vowed not to become a narrow-minded pre-med moron, a label designed by some liberal arts students when they wanted to lord their intellectual superiority and breadth of outlook over pre-med grinds.

Martha, I was told, loved her high school experience, and she excelled in all classes. Although not a natural intellect like John, her perseverance and hard work garnered her straight A's. John said he didn't understand why she was so driven. I looked at him for a long time after he said that and he finally caught on I was mocking him, since he was similarly driven. We both burst out laughing.

By a huge stroke of luck, I got a job at the *Cincinnati Enquirer*. One of their world-beat reporters left to work for the *New York Times*, so they had an opening, and I got a significant raise. I snatched the job up like a hungry junkyard dog. I moved to Cincinnati at almost the same time as Jack and Sarah. My boss at the *Star* had always appreciated my reporting and writing skills. He let me know he was most unhappy with me for leaving, but even so, he arranged a nice sendoff party when I left and gave me a warm handshake on my last day.

I found a neat bohemian apartment on Mt. Adams, a neighborhood close to downtown Cincinnati and my newly adopted paper. Named after our second president, it was a jumble of ancient houses tossed haphazardly across the rocky hills jutting up from the Ohio river. I had a great view of the city and the Ohio River and, for me it had an added benefit of being near Cincinnati's Art Museum and the local artist community. Young artists, musicians, writers, and theater people populated Mt. Adams, so I made friends quickly. Jack envied me, comparing my bachelor freedom with his own heavy responsibilities.

~~~

"Cyrus," Jack said on the phone, "we've moved in and would like you to come for one of Sarah's delicious dinners. I landed a job with that tire company I told you about, remember? Dayton Tire. They have a store about ten minutes from our apartment. Things seem to be falling into place.

"Sarah's found a presbyterian church here in Clifton and auditioned for their choir. She of course was immediately and enthusiastically invited to join.
~~~

It's an exceptional choir with over thirty singers. The director of music at the church teaches voice at the Cincinnati Conservatory of Music. She's real excited about it."

I was happy that Jack was positive about his new job. The family seemed to be well established in their new lives when I arrived for dinner on Friday evening.

When I gazed up at their yellow brick building, I saw three apartments on each side of a center-entrance, framed by heavy iron and glass doors leading to stairs with dark carved oak bannisters and balustrades. Each apartment had a bow-shaped porch in front with black wrought-iron grillwork firmly planted in a thick cement floor.

The building had a distinctly German character, solid buff brick, sturdy and functional, mounted on a steep inclined street where there must have been no building codes. It must have been built early in the twentieth century. No one would have called it a handsome structure, and surrounding buildings didn't relieve the austerity of this small stretch of housing. Across the street was a large Tudor-style red brick apartment building with maybe seventy-five units. Beside it was a large single-family Victorian frame house, seemingly out of place but probably one of the original houses on the street before apartment construction took over the neighborhood. It was odd, too, since most of Clifton, especially here, was quite residential with some very upscale homes.

When I went into their first-floor apartment, it was much more spacious than I expected. Sarah's ubiquitous upright piano was in the parlor, and we would surely gather around it for some singing during my visit.

"Welcome!" Jack yelled. "Can't believe we're all together again. Let me show you around." His joy at seeing me after so many months' absence was palpable. As we began a tour of the apartment, Jimmy called out from the corridor leading to the bedrooms.

"Wanna see my Zorro suit?"

"Sure!" I answered.

Jimmy came out wearing his black Zorro mask and a makeshift costume, with a short narrow wooden sword, thankfully blunt. He'd used Sarah's eyebrow pencil to smudge a mustache on his small upper lip.

"So, are you gonna make sure the bad guys pay for their crimes?" I said as I knelt beside him.

"Yessiree, they're gonna be sorry they crossed me!" he practically screamed.

"Okay, Jimmy," Sarah called, "time to wash up for dinner. Be sure you get all that black stuff off your lip."

"Little brothers are such a pain in the neck," John said when he appeared out of his room. "I have to sleep in the same room with that little brat."

"How's college treating you?" I asked, ignoring his big brother supercilious comment.

"I love it. Did you know I got elected class president?"

"I heard that! Congratulations. Pretty good for a transplanted Hoosier, I'd say."

I turned to Martha, who had materialized from her room. "And how's your school going?"

"Just fine. I'm taking Latin, geometry, and advanced physics. My entry tests showed I had potential in those subjects."

"Okay, say something in Latin for me," I said.

"Gallia est omnis divisa in partes tres," meaning 'Gaul is a whole divided into three parts.' Did you learn that in high school?"

"Can't say that I did. We didn't study any foreign languages in Vincennes, even though the town has a French name. I'm glad you're taking Latin even though it's called a dead language. It's the origin, the root, of all romantic languages."

After dinner we all gathered around the piano. Jack chorded some current songs:

> "Back in the Saddle again"
> "You tell me your Dream I'll tell you Mine"
> "Over the Rainbow"
> "You Are My Sunshine"
> "Paper Moon"
> "When you Wish upon a Star"
> "Night Train"

It was a bigtime songfest.

I was impressed with how much joy there was in Jack's voice when he was singing. He was pitch-perfect and his mellow baritone blended well with

Sarah's soprano. John had a sweet tenor voice and Martha was a solid alto. Jimmy hadn't yet developed any singing skills and he didn't seem interested. That would come later, along with violin lessons and the development of interest in classical music.

~~~

It was only six months later when we met for lunch that Jack told me "We're moving again. We found a house on Ludlow Avenue. Much more room and Sarah can walk to get groceries. She says she feeds us on a dollar a day! Don't know how she does it. John can hop the same streetcar he's always taken to get to UC – it comes by about a block from the house -- and Jimmy can walk to his school. This house even has a garage for my car."

"How's that car running? It's getting pretty old, at least for you," I said, knowing Jack bought new cars every two years.

"Well, it's a Ford and now that John drives, I'm keeping it a while longer since he's a kid driver and you never know what's gonna happen when they get behind the wheel! I taught him how to operate the vehicle, but I can't teach judgment. That car is vital since I use it for work and everything else. Sarah's a good driver, so I don't worry about her. But John, well, I don't know."
~~~

"I'm still driving my old Plymouth coupe. I may have to get a newer car now that I live on Mt. Adams. The hills around here are steep, so different from Indiana where everything's flat. What kind do you suggest?"

"Ford. Can't go wrong with them. Not exciting, but you probably don't care about that, right?"

"No, you're right. For me a car is only useful to get from point A to point B. I'll have to consult Sarah on color since she's the interior decorator in the family. How's that going for her?"

"Pretty well. I sometimes go with her to a client's home to help her hang the drapes she's made. I feel a little like a fifth wheel, but I don't want her up on ladders. Some of her clients are kind of snobbish too. She's very sensitive about that, but she never lets on."

"She still singing in the church choir?"

"Yeah."

His short answer caught my attention. Is this jealousy raising its head again?

"Do you go to that church?" I asked innocently.

"Used to, but I got into a big argument with the minister. He thinks because he has a DD, that's Doctor of Divinity, that he's hot stuff. So, I never go. Martha goes to the early service and Jimmy goes to Sunday School. John and I stay home."

"What was the argument about?"

"Freemasonry. He started railing on about it being a cult. He doesn't know beans about it but that doesn't stop him from bad-mouthing it. I tried to explain it to him, but he just looked down his nose at me, like I'm some kind of moron. I don't like his attitude. Sarah thinks he's wonderful. He treats her like a queen. That pisses me off too. I sometimes wonder if they have something goin' on."

"Sarah? Not a chance. She loves you unconditionally. And don't you forget it!" I don't often speak to my brother sternly, but to suspect Sarah of anything like that was just unfair and crazy.

"Okay, okay, sorry I brought it up. As a matter of fact, I didn't bring it up, you did." Jack was gaining a full head of steam. "So, I'd thank you not to interfere in my married life!"

"Jack, Jack, I'm not interfering with your married life! Calm down."

Jack headed toward his liquor cabinet, poured himself a generous glass of bourbon and before he put the bottle back, he looked at me and said, "Want some?"

I decided to join him this time. I'd heard that it wasn't good to allow an alcoholic to drink alone. But was I enabling his drinking? Hard to know sometimes what to do.

"I'm sorry," I said.

"Me too. I'm super sensitive these days. Work isn't great, and John is giving me a hard time about things. Now that he's a "university man" he finds my lack of education, what, embarrassing? Or he sees me as less a man than all those intellectuals he associates with now. And look at this house! It's a dump. I wish we could buy a new house, have Sarah decorate it with her good taste, and have people give us some respect."

"This house isn't a dump! It's very livable and in a nice neighborhood. Remember, this country is still in a depression. You're doing so much better than a lot of people. So, buck up, brother. A lot of people love you."

I could see his eyes watering and his lips twitching. I reached over and put my hand over his. This released a flood of tears, totally unexpected. We sat together for a few minutes until he gathered himself.

"Thanks, Cyrus. Sorry I popped off at you."

Living alone as I do is uncomplicated. Family life is not. It seems to me that all the desires and needs of family members are alternately hidden and revealed, often surprising everyone when a meltdown occurs at times when all seems calm. I chalked Jack's eruption up to an accumulation of recent frustrations embedded in his recurring disappointing expectations.

Chapter Twenty-One
Remember Pearl Harbor

1941

Dateline: March 11,1941

*Roosevelt signs Lend-Lease Program
Intended to Bolster Britain's Defenses*

Dateline: May 27, 1941

*Roosevelt Declares Unlimited National
Emergency*

Dateline June 14, 1941

*Roosevelt Freezes All German and Italian Assets,
Sends Consulates Back to Germany, Italy*

Dateline: July 27, 1941

Roosevelt Orders Seizure of All Japanese Assets

Rumors of Japanese assault on Hawaii began in late January when our national intelligence agents exposed clues that Japan was planning an attack. These troubling reports continued through the summer.

A controversial Army colonel, Billy Mitchell, had boldly predicted in 1934 that Japan would attack Pearl Harbor by their air force. Military strategists knew our territory of Hawaii was vulnerable.

But no one could explain why Japan, that little island country-- someone called it a "papier-mache country" -- would dare to engage with our mighty United States. What casual observers of world affairs didn't appreciate was that Japan had been in a decades-long competition with China for control of the western Pacific region.

I was asked to cover this developing story, which I eagerly accepted. When I told Jack about it, he became unusually reflective.

"I hope the Japs don't do something stupid like that," Jack said. He gazed away, choosing his next words carefully. "I have such strong feelings about getting into another war, but I'm conflicted about this one. If the Japs do start war with us, we'll have to respond." He lit up a cigarette and continued.

"Ever hear of the America First organization? Lucky Lindy is one of their spokesmen. He's been opposed to getting into war with Germany from the start. Some say he's a Nazi sympathizer. He blames Jews in this country for trying to push us into it. But what he doesn't even mention is the ugly fact that European jews are being brutally exterminated by his Nazi buddies. Of course, American Jews want us to get involved. Remember what John Donne said? 'Any man's death diminishes me because I'm involved in mankind; and therefore, never send to know for whom the bell tolls; it tolls for thee." We can't stand idly by while these atrocities are going on. As much as I hate war, I think we've got to resist Hitler and, if it comes to that, Japan too."

I never stop being astonished by Jack. Just when I think I understand him, he pivots away from his older, long-expressed opinions. Of course, I agreed with him. We were morally obligated to oppose this "sea of troubles."

"Churchill's been goading FDR to help England hold off Hitler and his thugs," I said, "but so far Roosevelt has said no. He knows Americans don't relish their young sons going to war. But Roosevelt's a crafty guy. In his heart he knows we gotta help the Brits. On my reporter's network there's buzz about covert plans to support England by a work-around called Lend Lease. Supposed to be signed into law before summer. That means...." I trailed off.

"I think we've gotta get in," Jack repeated. "If this madman takes over Europe, he'll set his sights on us. U-boats have already been spotted all over the east coast. You know we'll be next if Britain falls. Then when you add the wild card, Japan..."

On a fateful Sunday, December 7th, 1941, the Japanese navy, without warning, attacked and destroyed our naval installation at Pearl Harbor, Hawaii. Roosevelt would call this "a day that will live in infamy."

On that day, I went for an afternoon visit with Jack's family in their new digs on Ludlow Avenue. John brought Pauline Gormley, a young woman he'd met in his art class, to meet his family. Pauline was a talented artist who worked with oils. It wasn't long after they met that she had John posing for his portrait. That portrait would remain in the family long after his love affair with Pauline was history. It captured him in his post-adolescent sensuality, wavy auburn hair framing his angular face and bold jaw, dressed in his signature sweater and open-collar shirt.

She'd introduced him to the Beaux Arts Club, a group whose members were distinctly unlike pre-med students in John's classes. Some were visual artists like Pauline, others were writers, sculptors, and musicians. John felt most comfortable with the musicians because of his own musical skills and interests.

But December 7th, 1941, was an inauspicious time to introduce her. Jack was in a foul mood. Sarah was tiptoeing around him to avoid setting him off. He'd been drinking since the night before. It wasn't long until I discovered the reason for his ill humor: John had an accident with their car the night before.

"That's the last goddam time you get to take my car on a date, or anything else. What the hell were you doing? Have your arm around her?" rudely pointing to Pauline. "You took your eyes off the road, the first rule of driving! I told you that over and over when I was teaching you to drive. Now I don't have a car for god knows how long while we get it fixed. And insurance doesn't cover you, so it's out of my pocket."

Naturally Pauline was mortified being dropped into a family whose patriarch was drunk and in a rage. John was paralyzed in fear and embarrassment.

Jack was totally out of control. I didn't hear John's side of the story until later, but his excuses didn't matter in this atmosphere. It's true that Jack's car was crucial for his job. He'd not be able to make sales calls until it was fixed. "If I don't have a car, I might as well pick shit with the chickens!" he yelled.

Silence filled the room, no one wanted to pour gasoline on this roaring fire. Minutes passed, everyone stealing furtive glances at each other, then at Jack to see if his level of anger had subsided.

In this quietude, all that could be heard was low volume music from the Philco radio in the living room. But then, all at once, the music stopped, and an excited voice broke the calm. If we'd been talking, we'd have missed the announcement that would change our lives forever.

"We interrupt this broadcast for a special bulletin from Washington, D.C. We've received news that there has been a massive attack on the naval base at Pearl Harbor, Hawaii. Nearly all the U S naval fleet at anchor there has been destroyed by a Japanese air raid. It's too soon to know the extent of casualties but we'll have a report at our six o'clock news hour."

"Good God, now we're in for it," Jack moaned.

"Where's Pearl Harbor?" Jimmy asked.

"In the Hawaiian Islands, way out in the Pacific Ocean. Thousands of miles from here, Jimmy." I told him that to assure this young lad that we were in no danger. "They're territories owned by the United States."

The mood changed from anger to fear. Jack, now abruptly sober, looked first at his son and Pauline, then at Sarah, Martha, and Jimmy. When he looked at me, he asked, "Did you know about this?"

"We'd heard rumors for some time. But this is as new to me as it is to you. I felt if this happened it would force our hand to enter the war."

Sarah's hand went to her forehead, a familiar sign of distress.

"What do you suppose it means for you?" Sarah said to her nineteen-year-old draft-eligible son.

"Don't know for sure. Probably military service. This changes everything."

"Martha, you have one more year in high school. What then?" I asked.

"How should I know? This is so terrible. How could God let this happen?"

Everyone then dispersed to their own private space to absorb what had just happened. I went back home to Mt. Adams and listened to radio analyses of this momentous event. These went on all evening. I wasn't surprised when my editor called me around ten PM to call me to the newsroom so we could publish a front-page editorial about the "sneak attack," as it would become known, on Pearl Harbor.

The next day, Monday December 8th, President Roosevelt addressed a joint session of congress. In somber tones and with steel in his voice, he said,

"No matter how long it may take us to overcome this premeditated invasion, the American people, in their righteous might, will win through to absolute victory. I believe that I interpret the will of the congress and of the people when I assert that we will not only defend ourselves to the uttermost but will make it very certain that this form of treachery shall never again endanger us.

"Hostilities exist. There is no blinking at the fact that our people, our territory, and our interests are in grave danger. With confidence in our armed forces, with the unbounding determination of our people, we will gain the inevitable triumph, so help us God. I ask that the congress declare that since the unprovoked and dastardly attack by Japan on Sunday, December 7, 1941, a state of war has existed between the United States and the Japanese Empire."

At 441 Ludlow Avenue, in early afternoon on Monday, Jack returned from getting a report on the damage to his car.

"Well, we're lucky this time. The only damage is the front right wheel is out of alignment."

"That's a relief," John said. "What's the toll?"

"Thirty-five dollars," Jack said sheepishly.

"I'll pay for it," John said.

"That's all right, John. I'll take care of it. Sorry I got so worked up about it." Jack turned and walked into the other room to avoid further embarrassment.

Chapter Twenty-Two

Boogie-Woogie Bugle Boy

1942

"CYRUS, I HAVE NEWS."

It was Jack calling in April. I shuddered, fearing the worst.

"We just bought a house a few blocks from Clifton School where Jimmy goes. Whadaya think about that?"

Greatly relieved, but astonished they could afford a house, I said "That's terrific news! Congratulations! Tell me about it."

"Just built, $12,500, a real bargain. Living room, dining room, kitchen, half-bath, and bedroom on the ground floor, two bedrooms and a full bathroom on the second floor, a full basement, and a front entry garage under the house. Sits on a rise. Nice front lawn and a big hill in back abutting a large stand of trees. It's beautiful! Tudor style, brick with diagonally crossing front wooden gables."

"Wow! When do you move in?"

"Right away. Mr. Tidball, the realtor, told me the price was so good because a prospective buyer backed out at the last minute, and it was the last house in this development. His company needed to move it quickly to focus on other properties. As soon as we sign papers and a bank approves a mortgage, we can move in."

Jack and John rented a truck and loaded their furniture on a rain-soaked day in May. Everyone was upbeat despite bad weather. Jack and Sarah took the downstairs bedroom, and Martha chose the front bedroom on the second floor. John and Jimmy shared the second bedroom upstairs.

In the weeks following, other life events moved rapidly. John told us that the Army was hurrying pre-med students with good grades into medical school without completing their undergraduate degrees. The Feds created the V-12 program to accelerate doctor's education in the armed services in anticipation of shortages. John and all his medical student classmates would move into newly created barracks in McMicken Hall, the dusty old Gothic structure dominating UC's main campus.

The Army wanted to highlight the students' commitment to the war effort, so they marched in formation each day from McMicken Hall to anatomy dissection labs and lecture halls at medical school buildings on another part of the campus. In the evening, they marched back to McMicken. They ate free breakfasts and dinners at the Student Union on

UC's main campus. Their medical school curriculum was shortened to three years to rush them into active duty overseas and domestically.

I was with the family after they'd moved into their new home. Martha organized her closet and chiffonier, reveling in her spacious room overlooking the front lawn. Sarah arranged furniture and a closet in the marital bedroom. John wrestled two large duffel bags filled with Army uniforms and boots into the living room and emptied them on the floor. Jimmy watched with a fourth-grader's rapt interest in all things military.

"John, why don't you model your new uniform?" Sarah called from the kitchen. He protested mildly, but then took one of the duffel bags into the downstairs bedroom to change. He wondered if the uniform would fit. Everyone had been charged with submitting their measurements to the quartermaster. Most guys had no idea how to measure themselves for clothes, so it was a guessing game as to how they would fit. He came out with his uniform on. The fit was perfect. He could have been a poster boy for the Army. Jimmy's eyes shined as he viewed his big brother sporting his new Army duds.

"Boy, the military's come a long way since I was in. How did you know your measurements?" Jack asked.

"I had some help," he smiled, looking at Sarah. "After all, with a seamstress in the house it would be foolish not to use her services."

~~~

Newspapers covered war stories extensively, but there was little good news. We evacuated our troops in the Philippines and suffered costly early combat failures in Europe. Despite these losses, American propaganda was in full swing with most citizens caught up in patriotic fervor. People snapped up War Bonds as soon as they were offered. Citizens dutifully carried scrap metal to collection centers across America to be repurposed and turned into weapons of war.

"Cyrus, my heart ached the other day when I watched Jimmy dragging his little wagon up the steep hill to school, loaded with metal hangers, tin cans and discarded metal," Jack told me. "What's our country coming to when it asks ten-year-old kids to strain their guts pulling loads of scrap metal to school for the war? What lessons are kids learning from this? They know this metal is being forged into guns, tanks, and ships to kill people."

"Wonder what Papa would say?" I said. "He was an outspoken pacifist, wouldn't even allow us to have toy guns, remember?"

"Yeah. I wonder what he'd say about a lot of things these days. The world's so screwed up." Jack folded his arms across his chest. "But you know, we've got to stop what Hitler is doing. He's the worst human being in history if you can call him human. We're the planet's
~~~

only hope to block him and his barbaric soldiers." I could only imagine what other thoughts were in Jack's mind as he watched his handsome and gifted son pack his uniforms back into his duffel bags.

"It's a real balancing act. We're way behind in everything—battle-ready troops, ships, planes, tanks, guns. Military equipment needs metal, so these scrap metal drives must be needed.

"John, what do you think about all this?"

John snapped the drawstring tight on his bag. He paused before answering. Then, in his deliberate and analytical way, said, "So many guys my age and younger will die or get injured while I'm privileged to go to medical school, at government expense, no less. It's unfair. I guess that's the way the world works, though. Serendipity," John said. "I worry about civilian casualties too, what the military calls 'collateral damage.' It could reach all the way to right here.

"Horrendous things are going on in Europe. We're lucky, so far. Nazis are rounding up and killing Jews, dropping bombs every day on Britain, English families are sending their kids to the countryside for safety. Adults who stay in London practically live in squalid underground bomb shelters, smoldering fires in crushed buildings in the cities; it goes on and on. Much of the country is blacked out, fighter plane dogfights in the skies. What hardships we face here seem insignificant compared to Europe and England."

Sarah came into the room, wiping her hands on her apron, unaware that the conversation was so morose. She called out cheerfully, "Anyone hungry for dinner? I've got meat loaf, potatoes, and green beans ready." She looked at the duffel bags, then at all of us, and finally at John, and suddenly broke down in tears.

"We'll miss you so much," she said to him. "I don't see why they have to move all you guys into McMicken. You could still live at home, eat here, sleep in your own bed, and still go to school every day."

John got up, went to his mother and wrapped her in his arms, trying to comfort her. Jack and I rose, motioned to Jimmy, and went to the dining room table. I was relieved to sit down since it signaled an end to this dismal conversation. After Jack and Sarah brought dinner to the table, we bowed our heads to pray, not a usual practice for us, but the moment seemed right for prayer.

After a few moments of silence, the conversation turned to John.

"We haven't seen Pauline lately. Anything wrong?" Jack asked.

John didn't look up from his meat loaf.

"We decided to take a break. With everything so up in the air, it's difficult to see each other." I glanced at Sarah, wondering what she might know about this, but she was focused on her meal. I was curious to know whether that tumultuous scene here on December 7th had anything to do with this break, but I kept my mouth shut. I glanced at John. He was busy eating, clearly not wanting to get into any further conversation about his private life.

"How's the interior design business going?" I asked Sarah, shifting the subject away from John.

"Very well, thanks. The word is out, and I get calls nearly every week. I don't know how the war will affect it, but right now it's fine. Jack, tell everyone what you've done for me in the basement."

Jack finished chewing and said, "Well, I've watched Sarah tussle with the fabric at her sewing machine and I decided that what she needed was a large table where she could spread out her materials. So, I designed a chest-high table that now occupies most of her end of the basement. It's about 12 feet by 5 feet. It works very well."

"It makes my job so much easier," Sarah said. "Measuring and cutting drapery fabric was driving me crazy since I kept making mistakes that cost money. Now with this higher, bigger table and some new measuring devices I reduce cutting errors. I can also move the material around on the table easier."

"It sounds like the drapery and slipcover business is booming," I said. "I don't know how you do it, making things fit so perfectly."

"It's the old carpenter's rule: measure twice, cut once. And Jack is a big help. He sometimes brings chairs here for fitting, sometimes goes with me to people's houses where we measure couches that are too big to transport."

It occurred to me that Sarah's business had made it possible to buy this house. Jack was not, like so many men of his day, embarrassed that his wife was working and helping with the family's finances. Indeed, Jack was proud of her in many ways. Still, his jealousy was a nagging worry. He had recently declared that she couldn't sing in the church choir any longer.

Not only was he still mad at the minister over his attitude about Freemasonry, but he also suspected him of having designs on Sarah, which Sarah told me was simply not happening. Of course, not singing was a source of great sadness for Sarah, for she loved the release she got from musical expression. I knew Sarah was attractive to other men, but I believed she was faithful to Jack.

She certainly had good reasons to stray, I thought. Jack's insane jealousy, his bad temper, his drinking. She was, in my opinion, innocent of anything but being attractive. But she acceded to Jack's wishes, as was her pattern. Only she would ever know what she lost by not being allowed to sing.

Chapter Twenty-Three

That Old Black Magic

1943

"CYRUS, JOHN IS HAVING a couple of fellows over for Sunday dinner," Jack said on the phone. "We don't know them, but he's been friends with them for some time. John asked that his favorite uncle come so you can meet them too. Pauline introduced them to John."

Lee Spalding was a small willowy man, so quiet that when he spoke, I had to cup my ear to hear him. His self-effacing manner matched his soft voice. Fine brown hair hung loosely over his forehead. His steel-rimmed bifocals tended to slip down his nose and needed to be coaxed back into position by his long, slender fingers. He looked about thirty-five, surprising me that John would have a friend that much older than he.

His other friend, Bobby Rankin, couldn't have been more different. He stood six feet tall, blond, and even with a suit on, I could visualize a well-toned body, ready to play a round of tennis or touch football at any moment. He seemed closer to John's age than Lee. Martha was appraising his square jaw, wide-set clear blue eyes, clearly interested in this handsome man.

"Glad to have you both here. John has told us that the three of you have a common interest in music," Jack said to open conversation.

"Yes," Bobby said. "I play piano, and Lee is a fabulous organist. John told us he plays piano and led a band in high school."

"But I'm in a completely different league than these two," John protested. "These guys are classically trained and play professionally. Bobby plays with a local community orchestra and Lee performs nightly on the radio, a program, called *Moon River*."

"So, how did you meet? I understand that Pauline introduced you, but is there more to the story than that?" Martha asked.

"Yeah," John said. "Pauline took me to a Beaux Arts party, where I met Bobby and Lee, got to be friends because of our mutual interest in music, among other things. We've played some tunes together, but they're way out of my league. But I've learned from them."

"You said 'among other things.' What are those other things?" Jack asked, one eyebrow lifted a bit.

Bobby turned to John. "Your dad's very perceptive, John. Want to tell your folks what that is?'"

"Well, yes, that was one of the reasons I wanted us to have dinner together," John said. "There's this club we belong to. We're exploring some philosophies that are a little out of the mainstream.

"A little history here. Back in high school, Bible stories sounded ridiculous to me. I got more and more turned off by the religions I knew about. When I began reading about other ideas, I got very interested, wanted to look into it more deeply."

I watched Sarah. She stopped eating, hand on forehead, and paid close attention to John as he clumsily explained his interest in this "new philosophy." A devout presbyterian, hearing her son challenge the faith she held dear was making her fidgety. She kept glancing at Martha who shared many of her mother's beliefs. She was listening intently to her older brother, watching Jack jiggle his leg, crossing and uncrossing his legs and arms. I think Martha worried her dear old dad might burst into one of his tirades.

"What are these 'other ideas' you speak of?" Jack asked with the edge in his voice becoming sharper.

"Well, that's hard to summarize," John nearly whispered, fearing he was moving into dangerous territory. "It's a profound philosophy drawing on many ideas, especially from the seventeenth century."

"Sounds strange to me," Jack said. "Does this set of ideas have a name?"

"Rosicrucianism," John said.

"Well, tell me more about what they believe, what did you call it, Rosicrucianism?" Jack said, his speech becoming ever more clipped.

"I'll give you some pamphlets that explains it. After you read them, maybe we can talk more about it."

Lee broke in at this point.

"I sense this worries you," he said to Jack, watching as John became increasingly agitated. "To reassure you a little, it's something we're only exploring. We're curious about alternative philosophies and religious trends. This combines Eastern thought as well as some rejected ideas of other religions. It embraces esotericism."

"And what is that?" Jack said, getting more irascible.

"It's not easily defined," John said, his voice rising, moving his chair away from the table, glancing at Sarah. "I told you, I'll give you these pamphlets to read. Before we get into more discussion I'd like to wait until you read them. No more now though, please."

I'd heard a little about Rosicrucianism and knew that it drew on some of the ideas of Freemasonry, which Jack had embraced. I knew it was sometimes associated with alchemy, the "science" of turning lead into gold, so I had always dismissed it as bunk. It surprised me that John, studying medicine, could be interested in this. It seemed far from scientific. But I decided to reserve judgment until I knew more about it. The discussion petered out, but I felt the tension had not.

Dinner over, Jack thankfully broke the silence and suggested we have a little songfest. He asked Bobby to play a few things before we got into "mundane music," as he put it. Jack appreciated classical music when he heard it on the radio, knew a little about it from Sarah's involvement with classical choral works, but really had only superficial knowledge.

Bobby was as talented as advertised. He played an excerpt of a Bach partita, then swung into some Gershwin to ease the group into more popular music. Since we couldn't provide Lee with an organ, he just relaxed, enjoyed the show, and lent his voice to some of the songs he knew. Jack threw back his head and sang his old favorites, Sarah joining in with John, Martha, and me. Everyone enjoyed themselves as uneasiness over the prior discussion melted away. At least I thought it had.

But when Lee and Bobby left, John and Jack started in again. Sarah and Martha were in the kitchen cleaning up. I didn't enter the conversation, only watched their interaction and listened to the rising antagonism in their discourse.

"I thought you were interested in science," Jack began. "This stuff about esotericism is confusing. Sounds like a bunch of mysticism to me."

"Wait to talk to me after you've read more about it," John said with annoyance. "I'm early into this so I can't respond to your interrogation about it. I have some questions myself, so don't get bent out of shape."

"What do you know about Lee and Bobby?" Jack asked, changing the subject abruptly, revealing his suspicion about John's exotic new friends.

"What do you mean?"

"Well, what do you know about their families, where they come from, what are their personal lives like? What kind of friends do they have?"

"I don't know," John said, crossing his arms across his chest. "I don't pry into people's personal background. I enjoy their company, that's all. They're so different from my medical student friends. They talk about interesting things, places they've gone, Europe, South America, all that. It's a window into a world I don't know anything about."

"So, they got you into this Rosicrucian stuff? Are they really caught up in it?"

"I don't know what you mean, 'caught up in it.' They're exploring it, same as me. You make it sound off-color, or weird."

"It is weird. Sounds like a cult to me. I don't want you falling for a load of bullshit because it seems exciting."

"It's not a cult! Why do you jump to conclusions all the time? You belong to the Freemasons! Is that a cult?"

"Freemasonry has a spiritual foundation. They do community service. A cult is a different proposition altogether. A cult irrationally venerates a person or an object."

"Some people say Freemasonry is a cult. Secret handshakes and all that. How is that different from what I'm learning about?"

"Some upstanding people, such as Benjamin Franklin, and even George Washington, have been Freemasons. Name one person of accomplishment who's a Rosicrucian." A pause. "See, you can't name anyone."

"Read the pamphlets when I get them to you. Unless you don't want to learn about my new interest."

"I'll read them, and we can talk more about it then. Until then consider me a skeptic. And a suspicious one."

"I think we all ought to calm down until we know more about Rosicrucianism, Jack," I said. "I share your doubts, but I'm also open to hearing more about it."

"Well, he's not your kid!" he exploded. "I moved to this damned town so that John, Martha, and Jimmy had access to great educations, not for John to get hung up on some goddam mystical fantasy. It's not what I gave up my steady job for or why Sarah and I moved us again. I hate to have my son fall for some will o' the wisp crap when he should be attending to his studies."

John's face was beet red as he fumed on the couch, but he remained under control. I shouldn't have stuck my nose into this. Jack was right, John is not my son, although he's the closest thing I have to one.

"Okay, I'll butt out. Sorry." After a few beats, I said, "I better be going anyway. Tomorrow's a big day for me."

"What's going on tomorrow?" John asked, glad to have the drift of conversation move beyond anger.

"The Allied forces invaded Sicily a few weeks ago, the first time our men have been on European soil since the war began," I said. "Also, Hamburg has been under constant assault from British and American bombers. Really a major expansion in bombing of Germany. And, importantly, major setbacks in that dumbass Hitler's second front in Russia. They're reeling from winter losses and now retreating. These changes may be a turning point in the war."

"Well, it's about time. I thought when we got into the war it'd be over quickly," Jack said. "Nazis are resilient, though. Hitler may be a lunatic, but he keeps bulldozing his enemies for longer than I thought he could. When I heard "Der Fuehrer" -- Jack faked a German accent when he spit out these words -- "had opened a second front against Russia, I wondered why he'd forgotten about Napoleon's experience with the Great Bear of Russia."

"The Chinese say, 'we live in interesting times' when describing a bad turn of events," I said. "When we look back at World War II, I think we'll recognize that western civilization's salvation was a combination of Churchill's tenacity and Hitler's bad judgment. Say what you want about Winnie, his drinking and eccentric behaviors, he's dragged his little island nation through very dark days. Had Hitler listened to his advisors, he wouldn't have turned his attention to Russia before he'd beaten Britain."

"What's worrying me is whether our class will finish medical school before it's over," John said. "We still have a couple of years before we're actually doctors."

"I hope the war's finished before then," Jack said. "Then you can treat casualties without becoming one yourself. So many dead, so many injured. And entire communities wiped-out, all-over Europe and Japan. I thought World War I was horrible, but we didn't have anywhere near the aerial warfare, heavy artillery, and tanks we have now. How can those countries be rebuilt? It'll cost massive amounts of money. We're so fortunate here in the States that there's been no invasion."

The visit, by then, was over, and I was glad when I got home to Mt. Adams. But I was nagged by worry about Rosicrucianism. I resolved to dig into it and try to make sense of it.

~~~

In Europe things were happening so fast they drew my attention away from domestic concerns. In September, General Eisenhower announced that Italy had surrendered. In November, the big three – Roosevelt, Churchill, and Stalin -- met to discuss future military
~~~

operations. All hush-hush stuff, and the press was busy trying to keep up, although we didn't have much to report. That would come later.

"How are things with John?" I asked Jack a few weeks later.

"Fair to middling. We're still arguing about the Rosicrucian thing. And another thing has come to light. His relationship with Lee and Bobby has me worried."

"In what way?"

"It seems odd to me. Why would two older men be so friendly with John, who is ten years their junior?"

"What are you suggesting?"

"I think those two guys may be queers."

"Have you told John of your concerns?"

"No, can't bring myself to do it. I don't have any evidence, just a hunch, and I don't want to further alienate him by suggesting something that's not so."

"I could ask him about it."

Jack looked at me with thanks written across his face. "Would you do that for me?"

"I'll give it a try. He and I have always been able to talk. But if it turns out they are homosexuals, what then?"

"I don't know." He looked away, conflicted about whether he even wanted to know. "But if John is, it will affect him professionally as well as personally." He ran his hand through his hair. "Being a queer doctor, who's gonna come to you? And day to day life in our society is not easy for homosexuals." Jack pulled on his ear, trying to get these possibilities sorted out in his mind. "You know, he had a love affair with Pauline. I maybe messed that one up when I got so mad at him over that stupid little accident. So, he must not be abnormal."

"I don't think being homosexual is abnormal, Jack. It's just different." I said. "But you're right about society. You just spoke of homosexuality as not normal, and that opinion may be shared by most people. But it's been around since the beginning of recorded history. Michelangelo was homosexual, so was Tchaikovsky, Cole Porter, and legions of other famous and not-so-famous people. Many homosexual artists, musicians, and writers have contributed greatly to our Western culture. And an unknown number of ordinary people are homosexual, living good lives, but hidden from society. So, it shouldn't be considered abnormal"

"You're right Cyrus," he said quietly. After a few moments he continued. "I spoke from my own background, my own prejudices, I know that. But I'm fairly typical of our culture, and that's why I care so much that John doesn't have to endure animosity from the public. But here I am again, thinking about nosing in and trying to control his private life."

Listening to Jack assured me he was making a sincere effort to be tolerant. He'd always said, "judge not lest ye be judged," just like Papa.

"I'll put my conversation with John on hold then. Maybe it will resolve itself," I said, believing that doing nothing was the better course at this point.

We got together the next Sunday for dinner, another in a series of family get-togethers. After dinner we sang around the piano and then sat around and talked. John described his daily march to medical school.

"Here we are, a bunch of entitled kids, stumbling along beside a frustrated drill instructor who must wonder how he got this assignment, none of us giving a damn about whether we're in step or not. It's hilarious. We spend the first five minutes of class every day, giggling about it, like a bunch of schoolgirls discussing boys."

"Any other news from the medical school front?" I asked with a smile.

"Not so much from the medical school front, but you remember Lee and Bobby? They're both in New York City, with good jobs, doing their music. Lee's on television and Bobby is at Julliard. So, they're very happy."

"That's great news!" Jack shouted. Only I understood why Jack was so happy for the good fortune of two men he hardly knew. "Do you miss them a lot, John?"

"Well, not really. They were interesting guys, very worldly, sophisticated. I learned from them. But they're in world distant from mine. Medical school is consuming, so I haven't had much time lately to be with them. I certainly wish them well. When they're both famous I can say I knew them, but they probably won't remember me then."

Jack and I exchanged glances, both of us so happy we hadn't had the talk we'd discussed.

Chapter Twenty-Four

Rosie The Riveter

1944

I KNEW THAT MARTHA had completed two years of college when, according to Jack, her family's treasury was rock bottom. She had three jobs to help with her tuition but confided in me that she worried that her grades would suffer if she continued stealing time from studying.

"It makes me jealous when John revels in his medical school experiences. I know now I yearn to be a doctor too. But I can't afford it, and neither can Dad. Every time I bring it up Dad slaps the idea down." I saw this firsthand at one of our regular Sunday dinners.

"You want to do what?" Jack said when she talked about going to medical school. "Girls can't get into med school, and probably shouldn't," Jack began. "It's a man's profession. It requires stamina that women just don't have. Long hours, getting up to care for patients in the middle of the night. Then there's the issue of pregnancies and caring for your children. So, forget med school. Even if you could get in, I can't afford to pay med school tuition. Luckily, John's was paid for by the government. I don't know where we would've found enough money to pay for his tuition if that hadn't come through."

Jack still hadn't learned about Martha. No one, not even her father, would ever tell her what she could and could not do in life. She'd insisted on going to Walnut Hills, a public college preparatory high school, and won that battle.

"If John could go to med school, by God, so can I! You can't keep me from applying to med school!" she screamed into Jack's face. "I'm smart enough, and I'm tough enough to be a doctor! Who says girls can't be doctors anyway? Ever heard of Virginia Apgar? Alice Hamilton? Jane Wright? Have you ever heard of the Women's Medical College in Pennsylvania? Countless women have been great doctors. Why not me?"

Taken aback by her intense response, he answered in kind.

"I'm not supporting you going to medical school, either emotionally or financially," Jack shouted.

Martha leaped up from the table and stormed out of the room. Jack followed her into the living room, took her by the arm and whirled her around.

"Let go of my arm, you're hurting me!" Martha cried and grabbed his hand and bit it as hard she could.

"Godammit," he howled. Martha sprinted up the stairs to her room and locked her door.

"Jack, stop this right now!" Sarah cried, in an uncharacteristic display of opposition. "You can't treat your own daughter that way! You know how determined she is when you try to thwart her! That'll only make her more defiant!"

"Don't defend her! She can't go to medical school, and that's the end of it!" Jack retorted.

I watched Jack paint himself into this corner. What could I say to persuade him to reconsider his intransigence? But either out of cowardice or wisdom and not wanting to aggravate him into further anger, I stayed silent. Maybe once he'd had time to think about it, he'd relent. Martha told me later she decided right then that she'd quit college and get a job, doing something for the war effort. There was plenty of work available.

"Lots of women do men's jobs now. I'll work for a couple of years, save money, remove that obstacle without Daddy's help or blessing."

And, in characteristic fashion, she did exactly that. She moved to a rural community in southern Indiana where there was a government proving ground for testing ballistics. She rose quickly in the ranks, out-working everyone on the team, and became Team Leader of an artillery testing unit. Her aunt Agnes, Sarah's sister, also worked at the proving ground and let Sarah live in her small apartment rent-free, so she was able to save most of her earnings. I was so impressed by Martha's tenacity and grit. And grateful for her aunt's graciousness and support.

I admired her even more when she returned after the war, made up her unfinished college credits and applied to medical school. Jack still stubbornly refused to support her, but when she got her acceptance letter, he bragged about it to all who would listen.

He never formally apologized to Martha-- his pride wouldn't allow that-- but later, he hugged her and praised her warmly for this signal accomplishment. His second child followed his first to do what he was denied by fate. He couldn't have been prouder.

Chapter Twenty-Five

Paper Doll

1944

JOHN'S DAILY MARCH from McMicken Hall to medical school was a walk in the park compared to what went on in Normandy. The United States suffered enormous losses, much larger than anticipated in this widely publicized "successful invasion," but France was finally freed from the cruel iron grip of Nazism. A combination of good fortune and a decision made by the German high command saved Paris from devastation.

At home, inexplicable stabbing back pain shooting down both of John's legs during marches to and from medical made sleeping difficult and study even more demanding. He told me, before Jack or Sarah, so as not to worry them. I got to be the one who worried.

"Have you seen a doctor?" I asked.

"No, I don't want to be seen as a ninny. There are guys dying overseas in real war. To complain about back pain from short marches seems like whining. So, no, I haven't seen anyone."

"You should," I said right away. "You probably have something easily correctible. But it could also get worse and completely interrupt your education." I realized I was sounding like someone's old man, but I was concerned, and delay in finding out what was wrong wasn't a good plan.

"Papa used to say 'what you need is a diagnosis' when people came to him with an unexplained ache or pain. That's what you need," I said.

"Well, okay, maybe you're right. I'll see to it."

I didn't hear anything after a week, so I called him.

"Seen anyone about your back?"

"I mentioned it to one of my instructors. He told me to get a heating pad. I've been using it and it helps a little."

"That's no good," I said firmly. "Anyone could have recommended a heating pad. You need a diagnosis, remember what your grandpa said. Make an appointment with a real doctor who sees patients, not your instructor. You have access to one who sees patients?

"There's a student health service. I'll go there." A short pause. "And Uncle Cyrus?" Another pause. "Thanks."

"I want to hear from you as soon as you've seen someone, okay?"

"Yeah, okay."

Another week went by with no news from John. I was increasingly frustrated, then irritated, and finally very worried. Why was it that a kid who's studying to be a doctor won't get needed medical attention for himself? I called him again.

"You know why I'm calling, right?"

"I do," he sighed. "I do have an appointment, but it's not for another week."

"How's the pain?"

"The same. I'm tired of it. I'm also pooped because the pain is making me lose sleep. I can't stay awake in classes."

"Have you talked with your folks?"

"Not yet. I thought I'd wait until I had something to tell them. You haven't talked to them, have you?"

"No, but I can if you want."

"No, no, don't say anything to them. They're having enough trouble without my being a worry."

"What do you mean?"

"Well, Dad's drinking again. You know how that goes."

What the hell? What's bugging Jack now? I hadn't been in touch for several weeks and didn't know this. Damn. I'd better call Sarah.

"Okay," I said to John. "I'll call your mother and see what I can do. Call me after you've seen the doctor. Or sooner if things start going downhill. Okay?"

"Thanks again, Uncle Cyrus. I'll call you."

~~~
~~~

"Hi Sarah, Cyrus here. How're you? Haven't talked with you for some time."

"Glad to hear from you, Cyrus. I'm okay." I could see her face, one hand on her forehead. She didn't sound convincing. She was silent for a few moments, then said "The truth is, Jack's probably losing his job with Dayton Tire. His biggest client switched to Firestone. He must have gotten a better price on V-belts, Jack's main product line. He's real down about it. Angry too.

"Maybe hearing from you would pick him up a little," she said. "The other thing. He's back on the bottle." I could hear a catch in her voice and knew she was near the end of her rope.

"When will he be home? I'll call him."

"Thanks Cyrus. I'll tell him you'll be calling. Another thing," she stopped for a few seconds. "I'm seeing a divorce lawyer." Her frustration boiled over into tears. "I've had all I can take, Cyrus. He's gotten more verbally abusive, insulting, and accusatory. I don't really want a divorce, but I can't go on like this and maybe this will jolt him to come to his senses. Maybe this will force him to look at his behavior and try to change it."

I wasn't taken by total surprise, but I shouldn't have been, since I'd watched this marriage strain, now to a potential breaking point.

"I'm sorry, Sarah. If I can help this situation, you know I'll do anything you want. Talk to Jack, sit with both of you, whatever. Just tell me. Just so you know, I won't take sides."

"Thanks, Cyrus. You're always so helpful. I'm not sure where to turn. Let's just see how this goes." From her tone of voice, it was clear our conversation was over.

With a heavy heart, I trudged into the newsroom. There, reporters were celebrating good news: defeat of German forces in Belarus, a huge setback for Nazis, a turning point. But this hardly cheered me up. Worries about your loved ones close to home crowd out triumphs or disasters in a distant world. As I thought about Jack's descent back into the black hole of drunkenness and how it would affect the family, everything else seemed unimportant. John's back problem added to my melancholy. What could that be? I tried to tell myself it was a simple muscle or spine problem. A lot of people get low back pain. And he was twenty-four years old, slim and trim, in excellent physical condition. He used to be star quarterback on his high school football team, for god's sake. Why am I so worried?

"Hello Sarah. Cyrus. Is Jack there?"

"Hello Cyrus. Just a minute."

"Hi. How you doin'?" Jack said, completely unaware of the reason for my call.

"Well, I'm surviving. How about you?"

"Life stinks, but other than that, I'm just fine," he said, dripping with sarcasm.

"What's up?" playing dumb.

"They gave me notice at work. I won't go into details, but in two weeks, I have no job. We have a little in the bank, but it won't last long." He let out a deep sigh.

"What happened? I thought your job was secure."

"I got into it with my boss. He's never liked me, has always looked down on me, calls me an Indiana hick. So, the last time he started criticizing me, I let 'im have it with both barrels. Those sonsofbitches! I've worked my ass off for them, but as soon as sales start to slip, which is not my fault, they fire you! What kinda people do that? I'm disgusted with the world and all the goddam people in it."

"Hold on, Jack. Not everyone is bad. I'm here, Sarah's still in your world, you have a lot of people who love you. Count your blessings, man!"

"Well, that's another thing. Sarah's seeing a lawyer. Tells me she's had enough, wants out." I could tell he was nearly crying. "Hard for me to see a way out of this, Cyrus. What am I gonna do? No job, mortgage payments due, living expenses. Sarah's occupied with her little business, but she doesn't bring in enough to keep us afloat. And if she carries through with her crazy idea of getting a divorce...." His words became inaudible.

"You have a good work history, Jack. You'll find another job. The economy's improving these days. And about Sarah: that idea about divorce may pass."

"Yeah, right. Easy for you to say, you're fully employed, got no family, sailing right along."

His anger didn't even spare me. I worried about Sarah. Would Jack get drunk and hurt her?

"Jack, I'd like to help any way I can. Tell me what I can do."

"Not much, Cyrus," he said, his ire subsiding. "Just leave me alone for a while."

"Call me tomorrow. I want to help. If I don't hear from you, I'll call you."

After I hung up, I felt a rising level of anxiety. I decided to take the initiative and go after dinner tonight to have a face-to-face talk with my brother. And see Sarah, Martha, and Jimmy. It was Friday night, and this is when his drinking usually began.

I ate dinner at the Empress Chili Parlor downtown, near the Enquirer's offices. When I finished eating, I headed to Jack and Sarah's house.

Sarah met me at the front door. As I walked in, I heard Jack singing at the piano. I could tell he'd been drinking as his usual on-key pitch was missing. The other thing I noticed was his choice of songs.

He kept repeating a melancholy song. I looked at Sarah to gauge her reaction. Her head was down, her hand over her mouth, tears coursing down her cheeks. I put my arm around her and led her into the kitchen.

"Tell me what's going on here," I said.

"Oh Cyrus, he started drinking hours ago. He could barely sit down on the piano bench he was staggering so. And then he sings that awful song. I just hate that song. And he knows I hate it, that's why he sings it when he's drunk. Why does he want to hurt me so much?"

"He's drunk, Sarah, you know when he's drunk, he's not himself."

"Knowing that doesn't help," she said, her anger taking over her sadness. "When he's drunk it's like in that story 'Dr. Jekyll and Mr. Hyde.' It's like alcohol is the potion Dr. Jekyll drinks to turn into Mr. Hyde. He's so hateful when he's that way."

"Does he ever hit you when he's drunk?"

"No, thank God for that. But he's meaner than a rattlesnake. Curses me and accuses me of being unfaithful. And in the last line of that song, he's substituted 'simple minded' for 'fickle minded' to make me feel diminished. I don't know why he hates me so much! I've tried to be a good wife in every way, and I have been, Cyrus, and he treats me this way. Maybe I should go ahead and get a divorce."

"I know you've been a good wife, Sarah. When he drinks, it unmasks his mental problems. I think he needs to see a psychiatrist to get treatment for these delusions, this paranoia, before it takes him and everyone else in the family down. I'll try to talk him into it when he's sober."

I left Sarah in the kitchen and went into the living room. Jack had his head against the music stand on the upright piano. He was sobbing, tears dripping onto the keys.

"Jack, it's Cyrus. Let me get you into bed."

I put my hand under his arm. He slumped over, a bag of bones. Sarah came to help and together we got him into their bedroom and onto his bed. He was in a torpid sleep when we closed the door. We both collapsed on the couch in the living room.

"Sarah, I'll come by in the morning when he's sober and talk to him. I think he'll listen to me. I doubt that he'll be willing to see a psychiatrist, but I'll suggest it to him anyway. The other possibility is Alcoholics Anonymous. I'll check to see if there's a group nearby. Problem is, he's a stubborn man and may reject my suggestions. But this has got to stop. Call me later tonight if he wakes up and starts drinking again. I can come back."

It wasn't necessary for me to come back that night, but I went first thing in the morning. Sarah told me he'd slept in a drunken stupor until dawn. When he woke up, he had no recollection of my having been there or what had transpired. The blessing that comes to some drunks is amnesia for the night before. Jack was also one of the lucky alcoholics who never got a hangover. He was spry and active when he rolled out of bed on this new day.

"Cyrus, what the hell are you doin' here?" he said when he saw me sitting in the living room. "It's Saturday morning for God's sake."

"When I talked to you yesterday, I was concerned. You sounded real down. So, I came over to talk to you, see if we can figure something out."

This shocked him back to recalling he'd lost his job. It also stoked his anger anew.

"Bastards!" He spewed out the word with such contempt it took on a whole new meaning.

"I know you're angry, I would be too," I began, trying not to provoke him further. "I came over last night to see you. Do you remember seeing me last night?"

"You were here last night? No, I must be losing my mind," he said with his head down.

"You were drunk, Jack. Drunk, and singing a hurtful song about buying a paper doll to replace Sarah. You know the song I'm talking about?"

"Not talking about Sarah. Just singing a current popular song," he said. "I don't recall seeing you here. When did you come?"

"Right after supper. Sarah and I had to put you into bed you were so drunk."

He looked at me, bewildered. "How can that be? I don't recall that at all."

"That's why I'm here today. To talk to you about your drunken weekends. It's tearing Sarah apart."

"So, she's bitching to you about a few drinks I have on weekends? Maybe I should switch to a paper doll!"

I took him by the shoulders and shook him.

"Listen to me Jack! Stop this craziness! See what you're doing to your wife and family! It can't go on this way. You're ruining too many lives!"

I finally had his attention. And for the first time, he broke down and slumped in a chair.

"So much has gone wrong, Cyrus. The job thing is bad enough, but arguments with John over that Rosicrucian cult thing, seeing Sarah work so hard making drapes and slipcovers for Clifton snobs. And now she's seeing a lawyer. I shouldn't have kept her from singing in that church, but that meat-headed minister was lusting after her. And Martha drifting further and further away. Worry about the war-- it's all too much. I'm at my wit's end."

"Would you consider seeing a psychiatrist?"

"A what? Hell no. I can't afford it for one thing. Secondly, I don't want anyone outside the family knowing my problems. I have to solve them myself, be self-reliant, as Emerson said. Psychiatrists are for women with hysteria, not for men whose job it is to put food on the table, not go around whining about their lives."

I was pretty sure this would be his reaction to the suggestion of a psychiatrist. Now I wondered whether he'd consider AA.

"One other possibility is Alcoholics Anonymous. It has a great reputation helping men and women get off booze to change their lives. Would you look into that?"

"I'm not an alcoholic! I can stop anytime I want. I don't want to. It's the only thing that makes my life bearable. I'm not giving it up. And I don't want to go to a group of people, spill my guts to them. You can't trust other people. I sure as hell am not gonna do that."

This also didn't surprise me, but I was still disappointed. From what I've read about mental illness and alcohol addiction Jack's attitude was typical -- denial, mistrust, more denial. I decided to back off for now. You can pull a string, but you can't push it.

"Okay, Jack. I understand your reluctance. Just trying to help."

Arms folded across his chest, legs crossed, he was the picture of a defensive crouch. As I got up to leave, he relaxed slightly.

"Thanks anyway, Cyrus. I know you always try to be helpful. But this time, I'm gonna have to figure all this out on my own. Still friends, brother?"

"Of course. Call me if you need to talk."

I didn't sleep that night. The family I loved the most was coming apart. And I had no way to solve the problem.

Chapter Twenty-Six

When I Am Frightened

August 1944

ON MONDAY, I WENT TO Washington to attend a conference called "Dumbarton Oaks." This assembly of diplomats would discuss a framework for the United Nations. After all these years, it was a resurrection of Woodrow Wilson's fixed idea about a League of Nations to forestall future armed conflicts. It drew governmental representatives from the United States, Great Britain, France, China, and the Soviet Union to fashion plans for international peace.

As I flew out of Lunken Airport, I was so worried about the family it was difficult to turn my attention to work. I was going there to report on how national diplomats would address international challenges of keeping peace in a world full of potential and real conflict.

While there, the recently failed assassination attempt of Adolf Hitler was fresh in everyone's mind since the perpetrators were summarily killed the day after it happened. One constant in Nazi Germany was

Hitler's immediate scorched earth response to any threat to his power and domination. The other talked-about event was the horrifying Wola massacre in Poland. Nazi SS troops killed *fifty thousand civilians* in the bloodiest ever invasion committed during wartime.

The massacre of civilians by bombing raids continued unabated. With everyone emotionally numb and war weary, each horrendous event seemed now to cause less outrage because it was "not personal," as one observer pointed out. Another coined a phrase: "a single person's death is considered a tragedy. When thousands die, it's a statistic."

Once ensconced in my hotel room, I called John to check on his health and how his pain was. The phone in the barracks was answered by the duty officer. I asked for John and after a few minutes, he was on the phone.

"John, this is Uncle Cyrus, calling from our nation's capital," I said, using my most stentorian tones, hoping he'd get the self-deprecation. "Seriously though, I'm covering an important conference here but wanted to check in with you. How're you doing?"

"Hi Uncle Cyrus. Wow, that must be exciting. Are the head honchos there?"

"High ranking representatives. You know, US state department officials and their counterparts from other countries.

"So, how are you doing?"

"Well, I had a doctor's appointment yesterday. Had a full physical, x-rays of my back and a few other tests. Got another appointment next week to see what the x-rays showed and how the blood tests came out. He gave me some pain meds and they help a little bit. He told me I should be excused from marching.

"Now I take a taxi from McMicken to med school, but you know, it's embarrassing when I pass my fellow students marching along in columns. I keep my head down as the taxi passes them. But my commanding officer is being very decent about it, and more concerned about my health than I would have thought. I guess med students are considered valuable members of the armed forces."

"Well, you're getting a little closer to some answers. Call me next week when you know more. Gotta go now. The first session starts in 30 minutes, and I have to find my way around." I didn't bring up his parents' angst.

It was already September when I got back to Mt. Adams, and my first order of business was to call John, going through the duty officer on call at the barracks. When John came on the line, I said,

"Hey there, John. Uncle Cyrus calling. Checking up on you. Any news?"

"Yeah, got some preliminary reports."

"Stop right there, John. Where can I meet you to talk?"

"There's a tavern near here called Shipley's. We can find a table in the back room and talk there. It's on McMicken Avenue, near where I live now. Can you meet me there in about an hour?"

"I'll see you there."

Shipley's is a popular hangout for college students, a location I remembered having passed it many times. I walked past the long bar just inside the door where the familiar odor of beer and cigarettes washed over me. I found John camped out in a quiet back room. After we gave each other hugs and pats, we sat down and began the talk that I would never forget.

"The latest news is I have a lump in my groin they're gonna take out. I knew it was there but figured it was because I had a sore on my lower leg when I bumped into a file cabinet here in the dorm."

"What do the doctors make of that?"

"Nothing right now. They sort of agree with me that it's from the sore on my leg."

"How's the discomfort in your back?"

"Same. The new symptoms I have are feeling kinda weak and I'm sweating a lot when I sleep. They haven't told me what they think it's from. Maybe they don't know yet. I'm getting a little worried. When your doctor's vague about something, it's usually not a good sign."

"Well, I guess we just have to wait until the whole process is over with. When do you suppose they'll know what's going on? They give you any time frame?"

"No idea of when they'll know anything. Soon, I hope."

"Have you said anything to your folks?"

"No. Same reason as last time you asked. Dad's a mess. You know he lost his job, right? Mother's really down in the doldrums. I don't want to add to that."

"Anything I should be doing about them?"

"Don't think so. But don't tell them anything about me. I'll sit down with them when I have some real answers."

"When you say your father's a mess, what exactly do you mean?"

"He's a drunk!" he said with an angry pitch in his voice. "I hate the sonofabitch."

I'd never seen this side of John. He seemed to be boiling over from all the things he was dealing with.

"You hate what he does, John. I get what you're saying, but hate is a poison that consumes the person who holds onto it."

"I know, I know. But he's been such a … I don't know how to describe him. When he's sober, he's a different person, but even then, he has an attitude, always on the offense. Or maybe it's really his defense. He's so angry. Convinced everyone's out to get him. Has he always been that way?"

"When we were kids, no. But life has dealt him some bad cards. You know, his goal was to be a doctor.

When he was with Papa on house calls, he was never happier. He loved the medical experience, all its highs and lows. If Papa hadn't died, I'm sure your father would be a doctor. Your interest in medicine could be putting his desire onto you."

"I guess it has always been a sort of unspoken expectation. We never really talked about it," John said. "He's often talked about his father. I wish I could have the respect for him that he has for *his* father. But he and I have always had a tense relationship.

"When I was younger, he'd tell me stuff that sounded like slogans, I guess from salesman manuals. Things like, 'When a job is once begun, never leave it 'til you're done. Be the labor great or small, do it well, or not at all.' And 'ambition is the forerunner of success.' Fatherly aphorisms that kids laugh at behind their fathers' backs. I sort of scoffed at these and he got the idea that I thought he was telling me bs. That made him mad.

"And then this jealousy thing," John said, getting more animated as he poured out his frustration. "You know how jealous he is of men who crowd around Mother after she sings. The odd thing is that I think he's also jealous of me. Because Mother loves me."

He shook his head in confusion. "I'm her son, for crissakes, of course she loves me. She loves Martha and Jimmy too, just as much. And she loves him, takes care of him, defers to him in everything. I wish she wouldn't be so compliant.

"The other thing is our arguments about Rosicrucianism. I found its historical origins interesting, but I wasn't going to make it my guiding light. He was so adamantly opposed to my whole inquiry into it, calling it a cult and implying it was some nefarious plot. I was astounded at his extreme reaction to it. I don't get it."

I didn't know how to respond to John's outflowing of emotional pain. I put my hand on his knee as a show of understanding and we sat quietly for a time.

"I'd like to focus on your medical problem. What things worry you?"

His reply was immediate.

"There are so many diseases that can cause symptoms like mine that I can't sort it all out. One problem with being a medical student, you imagine you have all the diseases you study, and of course you don't. I gotta rely on my doctors to come up with the right diagnosis. Then I'll deal with it, whatever it is. I have no choice, do I?"

"We, as a family, will deal with it, John. You're not alone. As soon as we know what it is, we'll take whatever steps are necessary to get it licked. Okay?'

"Okay. Thanks. And thanks for listening to me. It helps a lot. You should have been a psychiatrist," he grinned at me. I loved this young man, my nephew who was like a son to me, and prayed his health problem was not serious.

Chapter Twenty-Seven

Lean on Me

Late September 1944

FINALLY, JOHN GOT SOME answers. But for some inexplicable reason, the lymph node removed from his groin hadn't been biopsied. One of the doctors at the Student Health Service, Dr. Doty, tracked down the specimen, mad as hell that it hadn't already been biopsied. Luckily, it hadn't been tossed out. Doty insisted that it be immediately prepared for microscopic examination. Results were pending when I talked with John.

"Why didn't they biopsy the lymph node when they took it out?" I asked, incredulous that such an obvious mistake had been made.

"Beats me. I thought that was the whole point of removal."

"Did you get any other information? Do they think the lymph node they took out of your groin and your back pain are related?"

"That's the 64-dollar question. You should have been a doctor, Uncle Cyrus."

"Not a chance. Your father wanted to be the doctor. I wanted nothing to do with it. Proves that we were fraternal twins, not identical. We're not very much alike."

"That's for sure," he said, embarrassing me, since he was having such misgivings about his father.

"I didn't mean anything by that," I said, trying to apologize for my faux pas. "Sorry I said that."

"Well, me too. Dumb remark."

"Call me as soon as you hear about the biopsy results. If you want, I could come with you when you go to the doctor to pull this all together."

"That would be great, Uncle Cyrus. That way you could pick up anything I might miss. Sometimes when you listen to a doctor talking, your mind goes in different directions, and you miss part of the message.

"Okay, then, I'll call you when I get the appointment."

Another interminable week went by before I heard anything.

"Hi Uncle Cyrus, John calling. I have that appointment tomorrow. Are you able to join me?"

"I'll arrange it. Where's the office?"

Around 2 the next day we sat together in Dr. Doty's office. We were ushered in right on time. Doty was in his mid-40's, balding above his forehead in a V-shaped pattern, and thin, almost cachectic. After introductions, he became serious, got down to business.

"First, let me tell you about the lymph node biopsy." He paused, and then said, "It's not good news. The biopsy shows Hodgkin Disease, a form of cancer." He stopped once more. "There may be other nodes in different parts of the body." He looked at John, then at me, to gauge our reaction. John looked stunned. I was devastated. No one spoke for what seemed like several minutes.

"Does either of you have any questions before I go on?"

"What is the treatment? The outlook?" I asked.

"I'm sorry to say, there's only an experimental treatment right now, being conducted in New York. We don't know the results of those clinical trials yet. The drug they're using is called P51, given by infusion."

"Is this an expensive treatment?" I asked, fully prepared to pay for it myself if necessary.

"It's part of a research program, so there's no charge once you get into the protocol. But if John is to be treated with this new drug, he'll have to go to New York. At least at the beginning. Once he's begun in the protocol he can come back here."

"How soon could he be enrolled?"

"Very soon. I've already talked with a Dr. Iverson at the New York Hospital, so it's only a matter of getting John there to start treatment."

"Do you recommend this?"

"It's the only treatment available. I can't predict outcome, though. It may slow it down, stop it altogether, or do nothing. We won't know until they analyze data when they're done with the clinical trial."

"John, what do you think?" I asked.

"Sounds like I need to go to New York and get started," he said, displaying his usual readiness for challenges. He looked at Dr. Doty and said, "I need to talk to my parents first, but only to let them know about this. It's ultimately my decision and I've already decided to go ahead." He looked at me to see if I had any further questions. His next question could have been mine.

"I'm curious about side effects of treatment. Can you fill me in on those?" John asked.

Dr. Doty was ready for this. Reaching into his desk he pulled out a sheaf of papers, handed them to John.

"This is a lot to read. There's a summary at the beginning. The bulk of the paper describes P51 in detail including side effects--there are a bunch. Most are typical for cancer treatments, you know, nausea, vomiting, headache, abdominal pain, hair loss. But read through this and call me with questions. As soon as I hear you're ready, I'll call Dr. Iverson and get things rolling."

We left Dr. Doty's office and went to a nearby coffee shop.

"Shall I come with you when you break this news to your parents?" I asked.

"I think I should do it alone. Dad might be angry I told you ahead of him and Mother. You know how he is. I think I can answer their questions."

"When he asks about telling me, what will you say?"

"Partial truth," John said. "I'll tell him you called me just to say hello and asked why I seemed down. I'll tell him I felt you ought to know about my illness since I'd be going to New York, and you'd wonder about that. I won't tell him you went with me to Dr. Doty's office. Could you call Dr. Doty and ask him to keep our little secret?"

"Good thinking. I'll call him when I get back to my office. Let me know how it goes with Jack and Sarah. If they want to talk to me, I'm always available."

"Thanks for everything, Uncle Cyrus. I really appreciate your help."

I was able to contain my grief until I got to my car, then the floodgates opened. It took me fifteen minutes to collect myself enough to drive back to the office. There were several messages waiting on my desk. The only one I answered right away was from Sarah.

"Hello Sarah, this is Cyrus. You called?"

"Oh hi, Cyrus. Yes. John called and wants to meet with Jack and me. Know anything about why?"

I was torn. I couldn't lie. But I didn't want to discuss this now, especially over the phone. I wished I hadn't returned her call.

"He has some health issues he wants to talk to you about. I'd called him just to touch base with him and he told me."

"What kind of health issues?" Her voice was unsteady as she asked.

"I'll be glad to talk to you after you've talked with him. It's a private matter. He'll have to tell you about it himself."

"C'mon, Cyrus, can you just give me a hint? Does he have VD or something awful like that?"

"No, nothing like that. Let's talk after you speak with him." I felt trapped. I couldn't reveal that her beloved son had cancer, that he had to go to New York for treatment.

"Cyrus, you obviously know more than you're telling me, I know you. Please. I need to know before he tells Jack, so I'm prepared to deal with the fallout."

"Sorry Sarah. This is one time I have to say no. As I said, we can talk after he meets with you."

The pause in our conversation underscored her disappointment and rising distress.

"Well, okay, but this makes me very nervous. I'll be on tenterhooks until someone tells me what's going on."

"I think he's coming over to see you tonight, so you'll hear directly from him. Call me after he's been there, and we can all talk."

"On an unrelated issue, which seems trivial now, is that I told my lawyer that I didn't want to proceed with divorce proceedings," Sarah said. "Jack and I had a heart-to-heart talk about many things and, at least for now, we seem to be doing better."

"That's such good news Sarah," I said, knowing this was the only good news in the air. "I'll talk to you later, then." I couldn't wait to get off the phone so I wouldn't spill the beans. I hoped she understood that I wasn't about to talk with her about what she desperately wanted to know. She put the receiver down gently, but I knew she was greatly agitated. I felt so bad for her. Now the only thing I could do was wait until this evening.

~~~

"Cyrus, Jack calling. You know why I'm calling," He hesitated, and I knew he was trying to find the right words to continue. "We wanted to get your take on John's terrible news. He was just here and told us."

"I'm utterly depressed. That's my take." I waited as the lump in my throat cleared and I could control my tears. "How's Sarah? How are you?" were the only words to escape my mouth.

"As you can imagine, we're both devastated. Sarah can't quit crying."

"Is John still there?"

"Yes, do you want to talk with him?"

"Sure, put him on." A pause as the phone was passed to John.
~~~

"Hi, Uncle Cyrus."

"Hello John. Should I come over?"

I could hear him asking them if I should join them.

"They said to come. I think it would be good if you came."

"Okay. I'll be there as soon as I can."

We all hugged when I came into the house. Tears were in everyone's eyes.

"Do you know anything about this P51 chemical, Cyrus?" Jack asked me right away.

"Only what John told me. It's my understanding that it's an experimental drug. Maybe it's described in medical journals, but even there it's probably too early in the trials for publication."

"Dr. Doty gave me twenty-three pages of information," John said. "I brought them with me. I read them over, and you're welcome to do the same, but there's not much hard data. A lot about side-effects. After all, P51 is a poison that can't pick out its target, so it's like shotgun scattershot. Medicine isn't very good about cancer."

"Do you feel like a guinea pig entering this drug trial?" Jack asked.

"Well, yes, but it's all that's available. Otherwise, Hodgkin disease is…, well, not so good. So, I'll go into this trial, despite the specter of side-effects. I must accept them if I dare hope treatment will kill it."

"Do you know how long you'll have to be in New York?" Sarah asked.

"Several days I think, but I'm not sure for how long or when. By the way, there's no cost for any of this. It's paid for by a grant."

"Will you be in a hospital, or will you have to stay at a hotel or something?" Jack said.

"Not sure about that. Probably hospital for a few days, but I don't know."

"Will you be able to continue medical school after the treatment?" Jack asked.

"Hope so. I'm due to graduate in May. I doubt the Army wants me with this diagnosis, so my internship can be anywhere, depending on my health."

"I'll come with you to New York," Sarah said.

"Thanks Mother. I don't know that'll be necessary. But I appreciate the offer."

I glanced at Jack. His expression was inscrutable. I wondered how he felt about her offer. It certainly caught me off guard. Her first thought was John, not her husband, Martha, or Jimmy. Could Jack understand that? Was this still another thing he would get jealous about? But wasn't this offer what any mother would make to a son with a potentially fatal disease? Jack remained silent, so we'd have to wait for him to reveal his feelings about Sarah's maternal gesture.

"John, we all love you, you know that," Jack said finally. "Anything that you need will be yours. I also want to go with you to New York. We can make arrangements for Martha and Jimmy. Let us know how you want us to help meet this challenge. Our common goal is to get you better." The question was answered. Jack had come through in this time of need.

I hadn't said anything, but I knew John understood I would also be at his side in whatever capacity I was needed. The last word was Sarah's: "'God moves in mysterious ways his wonders to perform.' I have great faith. Prayers will come for you from all kinds of friends."

John stayed with Jack and Sarah that night. I drove disconsolately back to Mt. Adams. My apartment, usually a place of comfort to me, did nothing to lessen the angst I felt. Only time would answer the questions we all had.

Chapter Twenty-Eight

New York, New York

JACK, SARAH, JOHN, AND I went by car to New York City to see the team of cancer specialists to evaluate John and begin his care. A woman from the church volunteered to watch Jimmy while we were gone.

When we arrived at The New York Hospital, I looked up at its ten stories, each level sporting identical windows, framed in cement sculpture. With its ancient gray Gothic façade, it seemed an unlikely place for a modern breakthrough cancer therapy. A most uninteresting example of architecture, I thought.

"Let's get started," Jack said, striding through the heavy front doors of the place where all our hope resided. He looked at Sarah and said, "Boy, I thought Cincinnati General Hospital was ancient, but this place takes the cake." Sarah wore an anxious look and had no response.

"I read up on this place," John said. "Some great doctors have worked and taught here, and their current roster isn't too shabby either. I recognized names of doctors who wrote chapters in Cecil's Textbook of Internal Medicine. It made me feel good that I'd have well-known competent doctors looking at my case. I was talking to Dr. Walter, UC's chief of medicine, who told me he'd trained with some of these guys at Peter Bent Brigham Hospital in Boston, you know, one of the big-time Boston hospitals in the Harvard Medical School's system."

John's anxious chatter was making Sarah even more nervous, but she was also feeling reassured that John was going to get the highest quality medical attention.

"I hope they're nice too. I hate it when doctors have a poor bedside manner. It's so important to patients to know their doctors really care about them," Sarah said.

We found the cancer treatment ward on the fifth floor. When we entered, a woman behind a registration desk waved for us to come to her.

"I'm Karen. Let me check to see if Dr. Iverson's team is ready to see you."

She returned soon and said, "Please come this way."

A long well-worn oak table anchored the middle of a conference room with matching armchairs on each side. A large gray-haired man in a starched white knee-length laboratory coat, a white shirt, and a red paisley bowtie, sat at one end of the table. He was busy shuffling papers in front of him. When he spotted us, he stood up quickly, smiled, and came around the table offering his hand first to Sarah, then Jack, John, and me. We all introduced ourselves, identifying our relationship to John.

"I'm Dr. Iverson. So glad you made it here, all the way from Cincinnati. How did you come?"

"We drove. I'm the chauffeur," Jack said.

"Glad to hear that long trip wasn't too tiring," Dr. Iverson said. He paused momentarily and then said, "The rest of my team will be in shortly. John, sit right here next to me. Mr. and Mrs. Lewellyn, and…" he hesitated, "and may I call you Cyrus? Please sit over here, indicating to his left. Turning to John, he said, "How are you feeling, John?"

"Well, about the same as I have for the last few weeks. Tired, got a lot of back pain. Also, I've been having night sweats most every night."

"We'll be taking a more detailed history when the team is all together, so you'll have an opportunity to tell us everything about yourself, your medical history and so on," Dr. Iverson said. "Then we'll get you admitted to the hospital, do exams, lab work, x-rays-the works. You know all about these things, don't you, John, since you're a med student. What field are you going to pursue when you graduate?"

I was impressed with this man's sensitivity and humanity. To ask about John's future plans was reassuring to us all, especially, of course, for John. As John and he talked, the rest of the team quietly assembled around the table. After introductions and brief conversations, we said our goodbyes with hugs and kisses, and tears from Sarah, before John left the conference room and was taken to an examination room to begin a series of evaluations.

We checked into a nearby hotel and found an Italian restaurant for dinner. We ate without much conversation as we each withdrew into our private space, not knowing what could be said to ease the anxiety of the moment. The next day we bade Sarah and John farewell at the hospital, where she would be staying on with him during the early phase of therapy. As Jack and I drove home we had sparse conversation as we both were subdued by the enormity of the situation.

Sarah called two days later once Jack and I arrived home.

"We've made it through these first couple of days," she said. "After some initial fumbling around finding veins for the infusion, things have gone well. John tolerated this medicine well, and according to the doctors, this is a good sign. But they warned treatment is in its early stages, and drug doses are small compared to what will come later. So, we'll see you on Thursday at the airport, okay?"

Jack was relieved to see them at Lunken Airport midafternoon on Thursday. Jack told me that John looked none the worse for wear and Sarah was glad to be home, but she looked quite tired. She hadn't slept

well at the hospital, so the first thing she did at home
was take a long nap.

Chapter Twenty-Nine

In the Bleak Mid-Winter

January 1945

AFTER SARAH AND JOHN got home, John moved into his old bedroom with Jimmy. He continued his P51 therapy every morning in the outpatient department at Cincinnati General Hospital. We all were glad he was home, but the downside was that the gargantuan task of caring for him fell to Sarah. She was his dietitian, cook, and nurse, giving him all his medications by injection. His skin had become dry and flaky, so she applied a lanolin ointment to his arms, legs, back and chest. She also had the challenge of handling, as best she could, the vicissitudes of P51 therapy side-effects. I spoke to her shortly after she began this new challenge.

"Tell me how you do it, Sarah. It must be hard."

"The hardest part is seeing him in such pain, especially during the dark nighttime. I've established a definite routine. When he wakes up and calls, I get up, boil water to sterilize the hypodermic syringe and needle, mash the tablet of pain medicine in a spoon, add sterile saline to dissolve it, put it in a syringe and take it up to him. I give the shots into different parts of his arms or legs each time. Then he gets enough relief to go back to sleep. And so can I. But it's exhausting. If Jack wakes up during any of this, he doesn't let on."

I wondered how long she could tolerate seeing her son suffering like that. But she was insistent on keeping him at home. Hospitalization was a separation she wouldn't consider unless it was absolutely necessary.

"You asked me how I do it. I've begun a regular course of action to help me through these times," Sarah told me. "I read my book of prayers, The Daily Word, first thing every morning. That little book is so helpful with advice, such as 'let your thoughts wander away from your problems, look for hope wherever you can find it, and do something that makes you happy.'

"So, to allow my thoughts to get away from my problems, I focused on anything that's right in front of me. I think some people call that 'living in the moment.' To give you a simple example, in the airplane coming home I wondered why seat belts are only in planes and not cars. I asked Jack about this, and he told me Barney Oldfield, the Indy 500 driver, had seat belts installed in his race car several years ago. Then, after staring off, lost in thought, he said that was an interesting idea. He's been searching for something new and different to do, something all his, not for someone else."

I asked Jack about this.

"Sarah's question started me thinking," he said. "It would be easy enough to fabricate seat belts for cars in my basement. All it would take is nylon belting and metal buckles, which I ought to be able to get from the same places the airlines get theirs. Sarah has a heavy-duty sewing machine she uses for her drapery and slipcover business. That would work to stitch the nylon belting to the buckles." His voice and pace of speech accelerated as he became more excited describing how this all would work. "Then I'd need U-bolts – I've seen them in hardware stores --to loop the belts through, fasten them together with sliding clamps, and screw the U-bolts through the floors beneath the seats. I'd then box them and sell them."

I felt Jack was in his own element, that of inventor and entrepreneur. This would give him a new purpose in life, and the best of it was that he would be sole proprietor of this new venture. He'd already taken a job as a manufacturer's representative for an electric motor company since he knew it would be some time before the fledgling seat belt business took off. His own business would be the best thing to happen to Jack in a long time. No one to answer to.

A few weeks later, he showed me his new "factory." He managed to procure the nylon seat belt fabric and set up the equipment for assembly, using a room that was formerly a coal bin in his basement. Then he installed various tools to measure and cut the belting material. He assembled a prototype auto seat belt and determined the size of boxes he would need to package them, ordered them from a local box maker, got labels with bright blue letters, "Super Safety Belts" and began assembling them. Within a month he'd made over a hundred.

He talked Jake Greenberg, the owner of a local auto shop, into installing them. Jake drilled holes through the floor of the cars behind the seats. He then pushed the threaded U-bolts through these holes and secured the screw ends with washers and nuts under the floor. Jack was working like a man possessed, happy he was distracted from worrying about John. This pleased Sarah, too, that he was occupied and not drinking.

The doctors rightly predicted that John would get weaker and lose weight, as Hodgkin disease progressed and P51 therapy would stunt his appetite and make him nauseated. A lab tech came weekly to draw blood to assess the degree of anemia and detect possible abnormal white blood cells. Dr. Doty made alternate day visits to assure Jack and Sarah that things were going as expected. It did little to reassure them, however, as they watched their son steadily lose ground to an inexorable foe.

Inevitably, John's toleration for pain faltered and stronger narcotics were needed. Dr. Doty sat down with John, Sarah, Jack, and me one Wednesday afternoon.

"Sarah, you've been doing such a good job caring for John all these weeks," he said, then turning to John said, "John, I've been following your lab reports and your general status. I've assiduously followed Dr. Iverson's protocol for infusion of P51 since you've been back."

He looked at us to sense how we were reacting to his words, and said, with steadiness, "Your continuing weight loss, lab results, and need for stronger narcotics persuade me that you now should be in the hospital."

Sarah sucked in a deep breath, Jack put his arm around her shoulders, and I held her hand.

"Is that the only course we have?" Jack asked, knowing the answer.

"I think it's the right thing to do for all of you."

Then John spoke up.

"Mother, you've been the best for these many weeks. I talked with Dr. Doty before you came in. I agree I need to be hospitalized. He's assured me I'll have a private room. Living at home has been disruptive not only to you but to Jimmy, whose sleep is interrupted every night by my cries for help. And Dad, it can't be pleasant for you to see your wife leave your bedroom every night to tend to me. I feel guiltier each day for putting you all through this ordeal."

"Her leaving our bedroom is only unpleasant because I think how much you need her to stop your pain," Jack said.

"I would do it no matter what," Sarah sobbed. John brought his face closer to Sarah's and said,

"I can't let you sacrifice your health, lose sleep, and worry about whether you're doing the right things every moment of your life," John said, holding his mother's hand. "The hospital people – I know a lot of them from medical school rotations, and they know me, they'll take good care of me. I'll be in good loving hands. So, try not to worry. And you can visit me as often as you want. They'll let you in. You and Dad are special persons to them."

I looked at John. He didn't shed a tear as he explained to his family that he knew he now needed the hospital.

"Dr. Doty, thanks for all your attention. I know you'll keep Mother and Dad up to date," John said.

"You can count on that, John. They've become my friends."

John had lost nearly forty pounds. I went with Jack and Sarah when John was admitted. The nurses greeted him warmly, but I saw that when they went back to their nurses' station, they wept. We all knew he was not the same man. His previously wavy hair was straight as straw now and his movie-star good looks had vanished. He was cachectic, a sick, about-to-die man.

After a few weeks in the hospital, he was coughing incessantly. We were called to the hospital one night when his coughing couldn't be stopped. They took x-rays, gave him morphine to control his pain and his cough.

This was the last time I saw John. He was diagnosed with tuberculosis, a common infection that finds an opportunity to invade the bodies of terminal cancer patients. Visitation was restricted to Sarah and Jack, who saw him every day, wearing surgical masks for their protection. Sarah and Jack were with John on his last night.

"The nurses were the best. They took such good care of him and cried with me at the end," Sarah said through her tears. "They were able to give him proper doses of narcotics that I wouldn't have been able to figure out. Because of drugs, he was not fully aware of his surroundings in his last hours, but I'm sure he knew we were with him until the very end. I'm thankful to Dr. Doty for recommending the hospital when he did."

Her emotional strength would be sorely tested in coming days. I spent most of my time with Sarah and Jack over the next weeks and saw how John's loss affected each of them. Sarah became agitated at times, compulsively rearranging John's clothes in his closet, talking to herself or to John.

At other times she was sad to the point of total inactivity, especially in the mornings when she felt she had to go into John's room just to look at his bed, hoping she'd been living in a ghastly nightmare. She stared endlessly at Pauline's portrait of John, haunting her from the wall in his room where it hung, asking him to speak to her.

She kept reliving the moments of his birth and early childhood, watching his little body grow, develop, take on challenges of school and bonds of friendships. She could hear his piano echoing from the past, his musical talent blooming in high school, together with his athletic prowess and intellectual curiosity. She had reveled in his success in medical school.

Reality would then creep into her consciousness and melancholy would overtake her.

Jack was nearly ruined by this loss. John's death resulted in behaviors I'd never seen in him before. He was stoic, as had always been his wont for all bad luck that came his way, but something else was at work. He seemed to have reached an inscrutable and profound reckoning with the world.

He became quieter, less mercurial, and something in his eyes was different- less frightened, less threatened. He was not morose or depressed but had somehow accommodated to this unthinkable loss. The death of his eldest son, who had vicariously fulfilled all those goals that had exceeded his grasp, was received with an acceptance that lay deep in some spiritual place.

The other remarkable change in Jack was his abrupt cessation of drinking. The day after John's death, he poured every alcoholic beverage in the cupboard down the kitchen sink.

Psychologists and theologians could have a spirited discussion about what motivated this epiphany, but everyone was thankful that this part of Jack's life was seemingly behind him. His demeanor and personality had undergone a metamorphosis without benefit of psychoanalysis, religious conversion, Alcoholics Anonymous, meditation or medication.

No one asked why or how he was able to quit, cold turkey, for fear of reversing this transformation. It was as though a surgical removal of a festering carbuncle had been performed by an unknown mystical being.

"This was the saddest day of my life since Papa died. Such an indescribable loss," Jack told me. "He and I had our disagreements, but he knew I loved him, and I felt his love as well. I'll miss him so much." He wiped his eyes and we embraced. I was crying too.

The next day, I was walking near my home on Mt. Adams when I spotted daffodils pushing up from flower beds in early April. The forsythia bushes were also blooming bright yellow flowers. Seeing new life emerging at the same time John's life ended reduced me to grunting sobs as I plodded along the hill. Life would go on, the flowers seemed to say, but it would never be the same for those who knew and loved John.

Chapter Thirty

In Paradisum

1946

THE ATTENDEES AT JOHN'S service crowded the Baiter Funeral home beyond its capacity. Many fellow students from his medical school class came, along with a cadre of medical school faculty. Lee Spalding flew in from New York and Bobby Rankin came from Chicago. Pauline, whom we hadn't seen since that awful Pearl Harbor gathering, came.

Her portrait of John was hung on the wall behind his open casket. Jimmy commented it was good to have that picture there, because the body in the casket was not his brother and the picture was. Several of John's high school classmates from Defiance attended.

People who knew him as a youth in Indiana packed the reception area. Sarah's friends from church joined the crowd and Jack greeted former customers and business associates with a personal warmth we hadn't seen in him for some time. He was touched by their sympathy.

Sarah picked Faure's Requiem as music to be played in the background. She told me it she felt it was the most peaceful of all Requiems, giving her great solace. She knew the entire score by heart. She'd sung Pie Jesu many times.

It took nearly two hours for the line of mourners to finish shaking hands and giving us hugs. No one in the family was composed enough to speak words of eulogy, including me. But others did want to say goodbye in public. One of his boyhood friends, George Shatner, who, incredibly, was also one of his current medical school classmates, rose to the occasion.

"Goodnight, sweet prince,

And flights of angels sing thee to thy rest," George began with Horatio's tribute to Hamlet.

Pausing to gather himself, he then told of their teenage years together.

"John and I packed newspapers in our shoulder canvas bags each morning before sun-up, for delivery in our town. We vowed then that we'd go to medical school. Little did either of us know we'd end up in the same class here at UC.

"John was as good a friend as any man could have. You knew he would be there if you needed him.

"But he and I had more in common than just delivering papers. John organized our high school band, which, I have to say, was terrific." I could hear a soft murmur of laughter, breaking up the somber mood.

"He played piano, I played trumpet and the rest of the band were buddies from our high school. But it was John who led us, picking the music, arranging the scores, encouraging us through some of the hard parts. That leadership was a prelude to his accomplishments in college and medical school.

"He was president of our med school class and, until his disease prevented it, marched with us to and from lectures and labs. His quiet courage as he battled Hodgkin disease was an inspiration to us all. We will miss him greatly." George sat down, wiping a tear from his cheek.

A man rose whom no one in the family recognized and took the podium next.

"My name is Myron Goldberg. I'm here to tell you about John when I knew him at Cincinnati General Hospital. I was a volunteer there helping out during the war. During John's senior year he had a lot of pain in his back. I understood there was no known cure. We didn't know what he had, but I'm sure *he* knew his days were numbered.

"He continued to go about his work and studies regardless of his condition. Many an hour, as I worked with him, I knew his pain was far greater than those to whom he was ministering. But he continued his work as long as he could be on his feet. The medical profession can be proud of a young man who, despite his short time among them, lived up to, and perhaps beyond, the oath he would take.

"All who worked with him from maid and porter to professors, loved him and sorrowed, knowing his time to be short among us."

The next speaker was the Chief of Medicine, Dr. Walter.

"John was a superb example of the kind of doctor this medical school cherishes. He heeded Sir William Osler's advice to 'listen to your patient, he's telling you the diagnosis.' He not only listened, but he empathized with patients, talked with them about their families, reassured them, held their hands when they needed that.

"Once they had John as their doctor in clinic, they asked for him to be their doctor from then on. His diagnostic skills as a clinician were uncanny for a student. His dignity when he became a patient himself was exemplary. His regard for others never flagged, no matter what their station in life was, no matter how sick he was or how much pain he endured. He will always be remembered for his humanity as much as for his professional skills. We will all miss him."

At the end of the service one of Sarah's friends from choir sang Malotte's "Lord's Prayer." For years after John's death, whenever Sarah heard this version of the Lord's Prayer, she could not suppress her tears.

There was no funeral procession for a burial because John wanted his remains cremated and scattered in a special place known only to him and his parents. When the service was over, the family went back to the house. Everyone was emotionally exhausted. We sat quietly in the living room for what seemed an eternity. What was there to say? Everyone's world was changed and each of us was altered in our own personal way.

Sarah was the first to speak.

"I have some food for anyone who might be hungry. I think it would be good if everyone ate something." So characteristic of Sarah.

~~~

In the fall of 1948, Martha entered the University of Cincinnati Medical School along with three other young women, Marge Klinger, Marilyn Goldstein, and Mary Griffin. They comprised 3% of that class, a tiny percentage, but more women than had ever been admitted before. Sarah knew Martha would excel in medical school as she had done in high school and college. Jack, who had tried to discourage her from embarking on this course of action, now spoke with great pride about his "daughter, one of only four female med students in her class."
~~~

Chapter Thirty-One

My Life Flows on in Endless Song

1947

IT TOOK A LONG TIME, but Sarah gradually centered on her interior decorating business, drawing satisfaction from measuring, piecing together and stitching fabric, some rough and some smooth, enjoying her act of creating. She returned enthusiastically to her joy of singing. She joined, with Jack's encouragement, the Clifton Community Chorus, a semi-professional singing group that performed both sacred and secular music quarterly.

Their first performance after she'd joined was of Mozart's "Requiem. This was a trial for her, but her inner strength sustained her through the performance. She told me she had felt a transcendent lift for having gotten through the emotional trial of singing this great requiem, composed just prior to Mozart's own demise. I admired her resilience and could only understand it in the context of her profound faith.

Why couldn't I have such a faith as hers? How does that happen in people, this abiding trust that a beneficent supreme being has a plan, impossible for mere mortals to understand. It worked for millions, maybe billions, of faithful worshippers of diverse faiths. Why not me?

~~~

Martha spent long days and nights studying, mostly at medical school libraries and labs. Sunday dinners with her became rare events because of her grinding schedule. But when she was able to come, we heard enthralling and thrilling tales from the secret world of medicine.

"We had this 'clinical correlation' lecture from a big-time surgeon last week," she began as we polished off a delicious chicken dinner Sarah had cooked. "It was about lung cancer. Fascinating. Dr. Siler showed slides of autopsied patients whose lungs just looked horrible-- big bulging tumors, large black sections of lung with no function." Sarah had her hand over her mouth as Martha described these ghastly pictures. Jack was fascinated, bringing back his early experiences with Papa.

"Well, this surgeon, who'd taken literally hundreds of lungs out of people, said something interesting at the end of the lecture. He said, in a very serious tone to the medical students, 'my advice to you is, if you smoke, stop today. You'll avoid getting cancer or emphysema. Because I'm convinced smoking causes lung cancer. That's one reason you should stop. The
~~~

second reason is that nicotine is in cigarette smoke. It's addictive. They don't tell you that in the cigarette commercials, where the actors, posing as doctors, tell of the so-called beneficial effects of smoking.

"Then he said, surprisingly, 'why take your money and buy stock in tobacco companies? Because people will go on buying and smoking cigarettes, because they're addicted, and profits will balloon for tobacco products.' When he finished with that last statement, he put his lecture folder under his arm and strode out of the amphitheater. He didn't address the immorality of doctors investing in a disease-inducing industry."

"Wow, those are pretty definitive conclusions!" Jack said. "I didn't realize research has shown that strong a connection between my Camels and lung cancer. I'm not sure I'm willing to accept this unless it's proven."

"A lot of articles now point to this connection, Dad," Martha said. "I haven't read any making such a definitive connection as the surgeon claimed, but it seems scientific publications are trending that way. So, Dad, maybe you should stop while you're ahead."

Jack smiled, then had a coughing fit, right on cue. We all laughed, but when we realized what we were doing, stifled our frivolity. Even Jack laughed. But we all were sobered by the seriousness of what Martha had said.

She then told us an interesting story, this time with an unexpectedly good outcome.

"I was on the psychiatry ward, assigned to a 35-year-old man, a withdrawn and extraordinarily sad patient. One with serious depression, according to his medical record. His history was that for the past several years he'd done nothing but lie around, sleep a while, then wake up still weak and lethargic. I did my best taking the history from him, but it was hard since he could hardly hold his head up. I did a complete physical exam and then gave my report to the psychiatrist attending who complimented me on my thorough evaluation. I soon forgot about him. He was one of dozens of patients I worked up as a student.

"A couple of months later I walked onto the internal medicine ward and a very excited man ran up to me, giving me a fright. 'Remember me?' he chortled. 'Saw you in the Psych Ward a while back. They thought I was a nut case until someone took an x-ray of my chest 'cause I was coughin.' Turns out I had a tumor of my thymus. They took it out, put me on some pills, and here I am!' Boy, was he a new man! Bright-eyed and bushy tailed."

"I don't understand," Sarah said. "What caused his depression? The tumor? I don't get it."

"Well, the patient thought removal of the tumor caused his improvement, but the thymoma is called a 'sentinel' lesion. That means it suggested the real disease, called myasthenia gravis, which is a defect in nerve and muscle connections causing weakness and lethargy. Further testing made the diagnosis. They started him on a drug that blocked a chemical causing his muscle weakness.

"I just love medicine!" Martha sang out. "I'm so glad I'm a medical student."

"I'm glad for you, too," Jack said, beaming at his daughter with admiration. After all his opposition, this was such an affirmation for Martha. "I was wrong being against your going," he said, surprising everyone at the table with his public apology. "Are the other women enjoying it too?"

"Oh, yes, and we've gotten to be such good friends. Birds of a feather, you know. Most of the guys in the class are friendly enough, but several give us a hard time, some are really nasty. They'll say things like 'you're depriving a guy from being a doctor. A man who would practice 40-50 years taking care of patients. You women will practice maybe 5-10 years, if that, and then start having babies. End of career for you. You four women are costing the general population of nearly 200 years of a practicing doctor.'

"I can put up with fellow students being obtuse. They're jealous, you know. What I really have trouble with is professors who hold similar disdainful opinions of women in medicine. They try to make us feel inferior when they look down their patrician noses at us, mere girls. During oral exams they intimidate by condescending attitudes and outright hostility."

"The fact that you're pretty probably doesn't help," Sarah said, feeling her daughter's pain.

"Yeah, and the ones who're not hostile can be annoying in other ways," Martha said. "They think they're irresistible to women by virtue of their being the great god doctor. They get fresh sometimes and need to be held off-- firmly-- or they'd love to take advantage of us."

"That was in my mind when I tried to discourage you from going," Jack said. "It was one of the things I worried about. But you're tough. I know how tough you can be," he laughed.

"I'm a red head, ya know? I must have some Irish blood. Come to think of it, how come John and I got red hair, anyway?"

"Good question, Martha. Must be the milkman!" Jack joked, and Sarah groaned.

"That's an old joke between us," Sarah said. "Fact is, my father had a red beard before it turned white. And my aunt Loane had red hair, so it's in the genes."

"Uncle Cyrus, what's going on in your life?" Martha asked, turning to me.

"Well, newspaper circulation is going up. I think upcoming elections are interesting everyone," I said.

"I think Truman's done for," Jack said. "I give him credit for ending the war, even though he used the atom bomb to do it. He also started the Marshall Plan. But he's such a country bumpkin. After FDR, the epitome of erudition. And Truman keeps pushing his daughter's singing career. I think she's awful. But Sarah thinks she's not bad and Sarah knows more about that type of music than I do. Barbershop is still my forte."

"I don't know anything about politics," Martha said. "I don't have time to read newspapers. Besides, no matter who gets in, it's the same old thing. A lot of talk and little do. They all speak in glittering generalities.

"I actually think our country is moving forward, Martha," I said. "Even though it seems slow, and I admit it moves at a glacial pace, but I think we have substantial new programs that improve people's lives. We've a long way to go but there's some movement."

"So, who's going to be the Republican nominee?" Jack asked.

"Oh, I think Dewey pretty much has it in the bag. And the election, too. Truman's definitely the underdog. At least as things stand today," I said. "But the thing I like about covering news is that you never know what's going to change things all around."

Chapter Thirty-Two

Happy Days Are Here Again

November 1948

EVERYONE COUNTED HIM out, including me. The polls predicted a stunning defeat for Truman. H.V. Kaltenborn, called the "dean of radio newsmen," broadcast on election day evening that Dewey had won.

He didn't anticipate a large surge of counted votes favoring Truman in the early morning hours. He was embarrassed to admit his error, but to his credit he did, when it was clear that Truman won. The *Chicago Daily Tribune* had already printed and distributed their morning edition with a headline announcing Dewey's win. There was plenty of embarrassment to go around in news reporting that night. Luckily, I hadn't made any predictions, but I was as surprised as anyone (except Truman) that he won.

"Well, what did you think about the election?" Jack asked.

"You first. What are your thoughts?" I parried back.

"Surprised as hell. I've never been impressed with that rube from Missouri. But I didn't like Dewey either. As someone said, he looks like the statue of a little groom on a wedding cake, with his silly mustache and dark three-piece suit. And his evasions. He never directly answered questions, just spouted platitudes. I also worried he'd try to eliminate programs like Social Security and get rid of TVA. I ended up voting for Truman. I liked his spunk. And that guy who yelled 'Give 'em hell, Harry!' sort of summed up my feelings once I got to know more about him. Not a bad guy after all."

"Well, I voted for him too. I got really disgusted about those southerners who walked away from Truman because he wouldn't go along with their racist attitudes," I said, warming to the subject. "Strom Thurmond is a narrow-minded and thoroughly despicable guy, in my opinion.

And then there's Harold Stassen. Talk about a stubborn sore loser. He didn't get the Republican nomination, so he ran as an Independent. Politics is getting stranger and stranger.

"What else is going on in your life?" I asked, taking a new tack on conversation.

"Well, the seat belt business is going nowhere. They aren't selling well, and I know why: the public simply isn't ready to accept the idea of being retained by a seat belt in the protective shell of an automobile, thinking that shell would provide the best chance of survival in a crash," he said. "Conventional wisdom is that being thrown clear of the vehicle at the time of a crash afforded the best opportunity to escape death. That's wrong and I'm sure future research will prove it."

So, Jack's brilliant idea had been a hard sell. His timing was wrong, and he had no platform to promote sales. Only a limited number of people ever heard, let alone accepted, his pitch. After several months, Jack stopped shoveling against the tide and stopped producing his brainchild. But in his later years he took satisfaction watching gradual acceptance of seat belts, and then shoulder harnesses, knowing that his "big idea" had actually turned into a "great idea" that was used in every car manufactured throughout the world.

"My job with the electric motor company has turned out to be pretty good," Jack said, after bemoaning the failure of his seat belt venture.

"Yeah, I heard that. Pardon for asking, but what do you know about electric motors?"

"I got connected to these guys when I sold V-belts for Dayton. So, I know more than you might think."

"No offense, Jack," I said, realizing I was not being as careful as I should be when dealing with him. "I just never heard of your interest in electric motors."

"No offense taken, Cyrus," he said, and I exhaled. I certainly didn't want to be responsible for any backsliding on his part. "I'm not getting rich from this, but it puts bread on the table.

"It's hard to believe, but Jimmy is sixteen, going to Walnut Hills," he said. "At Martha's insistence. You'd think she was president of the Alumna Association. She even sends them donations. Not much, she doesn't have much to spare. You know, she saved enough at her job at the government's Proving Ground during the war to pay her medical school bills. I gotta give her a lot of credit, she's a force of nature."

"How's Jimmy getting to and from school?" I said, recalling that was an issue when Martha first went there.

"Jimmy has a classmate from Northside whose mother takes her to school every day and they come right by our house. So, he hooks a ride. I've offered to pay her, but she says no, she'd be going this way anyhow."

"How's Sarah?"

"She's good. Drapery business is ticking right along. I help her hang them at client's houses. She's also singing in the church choir again. She loves that."

"I thought you didn't like the minister there."

"I didn't, but he's gone, thank heaven. They have a whole new administration, a new young minister. The choirmaster is still there, delighted to have her back. They do concerts around Christmas, Easter and Thanksgiving and, of course, weekly services. Sarah gets a lot of solos. I go when she's singing solos, a whole new experience for me, regular church attendance. Sarah still has a great voice."

The change in Jack is remarkable. He seems like a different man, more like the boy I knew growing up. Why, I don't know, but I'll take it.

Chapter Thirty-Three

Sixteen Tons

1949

CHURCH CHOIRS, IN MY experience, tend to have church members who love to sing but aren't so good, making them fodder for parody. But Sarah's choir was polished, singers all following the conductor, who led them with a minimum of theatricality.

"I loved it!" I told Sarah after the service. "I see why you enjoy singing when you're part of a choir that good."

"Well, you saw the finished product. Why don't you come and listen to one of our spirited rehearsals? You'll see why we're so good when you watch Dr. Heilman put us through the paces," Sarah said.

Sarah was so passionately committed to her choir that I was curious to know more about this corner of her life. So, on the following Wednesday night I sat in a pew near the choir loft and heard the interactions of the choir members and the Minister of Music, Harold Heilman. He and his wife Miriam both had studied lieder singing in Germany, where that genre was king. German composers like Haydn, Mozart, Beethoven, and later Schubert, Schumann, Brahms, Mahler, and Strauss, had composed hundreds of lieders.

"The Heilmans," Sarah told me "lived in Germany until 1938, when Miriam, increasingly nervous because of the rising influence of Nazism, told Harold she thought it was time to leave Germany before it was too late. They were in their early thirties when they came here, and Harold started teaching voice at the Cincinnati Conservatory of Music. Miriam was content to stay home, raise their new baby, and sing in her husband's church choir. She has a beautiful soprano voice."

With this colorful history, I was eager to observe Dr. Heilman, a large man with a booming bass voice, coal-black hair, and neatly trimmed beard, as he led the thirty members of the choir. Judging by the youth and talent of several members, I guessed they were his students he persuaded to be "ringers," paid singers, in his choir.

"Sopranos come in first, followed by the altos. Tenors and basses, you'll have to wait until the ninth bar to shine. So, let's go!" His enthusiasm was contagious, and singers energetically followed his direction. If one section failed to grasp their part, he would sing it along with them.

After the rehearsal most of the choir repaired to the Busy Bee, a nearby tavern. Sarah introduced me to Dr. Harold Heilman.

"Oh, you're Sarah's brother-in-law. She's told me about you, but I won't tell you what she said," he said with a chuckle. I liked him from the first moment.

"I tell singers that singing is therapeutic and I think they get that. Most of our singers tell me that choir rehearsals and the camaraderie they find in singing is such a release. There are few things that give such pleasure as raising your voice in song. Many also tell me that it's their central reason for coming to church."

As we talked, a tall fellow with a bass voice that sounded like hot fudge, came over to talk to Harold. He was visiting his erstwhile music teacher and had sung with the choir during tonight's rehearsal. They shared a few words before he left. I asked Harold about him.

"He used to be one of my voice students and was in town, so he came to see me. He's on a tight schedule so we arranged for him to come during rehearsal. He has a fantastic bass voice. His goal was not opera, not Broadway, but to become a country singer. He took the trouble to study with me and learn how to use his voice. He's done all right." His name was Ernie Ford.

Otherwise known as Tennessee Ernie Ford.

I came away from this rehearsal with a greater appreciation for Sarah's dedication to her singing. This was a vital part of her spiritual life.

Chapter Thirty-Four

Pomp and Circumstance

1950

COINCIDENT WITH JIMMY'S graduation from high school, North Korea invaded South Korea. The two Koreas were divided by a post-World War II treaty agreement between the US and the USSR. After that treaty, North Korea, under the influence of the Soviet Union, became a totalitarian communist state. South Korea, with backing from the US, became a democratic republic.

The United Nations General Assembly denounced North Korea's invasion and ultimately UN forces, led mainly by the US, supported South Korea. North Korea was supported by the USSR and China, making this essentially a proxy war between two Communist regimes and the United States. This put young men like Jimmy at risk of being drafted for military service with the chance of going to fight in Korea as soon as they graduated from high school.

"Uncle Cyrus!" Jimmy answered me excitedly when I reached him on the phone.

"Congratulations Jimmy! How're you feeling now that you're a high school graduate?"

"Top o' the world, Uncle Cyrus. Big day in my life. Now I can go on to UC."

"You'll tear up the place," I laughed. "Are you going to live at home like John and Martha did?"

"Oh yeah. I don't mind that. I don't think I'd enjoy living with a bunch of guys in a dorm or frat house. It's an easy trip from home on the streetcar. You know they call UC a "streetcar college" because so many kids get there that way. But Dad said he'd buy me an old car to get back and forth. That was his tradeoff for not paying for a place to live on campus. I hope to get a job on campus so I can park my car there."

"Are you applying for a draft deferment?" I asked, since right now, Korea was on everybody's mind.

"Didn't know there was such a thing. Tell me about it."

"Well, I don't know much about it myself. You must register for the draft, you know, so when you go to the Selective Service office to register, ask them about it."

Only five years after WWII and here we go again, I thought.

During his graduation celebration, Jimmy complained of a stomach-ache. At first, we thought it was simply overindulgence in cake, ice cream or cola. But it persisted overnight. In the morning Jack, Sarah and I took him to their doctor who examined him.

"Where does it hurt?" came the inevitable question.

"Down here," Jimmy said, pointing to his lower abdomen.

Doctor Linder gently prodded his belly, starting near the rib cage and proceeding toward his privates. When he reached the area beneath his belly button, Jimmy cried out in pain.

"When I press here," he said, pushing carefully just above his pubic bone, "does it hurt?"

"Not so much there as where you pushed before," Jimmy said.

Dr. Linder then placed his fingers in his lower right side. Jimmy again squirmed in pain.

"Let's get a blood count and then we'll talk some more," he said. He drew some blood into a tube, labeled it and sent it to a laboratory next door to his office on Clifton Avenue.

He nodded to us and said "go get yourself a cup of coffee while we wait for the lab results. Maybe an hour or so. Jimmy, you stay right here."

We went to Graeter's Ice Cream Store around the corner where we knew they had the best coffee and the best ice cream in the Queen City. Sarah was understandably nervous, but she tried not to let it show.

"I bet he has an appendicitis," she said. "Remember, I had that when I was pregnant with him. I came through it fine and so will he." We hoped she was right. Appendectomies were done routinely.

Unless the appendix had burst, I thought. After what the family had gone through with John, the last thing they needed was another serious health threat.

When we got back to Dr. Linder's office, he ushered us quickly into his consultation room.

"It's almost certainly appendicitis. His white blood count is way high, and the physical findings are quite suggestive. I think we ought to admit him to Good Samaritan Hospital and get that little worm out of him.

"I'll have Dr. Blank, a surgeon, examine him. I'm pretty sure he'll agree the appendix needs to come out. This operation only takes about an hour. Jimmy will spend a couple of days in the hospital, but he should be fine after surgery."

Sarah was smirking as we drove to the hospital.

"Maybe I'm the one who should go to medical school next. I knew it was appendicitis," she said with a smug smile.

Dr. Blank came out after the procedure to assure us that all went well. And he was right, Jimmy went home in a couple of days.

"I was surprised when Dr. Blank came to our house to take out Jimmy's stitches," Sarah said, a few days later. "Not many doctors do that nowadays. He was so gentle with Jimmy. He said Jimmy was well but should take it easy for a couple of weeks. No bike riding, jumping or anything that might open the wound now that the stitches weren't there to hold the edges together. We're so relieved."

In September Jimmy began premed at UC. He'd gotten his college deferment so he could go to school instead of military service, at least for the duration of his college years. But sooner or later, like all able-bodied young men, he would have to serve his two years. Some protested that going to college was draft evasion by the "privileged class."

There was some truth to this argument. College deferments came to symbolize the divide between the so-called "educated class" and the young men who became "grunts" in the Army and went to Korea, many never to return. We hoped that by the time Jimmy graduated in 1954, the Korean war would be over, so he'd fulfill his military obligation in peacetime and not be in harm's way.

When I talked to Jimmy about his career plans, he said, "I'm not sure about blindly following John and Martha into medicine. I'm also interested in a lot of other things, like English and history and philosophy. So, I'm taking a minor in English."

I was pleased, as I had advised him to cover his bets if premed didn't work out. I didn't want him to feel obligated to go into the "family business."

"If I end up going to medical school, I'm going to find the cause of Hodgkin disease and figure out how to treat it," he said. A naïve but worthy goal, I thought. "Oh, by the way, I got an old two-door Plymouth. It's got a gear shift lever on the floor! And even better news. Dr. Blank, you know the guy who yanked my appendix out, got me a job at the Student Health Service as a night attendant," Jimmy was very excited to tell me all this. "I have a parking sticker so I can park at the clinic any time. I work there overnight once a week. They have a sleeping room and shower room. The other guys who work there say they don't often get awakened during the night. The Health Service is there for students who feel sick and need attention, like for sore throats, ear infections, rashes. Sometimes male students get admitted to our infirmary and we look after them. There's a doctor on call for anything we think might be serious."

Martha, meanwhile, was going into her third year of med school, the clinical years. She was in heaven rotating through the different services: medicine, surgery, pediatrics, ob-gyn, psych, all the subspecialties. I asked her if she knew which field she wanted.

"All of them! I love everything about medicine. Maybe I'll be a GP. They deliver babies, then take care of them, do a little minor surgery, and a lot of internal medicine."

"Sounds like a lot of hard work to me," I laughed.

"No problem. I'm young and can do it all!"

At Sunday dinners we heard more gory tales of derring-do from Martha. On several occasions I thought this was not proper Sunday dinner conversation, but Martha was so excited to relate her experiences that no one considered telling her some of us would rather talk about the Reds' ballgame.

"I was assigned to the emergency department last month. Boy, is that place ever busy! One thing after another. You get done with one case and there's three more waiting for you.

"It's the auto crashes that scare me the most. Luckily, med students just stand back and watch. Blood everywhere, nurses and doctors scurrying about like squirrels, lots of yelling.

"There was this one awful case I tagged along with the intern to see. The cops led us to a gurney in the back hall with a sheet over it.

"After the intern pronounced the woman dead, which was the reason the cops brought him back to see the patient in the first place, he and I went to the doctors' room to talk about it. That's what they do, you know, when there's an upsetting case, they have a debriefing, a chance to talk about your feelings. The intern said he thought the cops got a kick out of watching us young inexperienced doctors get horrified at this kind of case. People are really strange sometimes."

I glanced at Sarah, wondering how this story was affecting her. She sat with eyes closed. I wondered what was going through her mind. It seemed to me we should avoid dinner table discussions about clinical cases. We should enjoy pleasures in life and exchange feel-good stories. I decided to tell Martha what I thought and pulled her aside after dinner.

"Martha, I'm glad you're enjoying your medical school experiences. It must be very exciting."

"Absolutely, exciting is the word."

I hesitated, not knowing exactly how to proceed.

"Do your teachers advise about the confidential nature of the cases you're seeing?" I finally began.

"Well, yes, they've told us not to discuss cases in public areas, you know, on elevators or in the cafeteria, where families of patients might overhear us."

"How about talking about patients you're caring for with your family?"

"Uh, no, they haven't talked about that. Hm. I think I know where you're going with this."

"I know you're exhilarated about your work, but I wonder if you've considered that cases like the one you described might be upsetting or inappropriate to us non-physicians?"

She flushed, looked down at her hands before she spoke.

"I'm sorry I described that auto accident case. I could see it upset Mother. I should have been more sensitive to her feelings. I'm truly sorry. It was thoughtless of me." She looked down and was about to cry.

"Listen, what's done is done," I said hurriedly, to forestall a flood of tears. "We all knew you told the story because you're so interested in your work. So, take this as a learning experience, not as a scolding. We all love you and respect you for what you're doing. I just thought I'd remind you that the family hasn't had the training you're getting to become inured to tragedies you see. Okay?"

We stood and I gave her a big hug.

"Thanks, Uncle Cyrus. I appreciate your telling me this. I should have known better. Should I talk to Mother?"

"Yes, just tell her we've had this little talk and that you'll be more careful in the future. She'll understand. She admires you so much for what you're doing."

I felt bad for her. She's still so young and vulnerable. But she's also strong, determined and committed to becoming a doctor. I knew she'd be all right.

Chapter Thirty-Five

What'll I do?

June, 1952

CINCINNATI IS LIKE A WET, hot sponge covering your face, one you can't seem to get free of. The muddy Ohio river, wider in Spring and early summer, seems to add steam to the air as it rushes to pour into the Mississippi.

The hot season, which stretches all the way from May to October and sometimes even later in the Ohio River valley, makes the medical school graduation convocation a sweaty affair, especially when you're wearing a long black graduation gown. Held in Nippert stadium on UC's main campus, it's hardly a personal event.

"I know it's a circus, but I consider it special, an occasion that happens only once in my entire life," Martha crowed.

She wouldn't recall much about the actual ceremony, so lost in the occasion was she. She clutched the diploma close to her heart, this fragile fragment of paper proving her accomplishment, as she went home for a family celebration. The newspapers noted that she was one of only four women graduates that year. Hugs were abundant all around when she walked in, as toasts to her future were raised and many happy tears spilled out.

"Well, you proved me wrong! I'm glad to have been so wrong. Gimme a big hug!" Jack said and embraced his daughter, tears of joy coursing down her face. And his.

"We're so proud of you," Sarah said as she held Martha close for several moments. "Now those dark nights of doubt and fretting seem far away, don't they?" Only Sarah knew of those nights of fear and trembling her daughter had. "And you graduated in the upper quarter of your class! That's really something!"

At the celebration back home, Jimmy was pouring glasses of juice, cola, and iced tea for the crowd, acting as waiter to prove himself useful. No alcohol was served -- Sarah's strict instruction. She didn't tempt fate with getting Jack hooked again. Jack didn't object. He told me he'd never consume alcohol again. He'd been dry now for four years.

I watched this tableau also feeling proud of this family, my family, my blood relatives. And envious. I remained a bachelor, and this was my only family, my anchor of love, and like all families, imperfect. I had seen this branch of the Lewellyn family tree pass through the Sturm und Drang of bullying, alcoholism, a variety of squabbles and the death of an adult child. But here they were, "bloodied but unbowed." Martha would soon be off to internship in Boston, facing new undefined challenges, this time alone, but with strength forged in a crucible of overcoming self- doubt and insecurity. She was ready, a veteran in calling up latent forces in her character.

Sarah moved around the room, greeting well-wishers, old friends and new, carrying a range of emotions in her heart. Martha's graduation must have stirred feelings she'd tried to keep under check—fear after Pearl Harbor when war came, the high of John's graduation from medical school six years ago, torment in the early stages of his illness, then constant ministering to him during his debilitating and ultimately fatal cancer. She didn't let her sadness show today, though, masking it with carefully cultivated cheerfulness, a hallmark of her personality.

I knew that in the back of her mind lurked the reality of Martha's looming departure, the coming emptiness of her absence. Since John's death, Sarah invested much of her energy in Martha's challenges and successes in medical school.

Jack was aware of this and accepted it without protest, a sign of his own conquest over jealousy. Jimmy was fourteen, so busy and preoccupied with his peer group that he hardly noticed his mother's focus on Martha. His father seldom paid much attention to him anyway, so this also went unnoticed.

After Martha settled herself in Boston, she wrote:

Dear Uncle Cyrus,

Boston is a fast train compared to Cincy. People here are always in a hurry, very abrupt when they talk to you, kind of rude, but also quick to laugh a lot of times. It's like they're high on something. They have strong views about everything, complain a lot about all kinds of things, like the T (that's their subway), city government, the school system, and, of course, traffic congestion.

As one woman said to me, 'Everyone here is entitled to my opinion,' and as I've found out, within 30 seconds you know what that opinion is, about politics, religion, local sports teams, whatever. Things we studiously avoided arguing about at home are right out there, in your face. For someone like me, it's kind of jolting. But I love being here. People's openness and honesty is refreshing.

Boston City Hospital is an architectural twin to Cincinnati General Hospital. The pavilions, as they're called, are laid out in parallel rows, just like CGH. In fact, I was told that the architects who designed this place were consulted during the planning of CGH. But Boston City Hospital is older than CGH and it looks it.

I'm living close to the hospital with a roommate, a girl I met at orientation. She graduated from NYU where she was one of about ten women in the class.

Maybe this is a trend! In the future, I bet women will get more and more seats in medical schools.

I start on Monday, on the medicine service. I'm a little scared, but so's my roommate. I guess all new interns are nervous.

Love,

Martha

Such a pleasure hearing from "Dr. Martha Lewellyn," my precocious and precious niece.

My newspaper assignment nowadays was to cover the presidential nominating conventions in 1952. The Republicans nominated Dwight D. Eisenhower with Richard Nixon as vice-president. Democrats nominated Adlai Stevenson with John Sparkman as his running mate. Although Adlai Stevenson ran a spirited, intelligent, and witty campaign, General Eisenhower, the hero of Normandy and World War II, running with the slogan "I like Ike," won easily in November. He pledged if elected to "go to Korea" to find a way to peace in this unpopular war.

Jimmy started his third year at UC. His commitment to medical school weakened and his grades showed it. Getting straight As in history, English and philosophy courses, but he barely passed his premed courses. Maybe two doctors in one family were enough, I thought, as I watched his interest flag.

"Seems you like liberal arts courses better than premed," I said to him when we met for coffee.

He squirmed a little when I said this, embarrassed that perhaps he might be disappointing a family so committed to medicine.

"Well, the truth is, I'm just not interested in chicken embryology and Mendelian inheritance," he said. "It seems so remote from what I think is important in doctoring. And physics! What an absolute bore studying the inclined plane. I'm much more interested in Spinoza, George Bernard Shaw, Shakespeare.

I believe aspiring doctors should learn about great ideas, creative ideas. Most of the premeds I talk to don't even know who Ezra Pound is or who wrote "*The Inferno.*" And they don't even seem to want to find out. All they seem to care about is to outdo their fellow pre-meds and suck up to the undergrad professors who write the recommendations for admission."

"That's reality, Jimmy. They have their eyes on getting into medical school. And that's okay. Cut them some slack. Most of them, if you got to know them better, are probably nice. And maybe they know more about the liberal arts than you think." Thinking about Martha, I said "Are there many women premeds?"

"Just a handful. They're treated badly too. I see now what Martha had to deal with."

"Speaking of her, have you heard from her?"

"No, she doesn't write much. I assume she's busy as hell. And she and I weren't that close anyhow. Nine years' difference is a lot. I'm still an annoying little brother to her. I give her credit though, for convincing

Dad to let me go to Walnut Hills. That was where I got interested in English lit from the likes of Miss Purington and Miss Hutchison and in history from Miss Ferdinand."

"If you don't go to med school, what's the alternative?"

"Grad school in English. My idea is to get a PhD and go up to a place like Kenyon and teach English, smoke a pipe, and wear tweed jackets with elbow patches," he laughed.

"I can't disagree with that fantasy," I said with a smile. "I'd like that myself. Problem is, college professors need to do things that require more than tweed and pipes. You must do literary research, publish papers on subjects you might find more boring than the inclined plane. Plus, campus and departmental politics can be brutal, according to some friends of mine who do what you're talking about."

"Well, I'll stick it out in pre-med and my minor in English and graduate. I have time to decide."

"If you don't go to med school and are undecided about grad school, you might have to go into military service. Deferments run out if you don't continue a course of study, you know, and then you have to serve your two years."

"Yeah, I know that. Maybe doing a stint in the Army would give me time to clear my head. See a little of the world. See how the other half lives. Might do me a bit of good."

"You'd go in as an enlisted man. You know that?"

"Yeah, that's okay."

I could see that he was swimming in a sea of confusion and had no clue what Army service would be like. The Korean War could be over if Ike goes to Korea and somehow finds a way out of that dilemma. But if another war breaks out in Southeast Asia or someplace else, and Congress still believes in the domino theory, then he could end up somewhere in a grave, god forbid. I shuddered to think what that would mean for Sarah, Jack, and Martha. To say nothing of me.

Chapter Thirty-Six

I Left My Heart in San Francisco

1954

THE KOREAN WAR ENDED in July last year. They called it an armistice, and no peace treaty was drawn up. The Korean peninsula was sliced in half at its midsection, with the De-Militarized Zone (DMZ), between North and South Korea. Threatening military installations line both sides of the DMZ.

In our peaceful corner of the world, planting of ivy, a ritual performed every year, celebrated graduation for UC's Class of '54. Jimmy, as class president, pressed the ivy roots into the ground as cameras dutifully recorded the event. He got his degree, albeit barely. Girls, fraternity parties and singing consumed most of his undergrad time. He flunked physics, the course he disliked so much, but he had enough credits to graduate anyway. A year later the United States Army inducted him as a private.

The "Cold War" was an uneasy peace. At Ft. Leonard Wood, Missouri, Jimmy moved through the eight weeks of basic training along with the rest of the "grunts," long marches to nowhere, crawling through underbrush, climbing wooden walls, shooting M-1 rifles at the range, and experiencing all the pleasures of boot camp. His second eight weeks were spent in clerk-typist school.

"Why am I being trained to be a secretary?" he wrote me. "It feels like a slap in the face to be reduced to such a wimpy job in the Army."

But after eight weeks he changed his tune. The Army sent him to Sixth Army Headquarters at the Presidio in San Francisco, probably the best Army assignment anyone could hope for.

"I couldn't believe it," he wrote. "I got my orders and boarded a four-engine plane from St. Louis, bound for the west coast. I'd never flown anywhere before and the farthest west I'd gone before the Army was Indiana. I was so excited I couldn't sleep, so fired up I could hardly sit still. Then when the Army bus rolled into the Presidio, I thought I'd died and gone to heaven.

Our barracks building was a handsome solid brick building facing the parade ground. Standing on the parade ground I could see the Golden Gate Bridge, a magnificent red structure enshrouded in fog that Carl Sandburg wrote, "comes on little cat feet." We slept in the belly of the barracks, but I still felt exhilarated. And blessed."

Jimmy kept me posted on his explorations of San Francisco, Barbary Coast, the Hungry i, (where, he later bragged, he'd discovered Mort Sahl, the comedian), the Purple Onion, Chinatown, Golden Gate Park, and Nob Hill. These exotic experiences were ravishing to a high-spirited boy from the Midwest, creating appetites he'd never discovered before. But from his letters it was clear he was being pulled back toward medicine. He'd enjoyed his experiences at the Student Health Service at UC in college. It was almost as though his DNA now exerted its delayed influence. Jimmy had always been a late bloomer.

> *Dear Uncle Cyrus,*
>
> *Well, I think I'm succumbing to the pull of Aesculapius after all. I'm taking physics at the University of San Francisco, acing it so far. Then I'm going to apply to UC Medical School. Wish me luck.*
> *Love,*
> *Jimmy*

I'm sure my wish of good luck played no role, but he was accepted. He began med school after his Army discharge, but he left San Francisco with fond memories-- especially of his favorite bridge.

~~~

Martha—remember her? –just wrote me:
~~~

Dear Uncle Cyrus,

I'm in love!! I met this wonderful guy, also in training here at BCH. He's Chief Resident in Medicine. We're engaged and plan on getting married in Cincinnati next summer. He's entering a Fellowship in Pulmonary at the VA hospital there and I'll be starting my Residency in Neurosurgery back at CGH. He's already got housing at the VA which is a block away from the main hospital complex where I'll be working.

I'll tell you all about it when I'm back. How is your life going?

Write me when you can,

Love,

Martha.

They're all growing up. Martha is getting married. Jimmy is making adult decisions. I'm only growing older.

Chapter Thirty-Seven

It's a Good Day

1958-63

IN MEDICAL SCHOOL, no longer was he the diminutive "Jimmy." Now he answered to "Jim" or "James or occasionally to "Mr. Lewellyn." He walked on the same floors that John and Martha had trod more than ten years before.

He told me that the odor of formaldehyde from anatomy class cadavers clung to his clothes and in cracks of his skin long after he left the dissection lab. He described long hours spent teasing away fragments of flesh to lay bare the course of nerves and blood vessels and to show how tendons bound onto joints of glistening bones.

"Memorizing all that anatomical detail is driving me a little crazy," he said. "But it does focus my mind, disciplines me, even though I wonder how long after the exam I'll remember any of it."

He will always be "Jimmy" to me, and I'll continue to call him that. He offered to show me the anatomy dissection room and I politely but firmly told him that

I might throw up if he took me into that grisly place. It's a figurative proving ground for aspiring medical students. I'll look at doctors from now on with more admiration, knowing how they had to put up with those rituals of learning.

Jimmy and I lost touch during the grind of his medical school years. He was completely immersed in his studies, and I was more involved with newsgathering.

After the calm of the Eisenhower presidency, a storm was gathering. The USSR installed Khrushchev as President, Castro took over Cuba, space exploration by USSR and the US was born, and Alaska and Hawaii were granted statehood. In 1960, John Kennedy beat Richard Nixon for President by a paper-thin popular vote but with a 303/219 margin in the Electoral College votes. United States sent soldiers to Vietnam and US-Cuba relations soured. So, I was busy.

In 1961 Jimmy graduated from medical school and went off to internship in nearby Indianapolis.

"The internship advisors advocated for spreading our wings for internship to gain new perspective, then come back home with all the new ideas garnered elsewhere," Jimmy said. "Indiana University has a good urology residency, so that's where I'm going." I can't imagine why anyone would want to become a urologist, but to each his own. His first rotation was on the urological service. That changed everything for him.

"They fitted me up with a plastic apron to do my first cystoscopy with my mentor. What you do is slip a scope into the bladder and look around for problems," Jimmy said. "Well, after this first cystoscopy, I decided right then that urology was not what I wanted to do the rest of my life." He finished his internship still undecided about further training, so he accepted an offer from a family doctor to enter a Cincinnati family practice.

My journalism world continued to engage me. In November 1963 the world changed forever. The assassination of John F. Kennedy stunned the nation and the world. The unthinkable had happened. The killing of this young, handsome, and articulate president left an incredulous nation in near universal grief, even among his political opponents.

His many accomplishments included his confrontation with Nikita Khrushchev, who had installed nuclear missiles in Cuba, only ninety miles from the US. After a tense thirty-five days, a deal had been arranged whereby the US would remove missiles from sites in Turkey in exchange for the removal of similar missiles in Cuba.

In the US, the emerging civil rights struggle was taking root. No one knew where this would lead.

Chapter Thirty-Eight

Every Time We Say Goodbye

1965

"CYRUS, I'M WORRIED about Jack. His cough is much worse, and I saw blood in the toilet after he had a coughing fit."

I dropped what I was doing and went directly to their house. When I got there, Jack was sitting quietly in his usual spot, reading one of his favorite books of poetry.

"Well, Cyrus, good to see you. What brings you around tonight? Wanna have a trio?"

"Not tonight, Jack. I'll get right to the point. Sarah said you're coughing up blood. She saw it in the toilet."

"Damn, I forgot to flush. Well, yeah, I been coughing a lot lately, there has been some blood. I figured it would stop, though."

"Call Jimmy. He'll know what to do," Sarah said with insistence in her voice.

"I agree, Jack. Give him a ring. No point in having a doctor in the family if you can't call him when you need medical advice, right?"

With only small reluctance, Jack picked up the phone. It was clear that he was worried too, and knew he needed help.

"What's up, Dad?" Jimmy said after his receptionist told him who was calling.

"Well, Cyrus and Sarah are nagging me to call, but I don't want to waste your time. Here's the thing: I've been coughing, even brought up some blood last time I had a hacking fit."

"Who's your regular doctor?" Jimmy asked.

"Well, I don't really have one anymore. Doctor Ruhrwein died last year, and I never found another."

"Sounds like I ought to take a look at you," Jimmy said, trying to keep his apprehension inapparent. "Come to the office this evening. I'd like to listen to your chest."

"Oh, I don't wanna bother you," Jack said. "I know how busy you are. Can you just call something into Pahner's Drugstore, a cough syrup or something, so I can get some sleep tonight?"

"Sure, I can do that, but I need to see you first. I'll tell Ellie you're coming, and she'll fit you right in, okay?"

Jack didn't argue. I knew him well enough to know that although he'd never admit it, he was concerned. He'd always had what he termed a cigarette cough, and passed it off as something all smokers had, a normal thing. But now, with blood, the stakes were higher, and he knew it. This was different.

Sarah and I took Jack to Jimmy's office. Ellie quickly directed us into his inner sanctum. His well-designed office had a central hall with eight exam rooms on either side. In his consultation room was a large walnut desk, examination table, equipment for vital signs screening, electrocardiogram, diathermy machine for heat application, and scales. We sat in Naugahyde-covered chairs facing his desk. Ellie came in, asked Jack to strip down to his waist, gave him a gown, left quickly, and returned to take his temperature and vital signs, weighed him, and left again to tell Jimmy his dad was ready.

"I hope he comes in soon. It's really cold in here," Jack complained. "Why do doctors keep their exam rooms so damned cold?"

Jimmy came in promptly, hugged both of us quickly turned his attention to his father, asking about his cough, especially the blood.

"Bright red blood?"

"Bright red, for sure," Jack answered.

"Hop onto the exam table and let me take a listen."

Jack hoisted himself up and breathed deeply as Jimmy listened, moving his stethoscope all over Jack's chest, front and back. As Jimmy listened, Jack had a coughing fit. Jimmy handed him a tissue and Jack coughed into it. Blood and mucus.

"Lie down on your back, please." Jimmy said, in his full doctor mode.

He felt his father's belly, seemed satisfied there were no abnormalities after a few pokes, then asked him to sit up and get dressed. Pretty quick exam, I thought.

"Well, you got a lot of noise in the left side of your chest," he said. "And coughing up blood is obviously not good. I want you to go to Good Samaritan for a chest x-ray tonight. I'll call ahead. After the x-ray, wait there until I hear from the radiologist."

"Well, whaddaya think?" Jack asked.

"Probably pneumonia," Jimmy said, putting the best face on his findings. "Lots of it around this week. While you're at the hospital we'll get the lab to look at your blood count and a few other things, examine what you're coughing up. You can cough that up for the lab, right?"

"Easy. I cough all the time. But never had blood before. That seems serious."

"Blood in sputum can mean many things, Dad, but it's serious, no matter what's causing it. I won't know what's causing it until I see the x-ray, and even then, it may not be definitive. The lab may be able to tell us if your sputum has germs in it and whether we need penicillin, but I'm not sure of that yet. Talk to you later, okay?" He laid his hand on Jack's shoulder, looked him in the eye. "I love you, Dad."

"Love you too, Jimmy. Thanks for seeing me so quickly."

We dropped Sarah at the house.

"You don't need me for the x-rays. You can tell me what they find when you get home, okay?" I knew she was anxious and hated being in a hospital, bringing back memories of John's ordeal.

We went to Good Samaritan Hospital, got the x-ray right away, and then at the lab, Jack coughed into a cup, gave it to a woman with "Rose--Laboratory Technician" on her nametag.

"We were told to wait for the results of the x-ray. Shall I wait here or in x-ray?"

"Better to wait in X-ray. The radiologist will be reading the films as soon as they're dry, and he'll call your doctor."

"You know Dr. Lewellyn?"

"Sure do. Nice guy. Helluva doctor too. Is he your doctor?"

Jack sat up straighter and smiled broadly as he responded. "He's not only my doctor, but he's also my son," he bragged.

"Wow, you must be tremendously proud. He's very well-thought of here at Good Sam," Rose said.

Ruffling through six-month-old magazines in a medical office doesn't ease one's mind. Especially if the man sitting next to you is not just any patient, but your brother since birth, father of three doctors, and husband of the lovely Sarah Lewellyn. It wasn't possible to read Jimmy's face when he listened to Jack's chest or when he accompanied us to our car. He told Jack he'd give him the straight scoop when he had it.

Jack was uncommonly quiet, sitting there against the drab mint-green wall of the radiology department. Somewhere behind that lead wall a technician was developing the most important x-ray of his life.

"Jack, penny for your thoughts," I said.

"I was thinking of Horace: 'Death's boatman takes no bribe.' I'm scared, Cyrus. With my long history of smoking, coughing up blood makes me think of only one thing. Remember Martha telling us about that lung surgeon who told them to stop smoking because it caused cancer? I've thought about that many times, sometimes kept me awake. But think it ever caused me to consider quitting the smokes? Proves how stupid I am."

"Not stupid. Shows how you, or anyone, can deny what they don't want to accept. Happens all the time, in all kinds of ways. Besides, you got addicted to nicotine before we knew what smoking did to people. The more we learn about cigarettes, the worse they seem. And the ads made them so attractive. Movie stars all smoked, all our friends smoked, even doctors were featured in ads, so we all thought it must be okay. It was the social norm."

The X-ray technician was wiping his hands on his apron when he walked over to us. We both stood up.

"All done. The radiologist will be in touch with your doctor about the results. Any questions?"

"Yeah, what did it show?" Jack asked.

"I'm just a tech, I don't read the x-rays. Sorry."

"Any hints?" Jack persisted.

"You'll have to talk to your doctor. The radiologist will tell him what he thinks." The technician whirled around and headed back into the radiology suite.

"Are we free to go then?" I asked the tech.

"Yep. All done now."

"Why did we have to stay just to hear that our doctor would tell us the results. We could've been home," Jack asked, with a trace of irritation, before the technician vanished around the corner.

"We had to be sure the x-rays were of good quality, and we'd not have to take any more," the tech explained.

We all headed home around nine o'clock. We figured Jimmy would still be in his office and we could call him once we got home.

"So, how did it go?" Sarah asked. I told her what we'd been doing for the last few hours.

"You don't know anything more than when you dropped me off?" she said, disappointment and concern resonating in her voice.

"Afraid not. We need to call Jimmy to find out what the X-ray showed," I said.

"Anyone want coffee or tea?" she asked, slipping into her role as comforter.

"Main thing is to call Jimmy," Jack told her. He dialed up Jimmy's office, got Ellie on the line.

"Hi, Ellie. Jack Lewellyn. Is Jimmy free to talk?"

"Just a sec," she said. I heard the brush of her hand over the mouthpiece, then Jimmy's voice.

"Dr. Sander just called," Jimmy said cautiously.

"Yeah, your tone of voice doesn't sound good," Jack said.

"There's a tumor in your left lung, Dad. I think we ought to admit you to Good Sam in the morning, get a thoracic surgeon to see you. Sorry to be so blunt, Dad, but I know you always want the straight poop."

Jack seemed resigned. "No surprise, Jimmy," he said in a low voice. "Thanks for being direct. I was prepared for bad news. Just a minute, I want to tell your mother and Cyrus." He repeated what Jimmy had told him. I put my arm around Sarah, who was distraught but not crying. "What time should I go in the morning?"

"Around eight. I'll see you there. Keep your spirits up. We don't know enough to think too far ahead," Jimmy said in reassuring tones. "Does Mother want to talk to me?"

Jack handed the phone to Sarah. We couldn't hear the conversation but assumed it was the same one we'd had.

After Sarah hung up, she turned to us.

"Did he tell you anything about the growth?" Sarah said, with her hand on her forehead, fear creeping over her face.

"That's what we'll find out when the surgeon sees me," Jack said. He looked at me and shrugged. "Well, you gotta die of something, right?"

"Jack, this is not a death sentence. We've got to find out a lot more. Tomorrow's another day," I said.

"Jack, did Jimmy tell you more than you're telling me?" Sarah asked as she came over to Jack, putting her arm around his shoulder.

"You talked to him. You know as much as I do. I'm just looking at the facts. Coughing up blood, a tumor in the lung, years of cigarettes, what Martha told us that surgeon said. Putting it all together adds up to some pretty serious stuff."

Sarah took in a deep breath, then looked at both of us. "We've weathered storms before. We'll deal with this one too," she said with conviction. "God will see us through."

~~~

I left Sarah and Jack at the admitting office around eight the next morning, parked and joined them as he was sent up to a four-man ward on the fifth floor. The other three fellows were about his age, seemed to be in good spirits. Jack, in usual salesman mode, introduced himself to all three. But I could tell he wasn't in a mood to get into conversation. He withdrew into his world of uncertainty, aware of the existential threat from his tumor. Sarah and I recognized that he was trying to adjust to being just one more powerless patient.
~~~

A nurse came in and in and said, "Sorry to ask you to do this, but I'll need you to remove all your clothes, put them into this paper bag and slip into that gown on the bed. Tie it in the back," She smiled at Jack. "You'll get used to the breezes coming in from the rear. Dr. Schmidt will be in to see you shortly." Turning to us, she said, "You folks might want to wait outside if you don't mind."

After he had changed, we were allowed back into the room. Jack settled back in his bed, glancing around at the room, taking in all the medical paraphernalia hanging from the walls. I stayed while he waited for the doctor, and we idly chatted about the Cincinnati Reds baseball team. Soon, an enormous man towered over us both.

"Good morning, I'm Dr. Schmidt. So, you're Jim Lewellyn's father? Glad to meet you. Jim is a fine doctor." Jack smiled broadly.

"Thanks, I'm very proud of him. His older brother was a doctor, as is his sister. I'm proud of all of them. This is my wife Sarah, and my brother Cyrus."

Dr Schmidt smiled as he shook hands with Sarah and me, then returned his attention to Jack.

"Did I hear you say his older brother *was* a doctor?"

"He died of Hodgkin disease a few years back." Jack said.

"I'm so very sorry for your loss, Mr. and Mrs. Lewellyn. That must have been terrible for your family."

We all nodded in unison but said nothing. There was no fitting response, and we wanted to move ahead.

"I looked at your films. What I intend to do, with your permission, is biopsy that mass in your chest. We'll put you to sleep, and under x-ray guidance, we'll slip a needle between your ribs, get a sample, get the pathologist to look at it. When we know what it is, we can plan future treatment. We have scheduled that for around eleven this morning. I need you to sign an operative permit before we go any further. Do you have questions before you sign?"

Jack asked a couple of questions and then promptly signed the permit. Dr. Schmidt wasted no time concluding his visit. After he left, the overhead speaker came on.

"Dr. Lewellyn, please call the operator."

Jack looked at me with a beatific smile, eyes filled with tears, and said, "It's all been worth it to hear that. Music to my ears." Sarah dabbed a tissue to her eyes.

It wasn't long before Jimmy appeared in the room, came over to Sarah for a hug, then embraced his father.

"You okay? You look like every other patient in the hospital," he said, laughing, trying to lighten the mood.

"Well, I've been better. Be glad when this is over with."

"This procedure's not too bad, Dad. You'll be home by midafternoon most likely. Then we'll have something to go on."

"I'm gonna have to leave now," I said. "My editor is after me to get a story done and I'm behind. I'll call you this evening, okay? Good luck Jack. I know you'll do fine."

Holding back tears as I hugged Sarah and Jimmy, I shook hands with Jack. As I walked towards the garage, tears spilled out. This disease couldn't be good, no matter what the biopsy showed. It had to be lung cancer, what else could it be? Sixty-seven years old is not ancient in these times. I felt like a forty-year-old most of the time even though I was the same age as Jack. Damned cigarettes!

At his home later, Jack was resting when I got there. "Have any pain?" I asked.

"A little in the back where they went in with the needle. But it's not bad enough to take anything for it."

"I just stopped by for a minute to check on you, but I have to get home. Got another deadline day tomorrow."

"What's goin' on in the big outside world?" Jack asked.

"Well, plenty. I have to go to London. They want me to cover Sir Winston Churchill's funeral on January 30th. Big deal. This is quite an assignment."

"Now there's a guy who smoked cigars and drank all the time and he's lived a long time," Jack said. "Just goes to show you some people are luckier than others. How old was he?"

"Ninety-one. What an amazing life. A crusty old SOB, but he was a rock during WWII. Saved England. I'm honored to cover his funeral."

"I'm only 67. Doubt I'll make it to 91."

I didn't know how to respond, so I kept my mouth shut.

"When do you go?" Jack asked.

"This weekend. Flying TWA. I'm not fond of flying, but that's the only way I can get there in time. Sorry I won't be here for you, but I'll be right back after his funeral."

"Don't worry, Cyrus, I doubt anything is gonna happen all that quick."

~~~

Jack was right. I was back a week later, and Jack was the same. Churchill's funeral was immense. Every prominent national leader, or celebrity, or sports figure was there, from all over the world. And, of course, Royals from everywhere a monarchy still existed were vying for attention. I got lost in the crowd but was still able to write a pretty good description with my byline appearing opposite the editorial page.

When I got home, I heard that Dr. Schmidt had decided against surgery. "Tumor too advanced," he'd said. Radiation was prescribed. Jack could live at home
~~~

and get radiation as an outpatient. Sarah would take him for the treatments since Jack was told he couldn't drive during therapy, but she did it with her usual acceptance. Jack hated giving up his favorite activity of driving. He also hated giving up control of everything else in his life, but he had no choice.

As Jack went through radiation therapy, he shed weight dramatically. He aged weekly, I thought, as though years were speeding by. Weak and unsteady on his feet, it became increasingly difficult to manage him at home. "This tumor has made an old man of me," he said. He lost all appetite, so Jimmy came by on his way to hospital rounds each day and started intravenous sugar and mineral solutions to keep him alive.

It wasn't long before Jimmy said to Sarah, "Mother, we need to admit him. You've been a superb nurse for him at home, but now he needs round-the -clock care and pain management. We can't provide that here at home."

After he was admitted, I visited him daily. One night when I came in, he was talking. I looked around to see if there was anyone else in the room. There wasn't.

"I love riding in *The Canadian*. How long 'til we get to Vancouver?" I listened but didn't try to talk him out of his pleasurable drug-induced delirium. It was his last night.

~~~

"Cyrus, can you give the eulogy at Jack's funeral service?" Sarah asked. "No one knows him better. And you're a journalist. You use words all the time."

I steeled myself not to break down. I'd already cried daily since his death, so I reasoned that I'd passed that early phase of grief. But when I rose to speak, stirrings in my belly gave me pause. Thankfully, my control returned when I put my hands on the lectern.

"Although Jack and I walked different paths, our souls were never far apart. We shared life's peaks and valleys, not always physically together but always in spirit. We had only a few quarrels, a rarity amongst brothers, especially twins. We trusted and tolerated each other's eccentricities, shortcomings, and faults, loved each other. No one is perfect. There are no perfect people. Jack had his faults, as do we all. We forgive you, Jack.

"He yearned to be a doctor, like our father, the original Dr. Lewellyn. He understood what it meant to be a doctor, by proximity. Papa took Jack with him on house calls and shared his knowledge and ideas about medicine, how to care for, and about, people. Papa's premature death, when Jack was thirteen, was destined to prevent the fulfillment of Jack's greatest ambition. His education was denied, creating a lasting sore.
~~~

"However, he was lucky in many ways. His best piece of good fortune was marrying Sarah.

"The other gifts of Providence were his three children—John, Martha, and James. All good-natured, big-hearted, and driven by some obscure supernatural force to be physicians. Jack's dream to be a doctor was stolen by fate, but in some mysterious way, the seed took hold and blossomed in his progeny.

"Nothing gave Jack more pride than seeing them graduate from medical school. Nothing gave him more despair than losing his oldest son John to cancer at the height of his powers, having just finished his internship. But with Sarah at his side, they bravely grieved their loss and persevered. Because they had two other children and each other.

"Jack Lewellyn, we will all keep you in our hearts. Forever."

~~~

Jimmy and I met for coffee two weeks after the funeral. I wasn't sure how he would be coping. I wasn't sure how *I* was coping.

We settled in our usual spots in Gert's diner. I looked at Jimmy trying to gauge his mood and his eyes met mine, probably doing the same assessment of me. He spoke first.

"How are you feeling by now?"
~~~

"Still numb, saddened, trying to accept his absence. How's it with you?"

"Well, it's interesting what these last few months have taught me. Dad and I were fairly distant most of my life. Not in a bad way, but I never felt I knew him and never felt he cared much for me.

"You know, he and John had a complicated relationship. I know they loved each other, but they couldn't allow that love to show, that is, until the end of John's life.

"But I sort of floated through my young life, with my friends, the Boy Scout troop, the camping I did with them, school, you know, the stuff of childhood. I was a little afraid of Dad. He was this larger-than-life presence, and when he was drunk, he turned into another person, wild, out of control, angry. So, I sort of avoided him. Mother was always my rock of security. She was always there when I needed a lift, or a hug—reassurance that I was an important person to her.

"But in the days leading up to Dad's death, I really began to know and understand him. We talked during those moments when I started his IV, or took blood from him, plumped up his pillows or pulled him up in bed. We had interesting conversations, and I realized what a deep reservoir of knowledge and passion he had. It was a revelation to me."

It took all my emotional control to avoid breaking down, but I needed to, for Jimmy's sake. Having known Jack from his and my beginning was not only my privilege, but it had provided me with an insight into the real Jack that was available to no one else. To hear this affirmation of his worth from his son touched me deeply.

"I'm so glad you had that opportunity to get to know him. But it must have been hard for you. He was your father, for heaven's sake."

"It was like an epiphany. I don't think many sons have the rare opportunity of caring for their dying father with the kind of relationship I had. I was doing for him what he wanted to do for others, so it seemed almost like a vicarious fulfillment of his own aspirations. When he looked at me with those blazing blue eyes full of feeling, I felt we really connected for the first time in our lives. It was an important lesson for me, one that I'll carry for the rest of my life. Thanks to him."

"I can't tell you how proud he was of you. When I was with him that day in Good Sam when he heard your name 'Dr. Lewellyn' called over the hospital speaker, he nearly burst with pride and love. He told me that that moment made it all worthwhile."

That got to Jimmy. I didn't mean to make him cry, but I wanted him to know of that moment so he could carry it for the rest of his life. He reached across the table and took my hand.

"Thanks, Uncle Cyrus. I love you."

Epilogue

Back Home Again in Indiana

1966

COVERING THE STORY about JFK's assassination in 1963 just about did me in. I'd been a Washington correspondent for almost a year when that happened. I followed President Kennedy's entourage to Dallas, so I was an eyewitness. Since then, my enthusiasm for on-the-ground reporting paled. The stress, the misery I'd seen, the sorrow- it was more than I could bear. I asked for time in the op-ed department. After some deliberation my Editor gave me that opportunity. He told me I'd earned it, which pleased me enormously.

A few months ago, I was offered a position in the school of journalism at Indiana University in Bloomington. I met with the Dean of the school twice and the job seemed right for me. I would be teaching undergraduates, serving on the admissions committee, and still would have time and permission to write a nationally syndicated column. I talked it over with Sarah numerous times while deliberating the offer.

After Jack died, Sarah continued to live in the house she and the family had shared in Clifton. But recently Martha, who now lives in California, offered to have her come west and live with their family. She was hesitant to leave the "Old Homestead" as she called it, but after she and I talked about my job offer, I decided to decamp to Bloomington as Professor of Journalism. As she considered my impending departure, she decided to accept Martha's offer to join their family in California. I would be going home to Indiana and Sarah would rejoin her daughter.

This was a bittersweet moment for both of us. I agonized about leaving my Mt. Adams neighborhood, Cincinnati, and the *Enquirer*. I would miss the proximity to Sarah and Jimmy, the familiarity of the surrounding city and my colleagues at the *Enquirer*. Still, the opportunity to teach, live in an academic community that I already knew from earlier days, seemed ideal for this time in my life. I accepted the professorship at IU. Sarah sold her house and moved happily to be with her daughter's family in Napa Valley. Jimmy recently left his family practice in Cincinnati and accepted a Fellowship at Harvard Medical School.

With the family scattering east and west, I felt sad to be so far from them, but I knew they were content with their lots. And so was I.

Author's Note

GLIMPSES OF REALITY are draped on a scaffolding that props up this story of a twentieth century family. It is derived from the true story of a family I knew. But "knowing" other people and their relationships is invariably clouded by the fog of time, failure of memory and distortions of observation. These contributed in unequal measure to recording the vicissitudes of the Lewellyn family. Invention of most of the dialogue lends to this fictional caste. If Jack, Sarah, John, Martha, and the fictional Cyrus were to comment on the veracity of the narrative, they would have much to challenge. But alas, they all have passed.

Robert M. Reece

Acknowledgments

THANKS TO ALL WHO helped complete this family tale.

Special gratitude to Betsy Kyle Reece, whose editorial skill is only surpassed by her keen sense of story. Her encouragement and support when the going got hard were crucial.

Thank you to readers, Jim and Alice Liljestrand, Barbara Struna, Jack Mulkeen, David Kerns, Larry Ricci and Judy Singer, whose feedback was valuable in shaping the narrative; and to Jennifer Reece, whose insight into the historical caste of the novel is reflected in her cover design.

Thank you to Kathryn Galán at Wynnpix Productions for her patience, knowledge, and suggestions; and to Michael Grossman of eBook Bakery, for his sensitivity and graciousness.

About the Author

ROBERT M. REECE, MD, practiced, taught, and did research in pediatrics for over forty years, specializing in diagnosis and treatment of child abuse cases. He published nine textbooks, nearly fifty articles, and twenty-seven book chapters. He founded and was editor of *The Quarterly Update,* 1993-2017.

His other novels include *To Tell The Truth, Double Blind Double Cross, Strong Medicine,* and *The Lewellyns from Vincennes.* In 2024, he published his latest novel, *About Ben,* the based-on-true story of a medical student stricken with polio who becomes the pediatrician's pediatrician.

Learn more at www.robertmreece.com